In Aeternum

POLAR OPPOSITES

ALIYAH BURKE

Polar Opposites
ISBN # 978-1-78430-159-0
©Copyright Aliyah Burke 2014
Cover Art by Posh Gosh ©Copyright July 2014
Interior text design by Claire Siemaszkiewicz
Totally Bound Publishing

Published in 2014 by Totally Bound Publishing, Newland House, The Point, Weaver Road, Lincoln, LN6 3QN, United Kingdom.

POLAR
OPPOSITES

Dedication

To everyone who's been there for me, thank you.
While writing tends to feel solitary, I know I couldn't
have done all of this without your endless support. As
always, to the men and women who selflessly serve
this country. Thank you for your sacrifices! God Bless!

Chapter One

Christmas Island

"Ivan Vinokourov."

Biting back his groan of irritation at being disturbed, Ivan turned his head, tipping it to peer over the tops of his shades. A large, dark-skinned man stood there, powerful arms crossed and reflective sunglasses hiding his eyes.

"Yes?" *Who is this man?*

"I need a word with you."

"Must be important if you tracked me down here." There were around two thousand residents on this island. Most people who arrived here were outsiders — scientists or naturalists.

"It ain't about the color of the sky, that's for sure." He lowered himself to the sand beside Ivan, apparently uncaring about what it may do to his pants. Silk, from the looks of them.

"So, what can I do for you, Mr…?"

"Kevin. Kevin McNeal." He stared like Ivan should know the name.

Ivan didn't, and merely raised a brow.

"I work for an organization called Theta Corps."

He blinked. "Congratulations."

"We want you to come work for us."

Suspicion flared. "Why?"

"Your reputation precedes you."

And flew as if it had sprouted wings. Shifting on his chair, he stared out over the Indian Ocean and hooked his ankles. "What rep would that be?"

"Dedicated. Hard-working. Extremely smart, and one of the top physicists in your field."

"Reputations can be falsified."

"They can be. In this case, they're not, Dr Vinokourov. We know it's true."

"And how do you know so much?"

"I know more than you probably think. I know of your training by Dr Thompson and your work with Dr Jaydee Cassano on electrogravitics."

He shook his head. "Sorry, I have no clue what you're talking about."

"I admire your commitment to keeping it a secret but I know Valentino Cassano, and Theta Corps does its homework." He draped an arm over his raised knee. "You can deny all you want but we both know the truth. And that's why I'm here. We want you to work for us."

"What do you need?"

"A man of your talents would be extremely useful to our organization."

Valentino Cassano. Jaydee's brother-in-law. Nope. He didn't need to be close to anyone—be it location-wise or friendly—who was close to her right now. Ivan shook his head and rose, his momentarily discovered peace spoiled for the present moment. "Thank you, but I must decline."

"You've not heard what I have to offer you yet."

"No need for me to listen or for you to waste your breath. I'm not interested. Period. Good day, Mr McNeal." Ivan walked away and didn't once look back. He'd meant what he'd said—he wasn't interested. Why continue to torment himself with the knowledge of what he couldn't have or who he would never be?

He didn't return to his hotel room, it wasn't where he wanted, or needed, to go right now. Instead, he made his way down the beach. He shoved his hands in his pockets and tried his best to forget the name of the one woman he'd loved. Jaydee Amos.

No, that's not right, she's Jaydee Cassano now. He'd offered to marry her. He loved her. A foolish endeavor he now saw, for never had her emotions been as vivid as when they involved Giovanni. Part of him would always love her, he knew that. Nevertheless, it was past time for him to move on. Something else he knew.

Easier to say than to do.

It had been hard for him these past few years. To see the woman he loved married and with a family of her own. A family that should have been his.

Things fall as they do and there's nothing that said she was to be mine or nobody's. Again, words that were easier to say than necessarily believe.

He veered from the shore and onto one of the numerous walking trails. Perhaps a visit to some fissure caves would do him good. All he knew was he didn't need to go back and talk to some man who'd tracked him down.

Why me and why all the way out here?

It wasn't Bali, or Monte Carlo. Hell, it wasn't even Rio. It had been a deliberate choice for him to come here. And to have this man know about him and what he'd done, come here and track him down...? Yes, color him suspicious. He'd never heard of Theta Corps before. Didn't do much interaction in regards to Valentino Cassano. Sure, he'd seen the man a few times—he'd married Jaydee's friend Lexy. However, they weren't personally friends.

He nodded at some people who were meandering by him. This wasn't a gambling spot, or one for races. He had come here because it was for those who loved nature. He continued, stepping past others on the trail. Over half of this island was a national park.

Eventually he got lost in his musings as he explored and enjoyed his day. Passing by two women, he smiled at them, chuckled when one whispered to her friend, and giggled as her face flamed. Despite the blatant invitation in her gaze, he traipsed on, not wanting to follow up on her hollow offer. He needed something more than just sex and this woman didn't have it, which was why to him, it was a hollow offer. Ivan was at the point where he wanted more than just meaningless sex with a stranger. He wanted to feel some type of connection with them—more than just a physical one. That woman barely got a physical one from him.

It wasn't until later that afternoon that he headed back to his hotel room. He slowed when he saw a couple arguing on the trail. *Christ, can't you keep it private? People don't come here to listen to your bitching.* He moved to the other side of the trail to skirt around them when something hard clipped him in the back of the head.

Stars flickering, he dropped to his knees and peered behind him. No more arguing couple. They looked intent on causing him harm. The woman raised a gun, aimed it and pulled the trigger. He tried to yell but nothing left his mouth. Fingers on the side of his neck, he encountered the dart sticking out and swore moments before he succumbed to the darkness blanketing him.

* * * *

Santiago, Chile

The knock at the door made her pause. Bailey Hyde shoved home her boot knife and sighed. She tugged her jean leg over the black leather with a three and a quarter inch heel. A quick perusal of her attire then she moved to answer the person on the other side. She didn't check to see who it was — only one person knew she was here. He'd sent her.

"What, McNeal?" She posed her question once she'd thrown open the door.

"I need you."

"My every dream come to life," she said drolly.

He brushed by her, the fall of his silk shirt and pants perfect — the man never seemed to be a mess. He was her boss in the group she worked with. Theta Corps. Throughout the organization, there were smaller groups of people who tended to work together. Except a few who were loners and did one specific job — assassinations. And she was one of the best.

"You, Bailey, are such a charmer."

His words carried no heat and she took no slight at his sarcasm. She shut the door behind him then leaned against it. Arms crossed, she waited for him to let her know what the job would be.

"You know why I'm here."

"Social call?"

"Besides that."

"You've never come for a social call, I'm not buying it. Who do you want me to kill?"

He exhaled sharply. "No one."

She raised an eyebrow. "So this *is* a social call? I told you I was fine and didn't need to be pulled from work."

Kevin McNeal walked farther into her small place. A studio apartment, there wasn't much in the way of personal items. A few magazines purchased from the store, but nothing that had been addressed to her.

"We worry about our people, Bailey."

"If this isn't about a job, what are you doing here?"

He turned his dark head so they had eye contact. "I didn't say it wasn't about a job."

"You said — "

"I didn't want you to kill anyone."

She walked to the tiny kitchen then filled the coffee pot and turned it on. "I'm not following."

"I need you to go rescue someone."

She didn't even pause in getting mugs. "I don't do that."

"You do this time."

That statement got her to stop. She set the spoons on the counter and faced her boss. "I'm not the person you send to rescue someone. I'll go along to eliminate a target. But typically when people need rescuing, they need someone softer than I am."

"Not this time."

"What aren't you telling me?"

"A man we have been after was taken."

"So send in a rescue team. I'm not a team, nor part of one. I work alone."

"Not going to work. I need you. You'll be taken as well, not in the same guise but the plan will have you getting in. Then I need you to find him and get him out of there."

"Then what?"

Kevin blinked. "Then what, what?"

"What do I do with him after I get him out of wherever he is?" She turned back and poured the hot drink. "Where do I leave him?"

"You bring him to me."

Handing him a cup, she canted her head to the side before sipping some of her coffee. "Why?"

His brow converged. "You never ask why."

"I also don't do rescues. Apparently now I do, so I'm asking why."

"We want him to work for us."

"This captured man. You want him at Theta Corps?"

"He's brilliant. However, even if he continues to refuse coming to us, we still need to keep him out of the hands he's in now."

She grunted and Kevin sipped his drink.

"No wondering why we want him?"

"Not my department. Where is he?"

"All we know is somewhere in Madagascar."

She finished her coffee and put the mug on the counter. "'Somewhere in' is extremely vague, especially in a place that size."

"I have faith in your ability."

She narrowed her gaze. "What aren't you telling me?"

"The head of the group believed to have taken him has a fondness for women like you."

"Like me? Assassins?"

"Tough. Black. Beautiful."

"So you want to dangle me before him like bait and have him want to keep me closer. That way I can locate this person for you and get them out."

He smiled. "I love it how you don't have to ask a lot of questions." He put down his mug and walked to the door. "File's on your table."

Of course it is. She didn't speak as he left, just stared until the door closed behind him. Intrigued, she walked to the square table and sat before the file. She flipped it open and stared down at the picture of the man on the paper.

Handsome, sure, she wouldn't lie, but it was his eyes that snagged her. Such a pale blue, she wondered if it wasn't a trick of the camera. Rugged features and a quirk of his lips that made her hesitate.

A physicist. One held in high regard by his peers. Her eyebrows rose when she discovered his friend was the sister-in-law to Valentino Cassano. She knew Valentino's name and had met him three times. The group he was in was pretty damn legendary throughout Theta Corps. She continued to read and her expression hardened the more she realized why they couldn't allow him to stay in the clutches of whoever it was that had him.

Reading on, she went for a large ceramic bowl, which she then set in the middle of her table. As she finished reading each sheet, she placed it in there. When a few were accumulated, she lit them on fire, allowing them to burn down to nothing but ash. After dealing with the entire file, she got to her feet and took the dish to the sink where she dumped the remnants down the drain. Running some water after it, she cleaned out the dish then set it upside down in the adjoining side.

The plan formulated in her head and she knew what they wanted. She walked to her closet and opened the door. After reaching in for her black duffle bag, she stuffed some clothing in it then went out of the front, locking it behind her and striding away without a look back.

* * * *

Madagascar

Bailey walked from her hotel and took in the sights again. She'd been here for a few days and had wanted to get a look at where this would take place. So she'd explored and mapped out all she had needed to. With a deep breath, she kept on her path. Now the time had come for it to begin. To allow herself to become the bait so she could do her job.

I feel weird not having my sniper rifle with me. Or a knife or three.

She kept a steady pace along the streets of Antananarivo, heading for her destination.

The evening sun cast a soft golden glow about her as she smoothed her hand down her dress before approaching the club. Once allowed inside she walked through to the bar.

She ordered a cocktail and cast a look around. She found all the exits and noted the number of bouncers. A rope blocked off the entrance to the other portion. That was where she needed to go and in a few moments, her way in would arrive.

Right on time. She watched the tall man walk through. His silk suit fitted him perfectly. She wove around people to his side. He tipped his head and gave her a smile, even while he tucked her against him.

The man by the rope unhooked it and allowed her past with the one she walked beside where she found her target—Kadyr Hamidov.

He noticed her the moment she entered—his head came up and his gaze fixated on her. A slight smile tipped up the corner of his mouth. She gave him a wider smile in return then glanced off at something else while taking a sip of her drink. Extracting herself from her ticket into this part of the club, she perched on the end of a low velvet seat.

"You're new. I've not seen you here before."

She glanced up to meet the owner of the deep, smooth voice. Dark brown eyes watched her from below thick lashes. The man was good-looking. Damn good-looking.

"Never been before." Another drink.

He sat beside her on the wide cushion. "Kadyr Hamidov."

"Bailey Hyde."

"Are you here with him?"

She didn't even bother looking over at the man. "Nope. Just used him to get back into this part."

"Resourceful."

"I have my moments."

"And if it hadn't worked?"

She dragged her tongue along her lower lip. "Hasn't failed me yet. I have good"—she glanced down at her chest—"assets." A slight shrug. "I would have removed the man there and come in anyway."

"He's big."

She toyed with the rim of her glass. "I've found the bigger they are, the harder they fall."

"Feisty." His grin turned lecherous. "I like that in a woman." He slid closer to her.

She smelled the faint lingering whiff of his cologne. Nice. Masculine and slightly spicy. "Do you?"

"You seem like a woman who can handle herself."

"I am."

"Do you like children?"

She stroked the back of her hand down the side of his cheek. "We just met. Don't you think it's a little early to discuss children?"

His smile exposed straight white teeth. "Why wait?"

She chuckled and got to her feet. "Thanks for the laugh, handsome. I'm only here looking for a good time, not to get tied down with children." She waggled her fingers at him and began walking away.

Five steps from the rope, a callused hand grabbed her wrist. She peered over her shoulder with one eyebrow raised. "Yes?"

"A good time I can do."

She raked her gaze over him. "I bet you can." Bailey faced him fully. "Is this something we're doing here, with an audience, or are we going somewhere private?"

He waved off the two men who followed him. "Private. Definitely private."

Bonus. Linking her arm through his, she rested her head against his shoulder. "Can't wait."

"Boss," one thug said, only to fall silent when Kadyr waved him off.

"I got this, we don't need you for this."

The men gave her a once-over, their expressions telling her they were neither pleased with nor happy about their boss's decision. She also understood they would do nothing about it—he was, after all, their boss.

Kadyr dropped his hand to rest upon her ass. "Let's go sit down."

She allowed him to lead her back to where he'd been sitting when she'd first entered. Only this time, she was the woman closest to him, not someone else. His goons followed and retook their seats as well. Bailey didn't argue, more than content to wait and leave later.

Chapter Two

Ivan scowled at the shadow he couldn't shake. No matter where it was, he wasn't alone. Hell, he still wasn't sure *where* he was. Like clockwork at a certain time, he was shown into a lab and the door air-locked behind him.

The man who'd traveled with him went to the woman at the front of the room. Ivan was used to this as well. All he knew for certain was they were Chechen. Personally, he had no quarrel with that ethnic group but what he'd picked up on—aside from their dislike of him—was that they wanted him to build something. No one had spoken to him or had given him more than a grunt or gesture so far. They'd just showed him the lab, left him there for a while then taken him back to his cell.

Yes, it was a cell. Nothing more. Nothing less. His food, meager at best, wasn't at all filling. A shower was allowed once a week and since he'd had three of them, he assumed he had been here for at least that long. Before he'd woken up here, he'd had no clue as to how long he'd been out.

Deep in his bones, he felt today was different. The men were sharper, their mannerisms crisper. Like people were when expecting the boss.

The door opened and he turned in time to see another man walk in. Tall, muscular, with his dark hair pulled back to the nape of his neck. He wore a three-piece suit and the other two fell silent when he entered.

"Ivan Vinokourov."

"Yes."

His gaze darted to the three men who had walked in behind this man. They were large and carrying automatic weapons.

"Do you know who I am?" He posed his question in a heavily accented voice.

"No. What am I doing here? Better yet, where am I?"

"Madagascar."

"Why am I here? And who are you?"

"My name is Kadyr Hamidov." He stroked his goatee. "I find myself in need of your talents."

Ivan crossed his arms. "Talents? What talents?"

Kadyr's thin lips turned up in a slight grin. "No need to be so humble." He leaned against a spotless steel table. "Your knowledge of antigravity will be very helpful."

There was no need for him to deny it—anyone who had the ability to track him down on Christmas Island had to know what he could do. "What do you want from me?"

"I need you to build me a prototype that will be able to be used on people."

He furrowed his brow. "You're talking like you mean you're thinking jet packs. Or something similar."

Kadyr held his gaze. "Can you do this?"

"If I say no?"

The grin grew menacing. "I would make very sure that is what you wish to say. I have no use for a man who cannot help me reach my goal." He stood and tugged on the sleeves of his silk suit. At a snap of his fingers, a man handed him a folder, one that Kadyr placed on the shiny top. "Read this. Think on it. You will join me for dinner and give me your decision." Kadyr headed for the door. "And Doctor" — he pivoted back — "make a wise decision." The door closed behind him with a click of finality.

Ivan didn't appreciate the impending sense of doom settling about his shoulders like a dark, wet, woolen blanket. His shadow and the woman glanced at him before resuming their conversation. Ivan moved to the file and flipped it open. His natural inquisitiveness rushed to the forefront and he stared at the papers beneath his fingertips.

Sketches of different ideas. Jet packs. Drones carrying bombs. He drew up a stool and sat as he began to read.

Shit.

The more he read, the sicker he felt to his stomach. Dirty bombs being delivered by men with jet packs. Drones that could travel much longer and farther, not to mention more quietly, with electrogravitics technology attached to them.

"You are intrigued, no?"

Not the word I would use. "Who's building the bombs?"

"Not your concern," the woman said.

She walked closer and moved behind him, dragging her nails along his shoulders. He held still, taking note of the way his shadow watched him. *Okay, so this is Shadowman's woman, or one he wants. I don't need any more trouble — I think I'm in deep enough as it is.* He turned his attention back to the papers and continued to read.

He had no desire to help them but he couldn't lie and say she hadn't hit it square. He was beyond intrigued. To put that technology on something smaller for human use. Yes, he knew it had been on smaller things but as far as he knew it had never been directly attached to a person.

His fingertips itched to get to a marker and a whiteboard. Lifting his head, he glanced around before moving to the one he spied in the corner. Sooner than he had registered what he was doing, Ivan stood there and was writing on the board. Not until the chuckles sank in did he realize what he'd begun. Staring at them, he frowned.

"If you want me to work, you need to be quiet. I don't work well with people muttering about mundane things."

He faced the board again and got back to work. Ivan worked until his shadow told him it was time to stop and go to dinner. He cast a glance over his board, content no one would be able to understand what he'd put there. Not unless they had Jaydee hidden somewhere.

The mere thought of her sobered him. No longer would she be working beside him, keeping his mind sharp with how she examined problems and their project. No longer would he share a dinner with her, then a bed.

I should be happy for her. She's happy and she deserves it. So why do I feel so damn miserable about the entire thing? That's right, because I'm in love with her. Because I asked her to marry me. I wanted to be the one sharing life with her, not that goddamn arrogant pilot.

"Do not keep Mr Hamidov waiting."

"Wouldn't dream of it," he said dryly. Irritated, he walked to the door and waited. Neither of them neared him and he glanced back over his shoulder. "Am I allowed to leave now on my own? Or is there some reason you're trying to keep me late from meeting him?"

Shadowman glared at him and muttered something Ivan didn't understand. He shouldered him as he went by and Ivan hid his smirk. Following the complaining man, he held his tongue as they finally stepped from the interior halls to the fresh air of outside.

Ivan paused and looked up. The sun shined down upon him, warming him as the rays caressed his skin. Bliss. He had missed this.

"Move."

At the command, he began walking again, taking in the rich soil beneath his feet and the ocean breeze that flowed around him. They neared a large house and passed armed guards to reach an ornately carved white door. He scanned the area as the door opened and the gun at his back encouraged him inside.

Deserted. He saw no one, not even a maid or any other form of help. Through not so subtle nudges, Ivan soon found himself walking into a richly decorated formal dining room.

At the head of the polished, dark wood table sat Mr Kadyr Hamisov. His white suit had been tailored for him. A smile crossed Kadyr's face as he dabbed the corners of his mouth then rose.

"Good afternoon, Doctor, I trust you had ample time to think about my proposal." He waved Ivan closer. "Come, sit. Eat."

Kadyr was jovial and Ivan approached cautiously to take his seat.

"Leave us." Kadyr waved a ring-adorned hand.

The man—Ivan's shadow—vanished without a single word. Reaching for the nearest dish, Ivan waited for Kadyr to speak. Nothing came—Kadyr didn't say a word until Ivan had put food on his plate and had begun to eat.

"You have seen my lab. I can get you whatever you need."

The rich quail's egg got stuck in his throat. Ivan swallowed a few times and took some water. "Surely there are others who would jump at this opportunity. Why me?"

"We have some similarities, you and I." Kadyr dipped his spoon in his bowl. "Although you are Russian and I Chechen, we do have some."

He seriously doubted that. "Really?" he asked dryly.

"Yes. We are a proud people. We want what is best for them."

"And you think dropping dirty bombs on your enemies is what's best?"

An unsympathetic shrug. "There are always casualties in war."

"And you're at war?"

"We are always at war, Doctor, surely you know this."

"No, I don't know this. Who exactly are you at war with?"

The door opened and Ivan paused, a forkful of potatoes halfway to his mouth. A woman walked in and made her way to Kadyr's side. Ivan's mouth dropped. This woman could have walked off a pin-up poster.

Fuck!

She had short black hair and a large red flower over her left ear. Her mocha skin sparkled as if diamond dust had settled upon it. The red sateen top boasted a plunging V neckline and the attached black skirt hugged each and every one of her curves. The cuffs exposed her forearms and her black peep-toe shoes emphasized her legs.

She turned her head and stared at him briefly before dismissing him. Her hair was longer, just pulled back in a bun. She walked to Kadyr and bent to kiss his cheek. He patted her ass and smirked at Ivan.

"She is beautiful, no?"

"Very."

"She is unlike any other I have seen before. My woman."

There was no denying the proprietary claim he laid down. Ivan nodded, not needing to poach the woman belonging to the man who held his life in his hands.

He held her nearly golden gaze. "Nice to meet you, ma'am."

She sat in a chair beside Kadyr and popped a piece of fruit in her mouth. "And who are you?"

"This is Dr Vinokourov. He is going to help me build a few things."

Boredom crossed her features. "I see." She ate another piece of fruit and Ivan couldn't tear his eyes from the way her tongue ran along her lips after she chewed and swallowed. Not until she met his gaze and arched an eyebrow.

He cleared his throat and looked away. This was insane—in no world should he be thinking of another man's woman. He wasn't that kind of man. Even when it came to Jaydee, he'd backed off the moment he heard it from her mouth that she was in love with Gio.

He scowled. Gio.

Bastard.

Focusing back on his food, Ivan ate a few more bites while the pin-up chatted with his captor. As they spoke, he plotted. How the hell was he going to get out of here? He had no intention of helping this madman. However, he also had no wish to die.

He lifted his focus and found himself staring at the woman who was bending over, pulling something from a low cupboard. His cock stirred as he stared at the black material that was smoothed over her ass.

Ivan looked down at his food. He didn't need to exacerbate his situation by lusting after this woman. He didn't even know her name. There were a few that came to mind, however.

Lauren. Ava. Betty. Rita. Barbara. And of course, Josephine — for the 'Black Pearl' or 'Bronze Venus' and to some the 'Creole Goddess'.

He shifted in his seat, a meager attempt to calm his increasing lust for this woman. If she knew he ogled her, she didn't let on. Not even if it bothered her.

Kadyr cleared his throat and Ivan slashed his gaze over to him. Those eyes were dead.

"I'll have your decision."

"Not really giving me any choice."

"Sure I am. You have two options. Work or die."

The door opened and the armed men re-entered.

Some option.

Ivan placed his fork, tines down, on his plate and wiped his mouth. "Put me to work then."

Kadyr's sadistic grin didn't settle his gut or his mind. Ivan made his way to his shadow and allowed him to propel him out of the room. He could work slow and hopefully discover a way out of this conundrum he found himself in. At the door, he glanced back and found the vixen watching him with her golden eyes. It may have been his imagination or it could have been his own desire but he swore he saw one corner of her full red-gold lips tip up slightly.

The door slammed on his vision and he regretfully faced forward and continued on his way.

* * * *

Bailey propped her hip against the counter. Damn, he was handsome. Way more so in person than on paper. Ivan Vinokourov wasn't how she pictured scientists—pale, skinny and bespectacled. Sure, the photo had prepared her. Not.

No image did this man justice. Even having read his stats, she hadn't been equipped for the raw sexuality that rolled off him. If she had been into sleeping with random men, she would definitely have been all over this one.

She poured Kadyr his vodka then left him alone, trailing her hand along his neck as she left. Her heels clacked along the tile floor as she walked to the stairs and ascended to her room.

Once there, she propped up on one foot and removed her shoes. First one then the other. Holding them by the heels, she padded to the bed and tossed them down on the king-sized mattress. She rubbed the nape of her neck then went to the large window and stared out over the landscape.

She knew where Kadyr was keeping Ivan. At the right moment this week, she would take him and begin the extraction. This project had taken her much longer than she'd anticipated, but Kadyr was more suspicious than she'd figured him to be. She wanted to get home. All this being on a mission with a different aim as to what she'd been trained to do bothered her.

This was why she did what she did—being around people all the time wasn't her idea of fun. Give her the bush any day of the week over this. She blew out a breath and unzipped her dress as she turned from the view. Within moments, she stood beneath the pounding spray of the steamy shower.

Over dinner, she set her plans, all the while carrying on a conversation with Kadyr. The man truly was a charmer, for being the bastard he was. Finished, she rose from her chair.

"Another walk?"

"I like my nightly walks," she replied.

He gestured for some more drink and while a servant filled his glass, she walked to the door and slipped through. Outside, the warm air surrounded her. She nodded at the guards she passed. They barely looked at her. *Fools.* It worked to her advantage.

She stuck to her normal path, well aware that cameras followed her. To her, it didn't matter. She merely wanted to enjoy her nightly ritual. Back at the house, she went straight for her room and curled up in the corner chair with a book.

* * * *

Over the next few days, she got down the schedule of Ivan's guard. Mac was his shadow and rarely left his side, if ever. The day arrived and Bailey held to her schedule. In the evening, Kadyr left to tend to something—she didn't know what and it wasn't her concern—on the other side of the island. Using the opportunity, she got going. Tossing her purse in her car, she blew on her nails and strode back inside.

"Everything okay?" the maid asked.

"Fine, Tula. I forgot something." She made her way through the spacious house and went out of a side door. Immediately she headed for the lab. She entered and hugged the wall as she gazed around for Ivan.

He lingered in the back of the room, whiteboards on three sides of him. Blue letters and numbers broke apart the shiny white. His shirt hung, not tucked into his jeans.

I wonder if he slept here.

Aware of her limited window, she wasted no time in approaching him. He muttered to himself as he stared at the boards.

"Dr Vinokourov."

He held up a finger without glancing at her then wrote with his left hand on the board nearest. She ground her jaw. Another reason she didn't go after people. Patience with others wasn't her strong suit.

"Actually, *now* is preferable, Doctor."

His pale blue eyes met hers—heat surged through his gaze and her body. Ivan wore his scruff well and she had this insane desire to reach out and discover what it was like moving on his skin.

"What are you doing here?" He gazed past her.

"Getting you out. Let's go."

"You're Kadyr's woman."

"I'm a lot of things and I'm nothing. We need to move." She grabbed his arm—his nicely muscled arm—and drew him away.

"Who are you?"

"We don't have time for twenty questions. Walk beside me and keep your head down. At the car, get in."

"My stuff—"

"Is immaterial and not worth your life, Doctor." She opened the door and gazed around.

Clear.

He moved at her side, his loose-limbed gait something she would have enjoyed watching were the situation different. She slid behind the wheel as he joined her. Engine running, she shifted into gear and drove away. In her periphery, she watched him.

Ivan was a presence one couldn't ignore. He didn't speak, just sat there.

"Did you give them anything?" Bailey nudged more speed from the car.

"If I say yes are you going to kill me?"

"No."

An explosion rocked the area — she spied smoke and flames in her rear-view mirror. Ivan jerked around, staring out of the back before returning his focus to her.

"Who do you work for?" His demand fell. "Better yet, who *are* you?"

"Theta Corps."

"I told him no. Sending you — no matter how hot you are — isn't going to get me to change my mind."

Her curiosity got the best of her. Ignoring the fact he thought she was hot, she asked the question. "He? He who?"

"Kevin McNeal."

She whipped them into a run-down lot and parked the car. After getting out, she gestured for him to follow. "Come on. I know nothing about whatever you and Kevin discussed. I'm here to get you out. Nothing more. Nothing less."

They crept around to a small speedboat and she gestured him in. Bailey knew most people wouldn't dare touch something belonging to Kadyr Hamisov, which was why it sat mostly unprotected. She wasn't most people.

With no hesitation, she turned the key, bringing the engine to life. Once they were untied, she guided them out to sea. Behind her, loud shots pelted the water.

"What happens now?" he cried over the wind streaming past them.

"We get you home."

She checked her coordinates and held them on course. The shroud of darkness covered them and did so right on target. Thankfully some things were predictable, unlike the men at the dock—she'd underestimated their response time. She continually monitored around them. Assuming their ride was on time, the approaching crafts of his men would be too late.

"Get ready."

"We're in the ocean. What exactly are we waiting for?"

She rummaged through the storage, light clenched between her teeth. "Our ride," she mumbled. Withdrawing the can of gasoline, she then began dumping it over the upholstery.

"What... What are you doing?"

Bailey paused and looked over the bow as the water churned before splitting to allow the sleek black conning tower of a US fast attack submarine to appear as they rose. The sight was always so powerful for her. She thrust the can at him.

"Finish pouring." She went to the helm and checked the screen. Their pursuers were moving closer.

"Done."

She shouldered her bag, the strap crossing her chest, and moved them nearer to the large black silhouette. A flashlight shined on them and she blinked before it moved to the side, allowing her to see four armed men plus the one holding the light.

"Ms Hyde?"

"Yes, sir."

"Let's get you on board."

Three minutes later, she stood on the hull and watched the speedboat go up in flames. Then she and Ivan descended into the sub. The hatch closed and they sank below the surface.

"Chief Terry, ma'am. Sir. Cap would like to see you."

"Yes, sir." She didn't even bother looking at Ivan.

Her rescued man hadn't said anything since she'd had him pour the gasoline. He trailed her through the narrow passageways to the bridge.

"Permission to come aboard."

"Granted, Ms Hyde."

She walked close and shared a handshake with Captain Roger Woodson.

"Good to see you, sir."

"You too." He peered past her. "He something special?"

"So I've been told." She stifled a yawn and met Ivan's gaze. He watched her, not his surroundings, and, as before, his direct stare created a wealth of heat in her gut.

"You probably want to rest. I relegated a stateroom for you—it's the XO's. You'll have to share."

"Fine."

Ivan's remark shocked her.

"COB will show you to it."

Bailey gave a nod of thanks to the executive officer. She understood the difficulties of a woman suddenly being thrown on board a sub and didn't wish to create any tension for the men. "Thanks for the ride,

Captain." She walked out, hiding her smile as Ivan stepped right after her.

She thanked the COB, chief of the boat, as he opened the door to her temporary quarters. Then they were alone. Ivan stepped closer to her—his large body dominated the confined space. In the depth of his incredible eyes, she saw passion and a thousand promises. Promises she wanted to indulge in.

It wasn't her style. Nor her wont. However, at this moment, nothing else mattered. There was too much that sizzled between them to ignore. She removed her shoulder bag and dropped it on the floor. While she didn't have any condoms with her, she didn't care— she was on the shot and knew she couldn't get pregnant. His records, which she'd seen previously, had shown him to be clean as well, so there was no reason not to indulge. Ivan met her in the middle. His strong arms banded around her and he held her gaze as their lips met.

Chapter Three

Ivan groaned as her tongue slid along his. Her taste—intoxicating. Were he asked to give it a name, he would say velvety peppermint. Smooth and cool yet warm, it wrapped around him in a way nothing had before.

Not even Jaydee.

She fitted into him like the perfect puzzle piece. Lush curves pressed into him. Tempting him. Luring him.

He burrowed his hands into her hair and held her tight, surging through her mouth. Her tongue danced and wove around his. She wrapped her arms around his neck as a small purr rumbled up from her throat.

Desire swelled and he rubbed his erection against her. She didn't back away. In fact, she pressed closer.

"Ivan." Her voice, a deep rasp, skated over his skin.

He loved his name rolling from between her lips. Ivan backed her into the door, tugging harder on her hair.

"Tell *me* your name," he ordered.

"Bailey Hyde."

"Bailey," he said, testing it on his lips. He liked it. Like the liquor that shared her name, she had a taste that flowed easily across his taste buds. Much like the drink, she was addictive.

Her moans reverberated through him and his cock jerked in his jeans. She lowered her arms and he inhaled sharply when her fingers trailed along his waistband. Bailey undid the buttons as he continued to dominate her mouth.

One. Two. Three. Four. And five. All were now undone.

She pushed his jeans down over his hips to pool at his ankles. He drew back, staring at her kiss-swollen lips for a brief second before meeting her gaze. Her golden eyes were dark with heated passion. It hit him low in the gut. The tip of her tongue snuck out and skimmed along her plump bottom lip. Ivan whipped off his shirt and allowed it to fall to the floor. Her grunt of approval preceded her hands touching his chest. He stepped out of his loafers and jeans before reaching for her again.

"You have too much on," he mumbled against her lips.

"Need help taking it off?"

He smiled. "No. I can do it just fine. Slowly. One article at a time."

"Too long." She pushed him back, ripped off her T-shirt, and shimmied out of her cotton pants. Her canvas shoes sailed in a different direction. "Now works for me."

"Damn, you're fine." His words left his mouth in Russian.

Her entire body looked to him as if she'd been dipped in luscious chocolate. His mouth watered at the prospect of tasting her. Everywhere. Her underwear were plain and unadorned. Didn't matter. A ten dollar set or an expensive purchase—he knew his response would be the same. Cellular. Visceral. Powerful.

Not even the scars sprinkled over her body could take away from her beauty. Ivan approached, reached between her full breasts and unhooked the closure. The white material fell away and he approved.

She hooked her thumbs in the waistband of her low bikini cut briefs and arched an eyebrow at him. "Change your mind?"

"Fuck no."

He stripped off his boxers, gaze remaining on her as she removed her final article of clothing. Her pussy, covered by close-cropped hair, drew his gaze. She stepped free and moved toward him.

Their mouths collided in a roar of craving. He couldn't get enough and the need that had calmed down slightly during the disrobing kicked back into high gear. Ivan grasped his cock and slowly fisted himself. She added her hand to his and he groaned.

Her touch was firm and warm. Up and down, she stroked his rigid length. He released himself and lifted her, pressing her back against the wall. She licked her lips and swiped her finger over the head of his cock, smearing the pre-cum with the pad of her thumb.

"I want in you."

She breathed hard while repositioning his cock to poise at the entrance to her pussy. He flexed his hips, their eyes locked, and drove into her. Her gasp was music to his ears. The feel of her velvet heat wrapped around him like a custom glove—heaven.

He leaned into her, pressing his lips to the base of her neck. She smelled amazing.

Bailey sank her short nails into the muscles of his back. She rotated her hips and her pupils dilated. "Yes," she hissed.

Ivan tangled one hand back in her thick hair and braced his other against the wall behind her. He began with slow, deep strokes. The fire in his veins grew with each heartbeat. The slickness surrounding him launched his need to another realm. Never had his reaction to anyone been so volatile before.

He liked it.

The sting from her nails digging into his skin spurred him on further. He leaned into her, his strokes quickening. His blood sang and he knew he wouldn't last long.

Her groans filled the air. She tightened her grip around his waist as her nails subsequently secured their position further. He captured one taut nipple, swirling his tongue over it. Her walls clenched around his cock as she gasped.

Right breast. Left breast. He paid both of them homage as he continued to thrust within her. The scent of her arousal permeated the air and it increased his desire.

She moved her hands to his head, threading her fingers through his hair. He gazed up at her when she pulled him back. Her eyes were wild with passion. He opened his mouth to speak and she shook her head. Ivan got it. No talking.

He could live with that. Still, surely screaming was allowed. And Ivan planned on having her cries reverberate off all the walls.

* * * *

Hours later, he stirred awake. Along his body pressed the soft curves of a woman. He smiled. Bailey. Their intermingled smells floated about the air.

She slept, using his shoulder as a cradle. The hair upon his skin was smooth and cool. She breathed slow and deep, resting her hand upon his bare torso. Ivan didn't even bother opening his eyes—there was no need to see they were together on the floor. It didn't matter where they'd ended up, there wasn't much room regardless.

They'd fucked on every surface. The desk. The chair. Floor. She stirred, rubbing against him, arousing him again.

"You're awake, why?" Her soft voice wove around him.

Sounds accented, perhaps Spanish. The accent was faint but he picked up on it—she hadn't had it before.

"Something woke me."

She closed her hand around his cock. "Something?"

"You could say that." He gritted his teeth as she slid down his body. Her warm breath, the forerunner to the heat of her mouth as she welcomed his cock between her lips.

Shit.

Bailey loved his taste. Salty. Male. She took more of him in, swirling her tongue around the large mushroom-shaped head. In her hand, he grew harder as she sucked and worked his length.

She bent forward and moved her hand over his shaft, her mouth having provided the wetness. Up and down she bobbed her head, her fingers drifting occasionally to tease his balls.

More. That singular word was the mantra in her mind. She craved more of everything. Tonight she was going for broke, for they had no future.

Ivan Vinokourov was her polar opposite.

He fisted his hands in her hair, his hips thrusting faster. She relaxed her jaw and let him set the pace he desired. She just enjoyed having him in her mouth. Alternating the firmness of her touch, she hummed as he increased his pace. Words she didn't understand spilled from his mouth. The emotion of them, she did.

"Almost there." The words were guttural English. They sounded forced.

She brushed off his attempt to draw her up his body — she wanted to taste his seed. Bailey grazed her teeth along his shaft. He trembled.

One final thrust, driving his cock deep, he came. Bailey kept him in her mouth until no more of his essence escaped. This time when he tugged on her, she went up and lowered herself onto his hard shaft. Capturing her lower lip in her teeth, she began to rock on him. She rotated her hips, rose and fell until she found a rhythm and speed she wanted.

Ivan laced their fingers then used his strength to tug her forward. Their lips met and she moaned into his mouth. He filled her and she closed her eyes, allowing the pleasure to wash over her. Unparalleled, it rocked her. She moved on him, breaking their lip connection. She took him in fully then lifted until just the head of his cock remained in her.

She gasped when his mouth closed over the taut nipple on her left breast. His teeth grazed it and she shuddered, her internal muscles clenching around him.

"Let go," he muttered, not releasing his hold on her flesh.

She listened. Bailey increased her speed until her own release poured over her. He followed her over the cliff and filled her with his seed. Momentarily, she held still upon him, hands now splayed on his chest. Beneath her palms, his heart pounded as hard as hers did.

"We need to get up. I have to see the captain."

Ivan narrowed his eyes and captured her hips in his large hands. "You know this man."

"Yes."

"How so?"

She began to rise only to stop when he wouldn't release his hold on her. "We've worked together before."

He held her gaze, his eyes burning with an eerie possession. It unnerved her and she climbed off him, not allowing him to stop her a second time. She made short work of cleaning up. As she fixed her pants, she glanced to her left and saw Ivan had followed suit.

"No need for you to come with me. Stay and get some rest. You'll be home soon." She shoved her feet into her shoes and pivoted to the door.

Ivan grabbed her shoulder, halting her. "That's it then?"

One eyebrow arched, she glanced back at him. "You expected more? Like what?"

"I don't know, perhaps a bit of an explanation as to why this happened?"

She shrugged. "Attraction?"

"I meant you and why you came to rescue me. Why anyone from Theta Corps did."

She opened the hatch. "I was following orders. That was my reason."

"Just following orders?" His tone had a bite to it.

"Yes." She stepped through and turned back. "I will see you in a while." Bailey shut the door in his face and strode off, nimbly avoiding the other men who traversed the tube. "Permission to—"

"Granted, Ms Hyde." The captain waved her forward.

She stepped closer, nodding at the XO and the COB before halting beside the man she'd come to speak with.

"Everything okay?" he asked, barely glancing down at her.

"Yes, sir."

"So you came just to visit?"

"I need to get word out to my boss."

"Where's your man?"

Her stomach erupted into flutters at those words. Her man. She could see herself with a man like him easily. They might not know one another that well but it didn't matter. She saw how he conducted himself. Cool. Composed. She liked that.

"I suspect the good doctor is sleeping."

"He knows not to wander?"

She shrugged. "Was I supposed to tell him not to?"

"Lord love you, Bailey. You do keep things simple."

"I find it best that way." She slipped her hands into her pockets and rolled her shoulders. A good bed and some uninterrupted sleep would be a godsend.

"We're not surfacing for a while but we're also not under radio silence. Go see Benson, he'll get the message out for you. I had some coveralls left in the room for you."

"Thank you, Captain."

He gave her a nod before responding to another's question. Bailey walked out and drew up when she found herself before the XO. He gave her a nod and she responded in kind.

"I appreciate you sharing your stateroom, Commander."

His smile was brief. "Orders are orders."

"Yes, sir. Please don't let us being there change your schedule. We can always hang out in the mess if you need your room."

"Yes, ma'am."

She sidestepped so he could move by her. "Thanks again."

"No problem." The XO walked away and she continued toward the mess. At the last moment, she adjusted her direction and went to the stateroom.

Ivan slept, the dark circles beneath his eyes telling her his experience had been more than he would admit. His blond hair tempted her to touch and the scruff along his jaw, she longed to nuzzle. Shaking off her increasing desire for him, she turned away. Allowing him to remain asleep, she drew on the poopy suit that had been left for her. It was a bit baggy, but with her clothes underneath it wasn't too horrible. She went to the enlisted mess and the room fell silent as she entered.

She glanced around before heading to grab a cup of what they affectionately referred to as 'bug juice' and drank it swiftly before getting herself some coffee. She took a seat off to the side. A couple of men raked their gazes over her and sent smug grins in her direction.

A combination of unoffended and unimpressed, she returned her attention to the cup in her hand. Although she expected the company when it arrived, she bit back her sigh of annoyance.

"What's a beautiful lady like you doing in a place like this?"

She leaned back in her chair, her fingers sprawled around the warmth seeping through her cup, and lifted her eyes to meet the sparkling green ones waiting for her. "How long have you been waiting to use that line?"

"Since I left port."

His smile showed youthful innocence and she shook her head in amusement. "First deployment?"

"Yes."

She had figured as much. Green. Cocky. He scooted his chair in a bit closer and she, well aware of the eyes watching them, waited to see what his move would be. After clearing his throat, he took a drink.

"Are you on board long?"

"Nope. Just catching a ride."

"So we'll be in port together."

She leaned closer to him. "I'll be gone by the time you are off the boat. You'll find someone when you get off." Bailey drained her coffee and stood. "Thanks for the company, sailor." With a small nod, she walked off, slipping away back to the stateroom.

She knocked lightly before pushing the door open. Ivan still slept and she observed him for a moment, taking in his rugged handsomeness. Who knew doctors were so sexy? She walked to the rack and reached out to shake him.

"Wake up, Doctor."

He rolled toward her and she fell prey to the intoxication of his gaze. That clear, pure glacial blue.

"How long have I been asleep?"

Christ, even his voice, deep and rasped, sent a tingle to her clit and nipples. She checked her watch. "A few hours."

"How long will we be on this thing?"

She watched his expression carefully. "Do you fear small spaces?"

"Fear? I wouldn't go so far as to say that. Not a fan, but not fearful."

Bailey held his stare for fifteen seconds before she glanced about them. "You'll be fine then. The time will pass swiftly and you'll be out of the tube."

He got up then stepped closer to her, his scent surrounding her and creating a purely physical reaction in her body. She swallowed back the moan threatening to escape. He was lethal to her.

"So what is there for us to do on here?"

"Nothing. We stay out of their way. When the XO wants his stateroom, we give it to him, even if it means sitting for a while in the mess."

His grin was brief but slightly possessive. "I'm all yours to do with as you see fit."

"Nothing will happen between us, Doctor. That was an anomaly, you know, an odd —"

"I know what an anomaly is, Bailey." He reached out and dragged his knuckles along her jaw line, eyes full of a blend of tenderness and determination.

Tiny sparks of desire lit her skin where he touched.

"I also know what was between us. If you want to call that an anomaly, then it's only because of the amount of passion between us. The connection. I *felt* you within me and that's never happened with anyone else before."

Hasn't happened with me before either. She ensured her expression remained bland. "Was is your key word. I came to rescue you. Nothing more. As soon as you're off this sub, I'm gone."

"Why?"

Bailey blinked up at the towering Russian who had invaded more than just her personal space. He'd left his imprint on her. "Why?" Her mind wasn't cooperating.

"That's what I asked. Why does this have to end once we land?" Another stroke of his fingers. "We have something unique and special, Bailey. You can't deny it."

Oh, yes she could. And would. Ignoring her body's determination that she give in to his lure, she ducked away from him and said, "I have to make a call. I'll see you later." She strode off and refused to glance back, even once.

Chapter Four

"Dr Vinokourov!"

Ivan drew up short at the sound of his name. Squinting through the thick fog that surrounded the wharf, he frowned when the shape materialized into the figure of the man who'd shown up at Christmas Island. Kevin McNeal.

The morning was cold and the clanging of buoys sent further chills through him. Ivan peered back over his shoulder to the black shadow along the pier. The submarine was impressive, no denying it. No sign of Bailey, though. She'd vanished when word had come down the pipe they were going to be docking soon. He hadn't seen her. Anywhere.

He waited until McNeal stopped beside him. "You know, last time I saw you I was kidnapped soon after."

"I am sorry about that but it was out of my hands."

"Where's Bailey?"

McNeal rocked back on his heels. "Gone, I suspect. Woman rarely sticks around once her job is done."

Ivan didn't like that. He wanted to see her. Hold her. Kiss her. *Get a grip and stop crying after her like a bitch.* His mental pep talk wasn't appreciated in any way.

"How do I get in touch with her?"

McNeal barely blinked. "You don't. Let's go. I have a car waiting."

"So, what, because you sent her to get me you think I'll join your little group?" They began walking up the long quay.

"I had no such thoughts. What exactly do you think our 'little' group does, Doctor?"

What he wouldn't give for a comfortable bed and a long, hot shower. "I don't think about it at all." Why would he? If he did eventually, it all came back to Jaydee and that hurt.

"Perhaps you should."

Ivan paused at the trunk of the black sedan. "And why is that?"

McNeal gave a slight smile, unlocked the vehicle and said, "Get in."

Ivan sank into the leather seat and buckled his belt. "Where are we going?"

"I have a hotel room for you. I'd like you to actually agree to hear my offer and not wave me off as you did before. Once you hear it, you can make your decision. Then we'll go from there."

"You're not concerned with what I may have done for the ones who kidnapped me?"

"Bailey said it had all been destroyed." He didn't take his eyes off the road.

Ivan tipped his head to look at the man driving. "She did?" He stared back out of the windshield and watched the way the headlights split the fog. Hell, he didn't even know where he was. They passed a guardhouse and continued.

"She did." Kevin's comment came after a few moments of quiet.

Ivan got it—this man wasn't a chatty person. They finished the drive in silence. He allowed the heat to sink in and banish the chill the dampness along the pier had created inside him. Not a single other vehicle on the road gave him a clue as to where he was.

Kevin pulled into the parking lot of a hotel and whipped into an empty spot. The two men climbed out and headed to the front of the building. Ivan followed him to the elevators and up to the fifth floor.

At room five twenty-four, Kevin unlocked the door and pushed it open before handing the key card to Ivan. "There are some clothes in there that will fit you. I'll be down at the bar once you get settled."

The man left without another word. Ivan watched him until he stepped into the elevator. Ivan locked the door behind him even as he took in the comfort before him. A very nice hotel room. A burgundy bedspread covered a king-sized bed full of pillows. Lying upon that were three suits and some other clothes, jeans and such.

Ivan picked through until he got what he wished to wear then he went to the bathroom and turned on the water. Staring at his clothing, he sneered as he removed them. They stank. He stank. Sure, there had been a shower on the sub but he'd needed longer than a quick one to get rid of the smells.

He stepped under the hot water and groaned in pleasure. Bracing his hands on the tile, he dipped his head, allowing the raining drops to cascade over him. He stayed that way until his tense muscles began to relax. Then he reached for the washcloth and lathered it up.

I wish I could have Bailey in a shower like this. I'd love to bend her over and take her in here. Or press her up against the tile wall and fuck her until neither of us can stand any longer.

His cock twitched and he didn't even fight the need, just curled his fingers around himself. The soap on his hand allowed him to glide with ease up and down his penis. He pinched the head of his cock then began stroking. Alternating the pressure and speed, he built up his need until he was ready to shoot his load. Eyes squeezed shut, he envisioned the woman who'd come to save his life and who'd given him the best sex he'd ever experienced. Bailey.

Ivan came with a low, keening shout. Thick ropes of his cum shot from his throbbing cock and landed on the wall in front of him. He continued jacking himself until none more came. Legs weak, he muttered a curse before cleaning up and getting out of the water.

Within ten minutes, he stood in the elevator and pressed the button for the lobby. Alone in the lift, he leaned against the wall and shoved his hands in the pockets of the jeans he had opted to wear.

He walked through the lobby and found the bar. Once in there, it didn't take him long to find Kevin. The man sat at a booth near the back. Ivan nodded at a waitress and made his way to sit opposite Kevin.

"I'm here. What's your spiel?"

"Drink?"

A waitress—the same one he'd nodded at when he walked in—stood at the table. She bent over, showing him her cleavage as she placed a bowl of chips and some salsa between them.

"Beer. A lager. Whatever you have on tap is fine."

"Coming right up, handsome." She smiled and walked off, an extra swing in her hips.

Ivan popped a chip in his mouth and waited. Kevin swirled the liquid in his glass. "Theta Corps is a group that operates to keep the country, and the world, safe from danger."

He ate another chip and fought off a yawn. That king-sized bed had sure looked inviting.

"We do things others can't because of red tape. We have a research department that I want you to work with. Your knowledge, as I said before, of electrogravitics would be invaluable to us. We need to provide our field agents with the best equipment. The newest tech. They're often in situations where they have no backup and no sure way out."

Ivan smiled at the server when she returned with his drink. Once she'd left, he took a sip. "And you want my knowledge?"

"Yes. The pay is astronomical. You wouldn't be in danger. The lab we'd provide to you would be state of the art. You can staff it how you want, if you decide you'd like other people to work with you other than the ones we already have. You need different equipment, ask and it will be provided for you." Kevin leaned forward. "You've heard the expression 'we'll spare no expense', I'm sure, Doctor. That's what I'm promising you. It would be your lab and you'd have carte blanche on what to put in it."

So sue him, he was beyond intrigued. "Why me?"

"I told you. I've heard about you from Valentino Cassano. Your name was second on the list behind a Dr Thompson, and tied with Jaydee Cassano."

"And what did Jaydee say?"

"We came to you first. She's a mother of triplets. We didn't feel she would have the time to devote to projects."

He leaned back and drummed his fingers on the table. "So Valentino told you to stay away from her."

Kevin shrugged.

Ivan contained his laughter. He knew those brothers and how closely they looked after one another's wives. "What's in it for me? I mean, why would I want to work for you instead of, say, who I was with before?"

"Because we're the good guys."

"I'm sure they think they are as well."

"They are out to destroy the world and create their own haven of chaos."

"I'm sure they'd say the same about you."

Kevin scowled. "What did they tell you to make?"

"Devices to drop bombs. Ones like jet packs to carry their men."

"See?"

"See what? They were honest. Can you promise me what I create or make won't be used to do similar things?"

His companion narrowed his eyes. "See, I'm a scientist, Mr McNeal. I know the stigma—geeky, nerdy, whatever—but never assume I'm stupid when it comes to how things work."

"I know what your IQ is, Doctor, and I wouldn't ever deem to call you stupid or assume you were lacking in mental capacity."

"Omitting the truth is still a lie. If I were to do this, I would want to know the exact application it would be used for. No matter what I worked on."

"Okay, I can see that happens."

"Where would I have to go?"

"We have divisions all over the world. Where do you want to go?"

"Russia?"

Kevin finished his drink. "We have one in Moscow and one in Vladivostok."

"Vladivostok."

"It can be arranged."

"I haven't said yes, yet."

"What will it take for you to say yes?"

"Bailey."

Kevin furrowed his brow. "I'm sorry?"

"You heard me. Is this near where Bailey is?"

"No."

"Where is she?"

Kevin shook his head.

"I want to be near her."

"What happened between the two of you?"

"None of your business. Where is she?"

Kevin scanned the room before resting his forearms on the tabletop. "Dr Vinokourov, let me tell you something. Bailey doesn't have an office like you or I would. She doesn't just work in one place."

"Why not?" He took another drink. "Not that it matters. I want to be by her. She's my deal breaker. If I don't get her—and I'm not meaning you have to tell her to marry me, I can win a woman on my own, but I need to be near her—then we don't have a deal."

"I told you, we don't have a lab near her."

He shrugged without remorse. "Money is no object you said, so build one. That's what I want."

"Same city she goes to will work for you? Well, one of them."

He didn't like the sound of that but he had to start somewhere. Perhaps he could hack into their system later on to find out where she was if it happened to be a different city. "Yes. I'll find her."

Kevin muttered something under his breath that sounded distinctly like he doubted it. "She's not going to be happy."

"Why? Is she married?"

"Nope. She's a private person."

"What does she do for Theta Corps?"

Kevin stood up. "I truly hope you know what you're doing, Ivan. I can't protect you from her. She's an assassin." Kevin McNeal walked off.

An assassin? Ivan didn't know how to process that immediately and so he remained there and drank. Perhaps this wouldn't go well.

* * * *

Santiago, Chile

Bailey grunted as she finished her pull-ups. *I hate these things. Hate them, hate them, hate them.* She dropped to the ground with a wince, her arms screaming in agony. "Have I said how much I hate these damn things?"

The warm sunlight streamed into her window hitting the numerous dust particles that floated through the air of the room she used as her gym. She wiped the sweat off her forehead with the back of her hand while she made her way to the waiting bottle of water and towel.

On her last mission—the one after Ivan—she'd tweaked her arm because it hadn't been strong enough and she realized her physical conditioning had begun to weaken. She wasn't willing to allow that to become an issue when she was out on another assignment. So she'd upped her program and currently was paying for it. Every inch of her ached.

She showered upstairs and dressed before sitting at her square table in boxers and a camisole. Laid out before her were bullets and gunpowder. For the next few hours, she made her own ammo, lacing them with poison. That way, even a scratch would take care of the job if she had a weak angle or a bad shot. With her gloves and mask on, she added the boric acid powder to each one before she pressed it.

The dust was irritating to mucous membranes and led to death. A death that could be immediate when swallowed. She would use this as a backup just in case the bullet didn't end up where she had intended.

Like that's going to happen. Bailey was a perfectionist and hated even being a degree off target. She worked hard to hone her craft, spending numerous hours at the range, fabricating odd situations that one day she might or might not find herself in. Anything to push her limits. High winds, extreme cold, whatever she could think up—she tried to create it and still find a way to hit her target.

Smooth jazz, more specifically Art Porter Jr, played in the background as she worked. This was her downtime. It relaxed her. One by one, she refilled her magazines and the bullet cases she kept. Normally it took one bullet for the job but Bailey much preferred to be prepared than caught unawares and needing more.

As she continued to fill, press and store her bullets, her mind traveled to the handsome Russian. Ivan. Dr Vinokourov. Her eyelids fluttered as desire washed over her and her hands trembled. Exhaling sharply, she laid down the items in her hand and took several deep breaths, trying to steady the pounding of her heart.

It had been so real, her memory of the experience in his arms. For a moment there, she'd been back with him, the scent of his skin all around her. Their mingled smells on the sheets and in the air.

For a scientist who spent most of his time in a lab, he sure had nice muscles. Being in his embrace had created one specific word to travel through her mind—safety. No, it wasn't the only word but never before had she been with a man where that word had made an appearance.

"Like it's going to do me any good to think about him. I did my job and we're done with one another. No matter how much I relive being in bed with him."

She'd spoken with Kevin a few times since she'd last seen Ivan and had made it a point not to ask about him. Her suspicions were up, however, because Kevin seemed to call more often than he normally did.

After sliding the .45s and the .357 back in their appropriate boxes, she pushed back from the table. Bailey cleaned up the boric acid, removed her mask then peeled off her gloves. Sure none of it had got on her, she lifted the boxes and walked to the floor safe, which currently sat open. Crouched, she placed them in their respective spots and double-checked all her other weapons. Knives, daggers, her sniper rifle, even two garrotes.

When she walked back into the kitchen, the floor was completely solid and no one would be able to tell there was a safe there. It took up four tile spots and so the outline was hidden in plain sight.

She had a few apartments all over the world and each one had a secret safe that held her gear. Identical items, for she had her favorites to use and wanted access to those no matter where she was deployed from.

Bailey poured herself a cold drink then set about getting ready to go out. She strapped on her weapons and tied on her shoes. There were parts in this city that were extremely dangerous. She had no intention of coming across as a victim anywhere she went.

After exiting her apartment, she locked the door and shoved the keys in her pocket. The sun shined down and she tipped her head back to enjoy the warm rays. All around her, the cacophonous noise from the city rose and fell as if conducted in its own opera.

She began walking, smiling at the children who played ball in the streets. When she slowed down along the market street and began looking for anything that might whet her appetite, her phone rang.

She retrieved it from a pocket and peered at the screen. McNeal. She typed her code and took the call with her earpiece. "Yes?"

"How are you?"

She picked up a chirimoya and tested it for ripeness. The lemony-vanilla custard taste was one she craved when away. "Am I needed?" Bailey picked six of them and the woman placed them in a bag for her. Money exchanged hands and with a smile, Bailey continued on her way.

"I'm merely trying to see how you're doing. It's not like you hung around when the sub docked."

"It wasn't common for me to go in and rescue anyone either. I don't like doing it."

"I need to see you."

"Aren't you in the States?"

"No."

Figures. She gestured for the loaf of bread she wanted and paid for that as well. "Same hotel as you were at before?"

"Yes."

"I'll be there in two hours." She ended the call before he could say anything else. "Thank you," she told the young woman who gave her change. "Good to see you again, Dulcinea."

"You were gone for a while," she replied with a slight smile. Dulcinea swiftly covered up the burn marks on her hand, which had been exposed, and readjusted her hair to hide the eye patch over her left eye.

"I went to visit some family," Bailey spoke the lie without blinking.

"We will have special in two days." A grin. "You come back then. Get good deal."

"I'll be back. Thanks for this."

"Bye, Bailey."

She waved and kept on going, shopping as she progressed. Twice she slowed and scanned the market. The most unsettling feeling skated up her spine. Being watched.

When she finally flagged down a cab to take her to the hotel, she sat where she could see behind her and made sure no one followed. Bags in hand, and only slightly less uncomfortable, she walked into the hotel Kevin stayed at when he was in town.

She watched him as he unfurled his long body and rose from the chair he'd occupied. His dark skin complemented his light linen attire. Kevin moved with a sinewy grace and she knew he could more than take care of himself. She kept her gaze fixed on his facial features. This wasn't a social call.

"I have a table for us."

She fell into step with him silently. There wouldn't be a big welcome—neither of them operated that way. She knew he cared about the men and women beneath him but as far as she knew—or cared to know—he was strictly professional about it. If he was with someone in the agency, she hadn't any clue.

They walked outside back into the warmth and settled at a table near the gate separating the outdoor café from the passers-by. Her purchases beneath by her feet, she waited for him to talk.

Kevin didn't speak until the time to place their order came. He ordered and once she'd given hers, they were again left alone.

"We're waiting on one more person. Two actually."

"Okay." She turned her gaze to take in the hillside dotted with numerous shanty buildings.

"McNeal," a man with a deep southern accent spoke.

Bailey looked over the guy who stood there. His body strong and capable. Unending muscles. She took more than one look. A dark billed cap hid his gaze from her and she wondered what color his eyes were. The way the jeans and T-shirt covered him nearly had her smiling. His woman was lucky. Or his man.

Beside him stood a woman with vibrant red hair. Her tanned skin was exposed, given the outfit she wore. A short white skirt displayed long toned legs and her black peep-toe booties with a stunning cut-out design highlighted them. They had a four and a half inch heel. Her shirt was black and silver.

And still... Bailey got the sense this woman was more than she appeared to be. Her eyes were sharp and assessed everything she saw. If Bailey had to put money on it, she would bet they were agents.

"Please, sit."

The newcomer looked at her briefly before complying with Kevin's statement. He sat on her left and the woman on her right.

Kevin peered around the table. "Bailey, this here is Anabelle Lee and her cousin Beauregard. They work for Theta Corps as well. With Valentino Cassano. Guys, this is Bailey Hyde."

She'd heard of them and gave them both a nod, one the redhead returned. Beauregard removed his hat. He had blond-brown hair and killer green eyes.

"Ma'am."

That there is a bedroom voice if I ever heard one.

"Heard of the both of you. An honor to meet you both." She fell silent when their food was delivered. While the other two ordered, she added salt to her plate.

They were alone again after the waiter left and she waited for Kevin to say what she was doing here, along with why they were here.

"I've heard about you as well," Anabelle Lee said.

All three of them watched her and Bailey ate a forkful of her sea bass before wiping her mouth and leaning back in her chair. "I don't do social calls so why don't we get to the crux of why you're here."

"We need your help." Beauregard held her gaze directly as he spoke.

"You need my help? With all the connections and equipment Theta Corps has at its disposal?"

"My cousin, her brother, is missing."

She flicked her stare to Anabelle Lee, whose expression had gone from bored and nearly flirty to cold and deadly.

"Missing for how long and why come to me about it? If you've heard of me, you know I—" Bailey snapped her mouth shut. She did find people occasionally.

Beauregard cleared his throat and leaned forward with an easy ripple of muscles. Bailey watched him, partially because he was just that mesmerizing and partly because she didn't know him.

"I know this isn't typically your thing but you know the area and we could really use your help."

She canted her head to the side. "Wait, you think he's here?"

"There was chatter." Anabelle Lee stirred her drink with her straw, the ice clicking and clanking against the side of the glass.

Chatter. Bailey understood. There was always chatter.

"Leave me a picture and I'll see what I can come up with." Bailey finished off her meal and wiped her mouth. "I have to go. It was good to meet the both of you and I'm sorry it was under these circumstances."

She made her way to the door, money left on the table to cover her meal. The redhead fell into step beside her. Outside the hotel, Bailey paused and looked up at her.

"Are you as good as they say?" Anabelle Lee questioned without any derision in her tone.

"How good do they say I am?"

"Stone-cold killer."

"Not really an indicative statement as to how good someone is." She shrugged and readjusted her hold on the bags. "Still, it's accurate. I am."

"Good. You find the ones holding them and we can't get back quick enough. I want you to kill them. All."

"You misunderstand, I'm not for hire. I work for Theta Corps. I kill sanctioned targets."

"These fuckers took my brother. I'll pay you whatever, even if it's to wound them and keep them until I get here. They will die and pay for what they've done."

Despite them being close to the equator, the ice in Anabelle Lee's tone made it arctic. Bailey nodded. "I'll be in touch." She walked away, no doubt in her mind the words she'd just heard were one hundred percent the truth. Whenever that woman found those who'd taken her brother, they would die. Moreover, it wouldn't be a pleasant death.

Chapter Five

Ivan stared out of the window of his new apartment. The past few months had been extremely time-consuming as he'd overseen the creation of his new lab. Kevin hadn't lied or even blinked when Ivan had sent in the sheets of what he wanted and needed.

The facility resided in the countryside and was built underground with an organic farm over the top of it. Locals came to work there and none were any wiser about what went on below the ground they farmed upon. It was truly amazing how much could be done when big chunks of money were involved.

The chime of his cell had him tensing. A specific ring for a special and unique person. He hesitated before he answered.

"Hi, stranger." Ivan spoke Russian, as he preferred to do.

"You have been avoiding me." She, too, spoke his native language.

"You have a husband and children."

Jaydee scoffed slightly. "Should I then insinuate that to mean *we* are no longer friends?" Her reprimand was obvious.

"Of course not."

"Then your reasoning for ignoring me?"

"We've gone substantial periods of time without speaking. We are both busy."

"Not when one of us is recruited by Theta Corps."

Of course she'd know that. "You've worked for different groups before."

She was silent. "You have changed, Ivan."

"Did you think I wouldn't after you turned down my marriage proposal?" He heard the lingering anger in his tone. Frustrated, he shook his head.

"We were friends."

"I know. But you're a wife and mother now."

"And capable of being a friend."

Ivan had to give Gio credit for this change in her. Prior to marrying that man, she never would have cared one way or the other if they hadn't spoken in a while. Her husband was good for her, he knew that. *Still doesn't make it any less painful she chose him over me.*

"I always considered you one, Jaydee. That will never change, but I needed space. Need space. I don't compartmentalize as you do."

"I understand. Goodbye, Ivan."

Their call ended and he lowered his cell back to his pocket. He stared at the wall and sighed before raking his hand through his hair. He missed his friendship with her but out of respect for her new life, he had backed away. Sure, some of it was his disappointment at losing her. But lately when he closed his eyes, it wasn't Jaydee who lay with him. It was Bailey.

His lips curved up as he smiled. Her memory always brought one to his face. He hadn't seen her yet and Kevin had said she had more than one apartment around the world so he couldn't promise when she'd be at the one in this city.

Ivan didn't mind. He was determined to find her. He relocated and sat out on his balcony, feet propped up on the railing.

An assassin. She wasn't what he pictured as one.

Granted, I've never met an assassin before so what do I know about what they should be like?

He'd had femme fatales or dark, swarthy people as shown in movies on his mind. Sure, Bailey could be a femme fatale but she didn't wear tight clothes as they did in shows he'd seen.

"I need to get a life." He stood and leaned over the balcony railing. His place was on the third floor and he overlooked the market. The vendor calls, food scents and more filled the air. Staring down at the crowd, his heart skipped a beat.

As if his thoughts had conjured her up, there she was. Bailey.

She meandered through the throng of people, bags in hand. A medium blue tight-fitting shirt bearing a vibrant pink flower had been paired with charcoal gray shorts. Her tennis shoes were a blend of gray with pink piping.

For a heartbeat, he hesitated. Could he be imagining this was her? She paused at the flower stall, talked and laughed with the woman and eventually pointed out a bouquet.

"Bailey!"

She never turned and he cursed, realizing she probably couldn't hear him over the crowd. He whirled and ran for the door, swiping his keys along the way. This woman—his reason for being here—was close. Ivan had no intention of letting her go.

He ran down the three flights and burst out into the afternoon, nimbly avoiding another tenant who was entering. "Excuse me," he muttered, pushing through the people as he hurried across the street.

Bailey lingered at the stall. Her hair hung in a thick braid down her back. He recommitted her to his memory. He moved up behind her.

"Hello, Bailey."

Their eyes met when she looked over her shoulder. Her golden gaze widened slightly before she smiled.

"Ivan. What are you doing here?"

He hadn't been sure what her reaction to seeing him again would be so this acceptance was a welcome surprise.

"Hopefully escorting you to your apartment." He took the bags she had in her right hand from her. "And catching up."

"Interesting," she uttered before turning back to the vendor.

He remained quiet as she paid and put the flowers in another bag. When she faced him fully, he worked hard to control his groan of desire. What was it about this woman that affected him so?

"Where do you live?"

"Why so anxious to discover my home, Doctor?"

He stepped closer to her and dipped his head so their lips almost touched. "Because I missed you and I can't give you a proper welcome out here in public." He grinned wickedly. "Well, I could, but I don't know if you'd want me to."

Her expression didn't change. She backed up and walked around him. "Come on then."

While not sure that was a ringing endorsement about her joy at seeing him again, he fell into step behind her until her ass was too much of a distraction and he walked beside her.

"What brings you to South America, Doctor?"

"I live here now." He sidestepped a young girl selling cloth.

"You work here? There's a lab here for a doctor of your abilities?"

"You know what I do?"

"I was given a file on you." She stopped and perused another stall, one of jewelry this time. He waited patiently for her to finish.

"So you know all there is to know about me?"

"Probably." Her comment was straightforward and matter-of-fact.

Ivan waited for her while she spoke Spanish to the woman and haggled for the earrings she ended up purchasing.

"How is it you know so much about me and I know so little about you?" He posed his question once they began walking again.

"It's my job to know about a target."

"A target?"

"It's what you were. My target. Granted, most times I'm sighting mine through a scope, but to me it's all the same."

"That's right, you're an" — he lowered his voice — "assassin."

"Does that disgust you, Doctor?"

"I'd be lying if I said it wasn't a bit unnerving but no, it doesn't disgust me."

They turned up another street and he noticed how people, while watching them closely, didn't try anything. *I wonder if they know her job as well.*

A few more winds and turns where he watched her share the food she'd purchased and give the earrings to a young girl. They eventually made it to a yellow building that she entered. She led him down the hall and through a nondescript door.

Her place was a cheery yellow. The hue was bright and reflected the sun that poured in through the windows and small balcony door. She placed her bags on the counter and he turned around, taking it all in.

Once his hands were free and she stood before him, he reached for her. Bailey stepped back with a slight shake of her head. "Talk first."

"Then what?"

"We go from there."

"So you're telling me what I felt in the sub was just me?"

"I didn't say that at all. I said talk first. I want to know the truth about why you're here."

All business. Like the woman who'd saved him from those Chechens.

"I told you, I work here now."

"For Theta Corps."

He nodded. She walked to the fridge and withdrew two bottles. After popping their tops, she handed one to him. Grateful for the drink, he took a long swallow of the fizzy beverage.

"They don't have a headquarters here."

"Kevin built me a lab here."

Her eyes narrowed slightly. "That farm outside of town on the east side. That's where it is."

"I'm impressed. How did you figure it out?"

She wiped the back of her hand over her mouth. "I've worked for Theta for a while now. Why here?"

"Why here what?" Lord he wanted to touch her. Revel in her smooth skin, her curves and taste the sweetness of her lips.

"Why did you have it built here?"

He glanced around and found the nearest surface. Once his drink rested there, he strode toward her, not slowing even at her quick step back. Cupping her face in his hands, Ivan kissed her. He ran his tongue along the seam of her mouth before she opened and he slid inside.

Her familiar taste hit him and he groaned as she did. Their breaths mingled and she pressed closer to him, her curves fitting perfectly against his body. When her arms wound around his neck, he allowed his eyes to close. Her whimper had him separating their lips by a hair's breadth.

"For that reason."

That is one hell of a reason.

It would be so nice to give in to the need raking her. She didn't understand how this one man could strip away all her common sense and make her think of nothing but the way he'd filled her as his cock had moved within her, and the rasp of his stubble upon the sensitive skin of her inner thighs while he'd masterfully eaten her pussy.

So why don't you? She didn't need her brain's commentary or to fall prey to her body's demand.

She couldn't. Not right now. With deep regret, she pulled away from him. Ivan retained hold of her arms.

He gazed down at her, eyes tumultuous with a wide range of emotions. Bailey cleared her throat and averted her head, severing their visual connection.

"Kind of a crazy reason to come to a country."

"Not really."

"You didn't even know I'd be here."

"He said you had an apartment here. Figured with an apartment comes the highly logical aspect you'd be here sooner or later.

McNeal has said a lot. "So based on that, you move here, not even with the knowledge of where my apartment is?"

"I picked near the market. Kevin said you liked the market. Figured my odds were substantial to find you."

I think I need to have a chat with McNeal about being so chatty when it comes to my living conditions. A short chuckle burst from her. "You're crazy."

His grin created flutters in both her belly and loins. "I'm a scientist and I prefer the term determined. Or hopeful."

"I thought as a scientist you dealt in tangibles." She crossed her arms. "Facts."

His eyes twinkled with what she would only describe as trouble. "I do. Fact one. You are sometimes an occasional resident of this city. Fact two. Living near the market increased my chances of seeing you again. Fact three. I am a man who's not felt what you made him feel in years, if ever, and I have no wish to lose that."

Ivan stepped back, his touch falling away and leaving her bereft. While a struggle, she managed not to reach out and touch him.

"Three facts."

"Would more make you feel better?"

"Not particularly." She rocked back on her heels. "Is that it?"

He arched an eyebrow. "Coldness won't push me away, Bailey."

"You expected me to be all over you?"

"Had kind of hoped for you to remember how irresistible you found me."

She couldn't help the grin spreading over her face. Ivan amused her like no other. "I do," she admitted. "Make no mistake about that."

"So then, have we talked enough?"

Had any other man spoken those words to her, she would have been pissed off. But Ivan had this air about him. She ran her tongue along the bottom of her top teeth. Raked her gaze over his firm body. *Why can't I indulge myself?* "Sure, no reason to remain chatty."

He ripped off his shirt and lobbed it to his left. "Chatty is fine. Feel free to vocalize just how much you enjoy what I'm about to do to you."

"Sounds promising." She removed her shirt. "I do hope you deliver."

His grin was sin incarnate. Ivan reached out and hooked his index finger into her bra. He tugged her forward. She went willingly. He plucked the flower from her hair, dragging it over the swell of her breasts, down the valley and across her belly.

Her gut clenched as need crashed over her. The silken caress of the petals tantalized her oversensitive skin. Locked immobile by his gaze, she witnessed his own increased breathing. His pupils dilated. The pulse on his neck kicked.

"Come here." His command fell from his lips like honey. Sweet and tempting.

She listened, stepping close and sliding her palms along his abs and around to his lower back. His warm skin heated her further.

Her clit throbbed in time with her heart, her nipples drawing tight. She dug her fingers into the muscles of his back as she wobbled.

"Ivan."

"I do love it when my name falls from your lips in that deep sexy moan you have."

If she wasn't careful, she would fall for him easily. So easily.

"Keep going and I promise, I'll give you more."

"That's a promise I intend to hold you to."

"Good." She yanked him close. "Let's get to it."

Ivan gently kissed the tip of her nose. He cupped her ass and lifted her, carrying her to the wall. The sunlight fell around them.

He pressed her into the solidness and made sure there was no space between them. His hard cock rubbed her pussy, the friction of her shorts heightening her pleasure. She leaned forward and allowed herself the joy of his taste.

Salty skin. Masculine taste. Heady and addictive.

Kissing down his torso, she repositioned her hands to the waistband of her pants. He captured one wrist and lifted it over her head. Ivan did a slow grind against her pelvis as he simultaneously positioned her arm above her head. Her breathing hitched as another moan slid free.

"Hands up."

Bailey released his pants and placed her other hand beside the one he'd put there.

"Hold the wall. Don't let go."

Lower lip firmly lodged between her teeth, she nodded. His smile created more trembling in her limbs. He brushed his knuckles along the tops of her breasts before he sank to his knees.

Head tipped so she could see him, Bailey waited impatiently. The tips of his blond hair were slightly lighter and she struggled against the urge to slip her hands in the strands.

He kissed her belly then unfastened her shorts. His breath fanned out over her exposed skin. The air, along with the normal sounds around her apartment, filled with the faint rasp of the material sliding down her legs. She held her breath as he removed her panties.

It didn't matter if people across the way could see them. Nothing but his touch did. He stood, fingers trailing along the outsides of her thighs. His gaze was hooded and sensual yet intense in a way she'd not seen before. She waited. He removed his own remaining clothing. His boxer briefs were the last thing to go. She dampened her lips as his cock burst into view. Long. Hard. Thick.

Her pussy clenched and she stifled a whimper of need. She wanted to touch him. Sink to her knees and take him deep in her mouth.

He said not to move.

Ivan reached out, cupped her and drove two fingers inside her wetness. Her cry ripped up from the bottom of her gut and her hips jerked forward.

"More!" A tremor overtook her. "Ivan! God, give me more."

His pistoned his fingers and she came hard. Legs weak and heart pounding, she depended on the wall she leaned against. Ivan withdrew and brought his hand to his mouth. Her belly tightened when his tongue snuck out and licked her juices from one finger.

"You, Bailey, taste exquisite." He placed his finger at her mouth. "Taste."

She opened and drew his digit in. His gaze darkened. When he pulled his finger out, she dragged her teeth along it.

"Wouldn't you agree?"

Bailey flexed her muscles and shrugged. "I prefer your taste."

He clenched his jaw and lowered his hand. Fisting his cock, Ivan used his thumb to smear the pre-cum.

"What are your feelings on mingled tastes?"

"Yes." Her response was breathy. "Inside me, Ivan. Now."

"Bossy woman."

"I'm a trained killer. Don't piss me off."

He placed the head of his cock against her. "Are you threatening me if I don't fuck you?"

She hooked a leg around his waist and rubbed. The move brought him closer. "Think of it as encouragement."

Another thick inch filled her.

"I don't need any of that to get inside you. I see you and I want to fuck you. Want to feel your heat around me. Your tight muscles squeezing my cock. Doesn't matter, day or night. I want to fuck you."

He lifted her and carried her to the windowsill. Each step pushed him deeper inside her so he sat completely buried when they reached the cushioned sill.

He wrapped his left arm around her shoulders and nuzzled her neck. Back and forth he thrust as he guided her left leg up so her ankle rested on his shoulder. His strong grip dug into her back. It was claiming. Possessive. Proprietary. She didn't mind in the least.

"Ivan!"

His hips continued to move, his actions keeping her teetering on the edge of the pleasure that waited for her. His approach didn't waver. He teased and tormented her, his cock sliding in then out, varying speeds and depth.

She buried her face in his skin and nipped as her rollercoaster of cruising between heaven and hell continued. He kept her craving until she wasn't sure how much more she could withstand.

"Ivan, please!"

"You don't get to rush me, Bailey. I've missed you and I plan on taking my time."

Ivan wasn't lying—he maintained a gut-wrenching pace. All her nerves burned as if they'd been dropped into a volcano. Her throat raw from her cries, she screamed in relief when he allowed her to go over and embrace what she'd sought.

Back bowing, she milked his cock and rumbled in pleasure when she felt his ropes of cum shoot into her. Ivan slanted his mouth over hers and kissed her. Their tongues slipped along each other and she shook from exhaustion. Against her chest, his heart pounded just as hard.

"Again," he muttered into her mouth.

She maneuvered her hand to the nape of his neck and lightly raked her nails along it. "Hell yes."

Chapter Six

The sunlight woke him and Ivan stretched with a groan before looking for the woman who'd fallen asleep in bed with him. She wasn't there. He was alone in the double bed.

Pity. His cock lifted the sheet and he ignored it, opting instead to roll free. He peered around the room and found his jeans. After pulling them on, he left the top two buttons undone and set out to find his woman.

I'm claiming her already? He nodded. He was. *I didn't move across the world to let her get away.*

He stepped into the main living area and found her putting away a tall black piece of machinery. "Morning."

"Sleep well?" She rolled up the newsprint that had covered the table and carried it to the trash.

"I did. What are you doing up?"

"I was working." She flashed him a smile over her shoulder. "Are you hungry?"

"I could eat." His attention went back to the press machine. "What were you doing?"

She washed her hands. "Making bullets."

Ivan froze at her words. *How easy it is for me to forget she kills people.* She spoke her words so casually, so matter-of-fact. While he pondered that thought, he joined her in the kitchen.

Bailey chopped up some fruit, the knife moving with swiftness. The sun glinted off the gold ribbons that she'd woven into her hair. There was something different about her.

"You're staring at me." She dumped the diced fruit into a bowl and reached for more. "Why?"

"There's something about you."

Her pink shorts with white stripes stopped high on her toned thighs. The white shirt hung loosely over her upper body.

"Different from before."

"I like to be able to relax between"—she paused when her cell rang and she glanced at it briefly—"my jobs."

Jobs. Assassinations.

She stopped chopping and lifted her head, gaze guileless. "What I do, it bothers you."

"Never met anyone so cavalier about killing."

She popped a piece of fruit into her mouth. "Is there a specific way I should be about it?"

Good question. "Nope. I just forget you, Bailey Hyde, are not typical. Not sure why I forget—most people I hang out with are different in one way or another."

"And you expected me to be typical?"

"You're not a scientist," he said by way of explanation.

If he'd wanted her to ask more questions, he was in for a world of surprise. He leaned against her counter and stole a piece of fruit for himself. For a while, the only sound was that of her chopping.

"For a minute there I forgot that not only scientists have their quirks."

She briefly met his gaze and blinked.

"You're such a one-eighty from the woman who took me out of that place, drove me out into the ocean where a submarine picks us up and we leave the motorboat burning. Everything about you was serious."

She twirled the knife in her fingers. "And it's bad I'm not serious now?"

He sucked the juice off his thumb. "Not at all. Just amazed how complete the change is."

Her eyebrows rose and fell before she flipped the knife into the cutting board. The tip embedded into the wooden block. Ivan shifted his weight, suddenly uncertain.

"Make no mistake, Ivan, just because I'm not dressed in cargo pants and a tank with guns attached doesn't mean I'm any less capable."

He crooked his finger at her. She approached as far as the counter would let her. "I'm not a fool, Bailey. I see what you do. I know you don't operate a sewing shop or sit in a lab every day as I do. None of that matters to me."

She canted her head to the side. "So what was the purpose of mentioning all this?"

"Just an observation, my dear."

She blinked and pointed to the cupboard to her left. "Grab the plates."

He did and followed her out to the small balcony where they sat at the table there. She placed the bowl of fruit down, returned inside then came back carrying some bread and yogurt.

"Do you want some juice or is coffee going to be enough?"

"Coffee is fine. No, stay, I can get it. You don't need to wait on me, Bailey. Eat. I'll be right back."

He stood in her tiny kitchen and poured the java into their mugs. He knew how she liked hers and added the cream and brown sugar. Ivan glanced around her place, the studio apartment. Happy, cheerful and nothing in it that would tell him more about the woman.

Like Jaydee's places. Nothing personal in those either.

He scowled, fiercely shoving away her memory. He didn't want to sit around and compare how alike they were. It wasn't something he needed to do. *It's not healthy.* Didn't matter, he still couldn't stop his brain from doing exactly what he needed it *not* to do.

Both women were slightly off, granted for different reasons. He didn't know much about Bailey's upbringing but he wanted to know. Did she have family? Siblings? Were they close? What did she like to do in her spare time? Most importantly, how the hell had she got involved with Theta Corps and the work she did with them?

Grasping the handles of the mugs, he blew out a breath then made his way back outside into the warm sun. Bailey looked up, a piece of bread in her hand.

"You okay?"

He set her drink down then sipped his. "Sure, why do you ask?"

"You have a haunted look about you, like you've seen a ghost or had a bad memory."

Ivan waited for the question but it didn't come. She didn't pry, just made her observation then let it go.

Like someone else.

Damn his subconscious. He didn't need its commentary. With a smile, he sat opposite her and spooned some fruit onto his plate. "I'm fine."

Her shrug was her answer. She went back to enjoying her food. Ivan joined her. The bread was warm and when he bit into a slice, it crunched lightly. *Perfect, just how I like it.* He had butter on his but noticed she ate hers dry.

"Tell me about you, Bailey."

She drew the piece of fruit on the end of her fork into her mouth and chewed it slowly. Moving the utensil in a circle, she swallowed.

"What do you want to know?"

"Everything."

"Not much to tell." She ate the last bite of her toast. "But if you really want to know I'll tell you as we go back through the market."

"Isn't that where I found you?"

She rose and picked up her empty plate. "Yes. Moreover, because you did, I got sidetracked so I didn't get all my shopping done. I'm going to go change. No rush, take your time." She walked back inside.

He grinned to himself and drank some more coffee. *Hearing things like that is good for my ego.* Ivan didn't rush. By the time he'd finished and had carried his dishes inside to her sink, she was sitting on her couch flipping through a gun magazine.

"You speak Spanish?"

She never looked away from the glossy pages. "Pointless to live in this city if I didn't speak the language."

"So you speak the language in every place you have an apartment?"

"I do."

"How many languages do you speak?"

She looked at him, eyes sparkling with laughter and tossed the magazine down. "More than two"—she rose—"less than ten." She grabbed her pack. "Ready?"

"Can I go to the market in just jeans?"

She flashed a smile. "You can go however you want."

"Give me a few minutes." He walked to her sectioned off corner where her bed sat and swiftly dressed in the rest of his clothing. "Now I'm ready," he commented, stepping around the shelf that gave her a small bit of privacy.

"Good. Ask your questions." She locked up after they had left.

"I asked about languages."

"And I answered."

"Sort of. Do you speak Russian?"

"No. Well, not more than a few phrases. I can catch a cab, get to a restaurant or hotel. And I can get to a restroom."

So no apartment for her in Russia. "Do you speak Italian?"

They stepped out onto the street. "I do.

"Have you been to the Vatican?"

"I have."

"I meant Vatican City."

She shrugged. "Oh, well, I've been there too. Hard to get to the Vatican without being in the city."

"What were you doing there?"

"It was work related."

He truly didn't know how to respond to that. *Time to change my line of questions.* "Do you have family?"

"If I do, I don't know about them. I was raised in a foster system." She stopped at a stall and looked over the vegetables. "I was in it until I reached the age of eleven."

"Then what happened?"

She picked up a few and gave them a squeeze test. "I met a man named William." Bailey looked at the vendor and got what she wanted.

"Who's William?" Ivan asked as they began strolling again.

"He works for the same people I do."

"They recruited you at age eleven?"

"*They* gave me a home then. I've been with them since that time."

"So you've not been away from them?" Flashes of Jaydee's upbringing hit him. Cut off at a young age, treated like an object and not a child who was allowed to have fun. Anger filled him.

"You say that like it's a bad thing."

"It is, Jaydee. You know how you were treated."

She stopped and grasped his arm.

"What?"

"I'm not Jaydee."

He couldn't read her expression. Ivan closed his eyes and groaned. "Shit, I'm sorry. So sorry."

* * * *

Bailey didn't appreciate the uncertain emotions that danced through her. The shower ran as Ivan used it. The rest of their trip through the market and the return one to her apartment had had a decided tenseness about it.

Who the fuck is Jaydee?

It hit her as she put away the last bit of food. Memories from the file she'd read. Valentino's sister-in-law. That woman was Jaydee Cassano. *She must be his one true.*

She may not like that fact but there it was. Nothing she could do to change it. Everyone had the one person who could get to them. Or so she had heard.

The screen on her phone lit up indicating an incoming call. She stared at the name, same one she'd ignored before. Not this time. Bailey reached for it.

"Yes?"

"I have a job for you."

She flicked a glance to the closed door, behind which Ivan was. "What is it?"

"What do you know of the group called The Watchers?"

"Not much. A home-grown terrorist group, although they prefer to call themselves patriots. They're the group which went after Cassano's wife." She readjusted and sat on her counter. "I thought the leader had been eliminated."

"Along with most of his faction."

She narrowed her eyes. "Most."

"Yes, exactly. Most. Someone who goes by the name of The Chief runs things now. They just took credit for the recent bombing. Did you hear about it?"

"Nope. What'd they hit?"

"George W. Bush Presidential Center."

"Texas?"

"Dallas, to be exact."

"Casualties?"

"Yes. It happened during an event there. The Watchers didn't even wait to take credit for it. They claimed it before the body count had even become official."

She snarled softly. Innocents always got hurt during war but it didn't mean she liked it. At all. Kids frequented libraries. Parents of children.

"Not sure why you're calling me. You said you don't know who this person is, so what is it you need me to do?"

"They made a few other declarations. Saying they will be striking again. Soft targets."

"They specifically said soft targets?" Her question was low and vibrated with danger.

"Yes. I'd like you to track someone down and bring them back to the States."

She hopped off the counter. "I'm not in the retrieval business, McNeal. I told you that before when you sent me after the doc."

"This person may very well be the key to bringing down The Watchers."

The shower shut off. "So send in Cassano or the ones he sometimes works with. What about some of Ethan's friends? He's the tech guy who never has a problem finding anyone. I know he's missing but surely he had people he was close to."

Ice coated her heart at the reminder. Her fingers flexed like she was readying to take a shot. No, take a life.

She knew of Ethan and liked him, what she'd heard of him anyway. He was the one from that particular group of operatives she knew the best. Him and his sister—crazy woman that she was, according to rumors—Anabelle Lee. She'd first met Anabelle Lee and Beauregard when they came down to ask for her help. She'd seen Valentino a few times but wouldn't say she *knew* him. Not that it stopped the stories that floated around about their prowess. The four of them were almost legendary, if she were to put a word to it.

"All feelers are out but nothing has hit, including the one to you. I didn't call for that. I need you to track this person down for us. I'm sending the file to your phone."

"Very well."

"Bailey?"

"Yes?"

"Do whatever it takes to get him back to us alive."

"Yes, sir." She ended the call and waited for the file to upload. The moment it finished, she opened it and began reading.

"Bailey?"

She glanced up, Ivan stood there wearing nothing but a blue towel. Water droplets ran down over his tanned torso, flowing along his defined muscles. He raised one eyebrow and she cleared her throat then looked away.

"Something you like?"

"You know that's the case." She closed the file on her phone. "Feel better?"

"I do. Could have used the company in the shower, though."

Her body trembled at the thought of sharing the space with him. "Sorry."

"Everything okay?" He approached her and stopped just shy of touching her. "You seemed a bit occupied when I walked out."

"Another job."

His face tightened. "I see." He crossed his arms. "When do you leave?"

"Soon. I haven't finished reading everything yet."

"Should I even ask?"

"No." She moved by him and went to the other side of the island counter, needing some space between them so she didn't only think about what it was like to touch his skin. Taste it. Kiss it.

"Very well." Ivan placed his hands flat upon the white diamond recycled surface. "So what happens now?"

She indicated her phone. "I finish my reading."

"I'll cook."

"Excuse me?"

"You have work, you work and I'll cook you a meal."

"You cook?"

"There are many things about me you don't know yet. I'm a damn good cook and I actually enjoy it." He shooed her out of the kitchen. "Go away."

Bailey shook her head as she walked to the couch. *Kicked out of my own kitchen. There is something wrong with this picture. And yet...* She gazed over her shoulder at Ivan. *There's something to be said about a hot-ass man wearing nothing but a towel in there fixing me food.*

Pulling up the file again, Bailey settled forward and focused on reading. Cairo. Egypt.

Bailey leaned against the back of her couch and chewed on her thumbnail. She needed to book a flight via London. Her Arabic was passable—she spoke some Egyptian Arabic. Enough to know if she was being screwed but not enough to pass as a native.

The man she sought was Klinehaus. Eric Klinehaus.

I would have thought a man with his name would hide in a Germanic place. But then again, I shouldn't assume anything based on names.

She memorized his picture and the information they had on him. It didn't amount to much. A few likes, and his scar.

Rubbing the nape of her neck, she dialed her boss.

"When do you leave?" McNeal asked by way of answering.

"As soon as you book me a flight. I need a stopover in London."

"Consider it done. I'll send you your info as soon as I make the arrangements."

The call ended and she dropped her phone on the armrest. Bailey pushed to her feet, went to pull her bag out then began to pack. She paused when the sensation of being watched hit her.

"Something you needed, Ivan?"

"Many things, but I wanted to put my clothes on."

"Pity," she said with a smile, facing him. "I like you this way."

Ivan gripped the edges of the towel and slowly released the tuck. She lowered her gaze and focused on his hands. *Remove the towel, please.*

"Bailey?"

"I haven't received my flight info yet."

He dropped the material and she licked her lips as a spear of longing pierced her. His cock rose, proud and thick.

"Which means?"

"You have time to put that to work." She crooked her finger, pleased he came in close enough for her to touch. So she did. And so did he at least until her phone beeped indicating the information had arrived.

When the information finally arrived to her phone, she left with her bag. Ivan still slumbered in her bed. There was no concern on her part about leaving him in her place and as the door closed behind her, she turned her attention to the task at hand.

Chapter Seven

Ivan stared at the whiteboard, his right hand cupping his chin, his left in the pocket of his lab coat. Something wasn't right.

If I could just figure it out. His concentration had basically been shit since he'd woken up to find Bailey and her bag gone. *I'm worried about her.*

Scrubbing his hand down his face, he grunted. After loosening up his shoulders, he once again stared at the equations. There was a way for him to make this work. *I just have to figure it out.*

Two of his assistants walked up and he gave them a nod.

"Everything okay?" he asked.

"We were working on the prototype of the warder."

He waited but nothing else came from the speaker. "And?" he prompted.

The blonde woman, Chrissie, shared a glance with her companion, Trick. Ivan didn't know Trick's real name and didn't care. The brunette was damn good at her job, she just didn't speak. Ever. She signed.

"Chrissy? Trick? What's going on?"

Another shared look between the women.

"I think you should see for yourself. First-hand."

He nodded even as he took one final look over his board. *Maybe a break will do me good.* "Let's go."

The women fell into step beside him. They were silent during the walk through the quiet corridors and to the elevator that took them down two more levels.

Once in that lab, he followed them to the bench table and stared at the items lying there. He lifted the thin silver band.

"What's wrong with it?"

He had to admit, he truly enjoyed being in one of the research and development sections of Theta Corps. It was more than what he'd been doing and allowed his crazy mind to fly free.

Chrissy rested her hip against the edge and placed her hands in the pockets of her lab coat. "Didn't say anything was wrong with it. Just suggested you come see for yourself. Put it on."

He closed it over his right wrist. A slight tremor moved through his muscles. "What was that?"

She shrugged despite her gaze flashing with excitement. "So it did happen to you as well, then. We don't know. We also can't replicate it. If it's in being scanned, it never displays it on the readouts. We've tried putting it on a pig carcass, nothing. Even tried —"

"Attaching nodes out here?"

Chrissy sat beside him. He peered between the women. Trick stared back. He knew she was reading their lips as well as listening.

"We can't get it copied, whatever we do. In the room, out here. I don't understand. We've all felt it."

In his periphery, Trick nodded.

"Have you tested it for its true purpose?"

"Not yet. We've been trying to isolate this peculiar phenomenon before we continue on with the testing phase."

He placed his hands on his hips. "Get a shooter. I'll be the guinea pig."

She furrowed her brow. "Are you sure?"

Trick's expression mirrored Chrissy's.

Not in the least. "Of course." He clapped his hands together. "Let's do it." *Quickly before I lose my nerve.*

Chrissy hopped off the table and headed for the phone on the wall. He heard her muttering as she went. The words 'insane' and 'bat-shit crazy' got a mention.

She's not far off.

Ivan headed to the test room and activated the cameras. He needed them all running if he were to figure out what was going on at first contact. Not to mention if it would affect the purpose of the bracelet. He removed it and placed it down then finished getting ready.

"Dr Vinokourov!"

He stepped back out and stared at the reed-thin man calling his name. "Yes?"

"Phone." He made the gesture as well. "Line six."

"Thank you." Ivan lifted the receiver and pressed the appropriate button. "This is Dr Vinokourov."

"It's Howland."

Ivan rolled his eyes. Howland was the head of Theta Corps' research and development division. Normally the pain in the ass remained in her office. Unfortunately, when she did stick her head into stuff, it typically got mucked up. He couldn't imagine what it would be like were she over the entire black op organization. Not what he wanted to find out.

He didn't know her first name. Nor did he know if anyone did. Perhaps she didn't have one, just Howland. Either way, he wasn't up to talking to her right now. There were more important things for him to do.

Be polite.

"Yes, ma'am."

"I want a status report."

He leaned against the wall. "On what?"

Chrissy returned with a man named Trevor in tow.

"I heard the warder worked. Why aren't they being produced in my lab as opposed to being still listed in the test phase?"

He peered through the window to the silver bracelet that lay where he'd placed it. Unadorned and plain. And supposed to protect the wearer from being shot. "Something else has come up. It's not ready."

"Don't try to bullshit me."

"I haven't the time or inclination to do such a thing," he stated truthfully.

"We need this to be operational."

"Until it has passed *all* the tests, it will not be signed off on by me or anyone else in my lab."

"Then why was I told otherwise?"

He tensed. "Is my name on the memo?"

There was a slight pause. "No."

"Then that assumption is on you, because I never sent it." Ivan returned the handset to its cradle. *Lord, I don't have time for this.* He re-entered the room and made his way to the back wall, swiping the bracelet on the way. "Let's do it," he said, facing Chrissy and Trevor.

She lifted her shoulders and blew out between her teeth. "Your call."

"Trevor," he said, meeting his collected brown eyes. "On three, go. Chrissy, make sure all cameras and sensors are running. Give me a thumbs up when all is ready and running."

"You got it, boss." Chrissy went to the table of monitors.

Ivan cracked his knuckles before donning a vest and ear protection. He then took several deep breaths while waiting for the go from Chrissy and for Trevor to take his position. Ivan scowled at the way his heart kicked up to a higher speed. The purpose of the bracelet was to repel the bullet and save the wearer.

"Make sure you don't miss," he said.

"I never do." Trevor stepped behind the shield wall without so much as a smile.

It didn't matter he knew where the shot was supposed to go. The fact he had to stand there and let a man shoot a 9mm at him filled him with nervousness.

The bullets were armor piercing. He wanted to know more about this new tingling when it was attached.

Behind Trevor, Chrissy gave him the thumbs up he'd been waiting for. Or dreading.

Aware of the sensors on his own body, Ivan placed the bracelet on his wrist and waited for the immediate tingle to go away. He took one more deep breath and flexed his fingers.

"When you're ready, Trevor."

The words had barely left his mouth when he heard the shot. He flinched, expecting the impact of the slug. It never came. The hair on his arms stood on end as an electrical current ran through him. Not like a painful shock, more as if hooked up to a TENS machine.

"Empty your clip," Ivan commanded.

Trevor never questioned him, just did as ordered. Not one bullet had hit him. Once Trevor had cleared his weapon, Chrissy entered with Trick behind her.

"It works!" she cried, her glossy red lips forming a wide smile. "What did you feel? Impact? What?"

Trick began gathering the spent bullets. Ivan held up his hand. "With the vest. I have to try without the vest as backup."

Trick showed him the plastic container holding all the slugs. Every one of them had been fired from a weapon. It wasn't like someone had a toy gun and had strewn bullets on the floor.

"Run tests, Trick." Excitement flowed through him.

She nodded and walked away.

"We need to begin analyzing everything. This was wicked."

Chrissy tucked some blonde strands behind her ear — one laden with earrings — and waggled her eyebrows, the gold post in one glinting in the overhead light. "I want to hear all about it as we go over the video."

"Absolutely, we can go over the vid while the results are compiling. Thanks, Trevor."

The man saluted him with two fingers then left. Ivan glanced at Chrissy before they headed to the table of monitors that waited.

* * * *

London, England

Bailey walked from the Tube to her destination. The sun shined brightly, broken up by a few clouds. Her steps slowed as she approached the Chelsea Physic Garden and paid her admittance charge.

The Chelsea Physic Garden was one of the gardens on a list referred to as poisonous gardens. And behind those walls was something she needed to pull her mission off in a successful way.

I would really like to know why Kevin thinks I'm cut out for retrieval. Sure, my success rate is perfect but then I have only done it once.

With a swift glance at her watch, she altered her direction and angled toward the Tangerine Dream. *No reason not to eat well while I'm here. Airline food sucks.*

She grabbed some salad, a lavender scone and of course a glass of their renowned, homemade Amalfi lemonade. Once she had her food, Bailey made her way outside to eat beneath the covered terrace.

After she'd finished her salad and had begun on her scone, a shadow fell over her. Bailey paused with the fork on its way to her mouth.

"Fancy meeting you here," she said, staring at the person standing.

"It's a small world." Anabelle Lee hefted one of the two mugs she held. "You need tea, not lemonade, with the scone."

Anabelle Lee lowered her lean, toned body into the seat opposite Bailey.

"Thanks." Bailey accepted the tea. "Spending your days in London now?"

Anabelle Lee grimaced slightly. "Hunting down leads."

She nodded. "I also have feelers out."

"Thanks. For meeting us in Chile as well. Every little bit helps and we appreciate it. I was surprised to hear you were here."

She enjoyed a bite of her scone. "Didn't realize I was on your radar."

Anabelle Lee held her gaze. "Everyone's on my radar."

Bailey knew that. Anabelle Lee made it her business to know what went on. With her brother's disappearance, it should have come as no surprise to her that Anabelle Lee's alertness had increased.

"How's your cousin?"

The first honest smile she'd seen since Anabelle Lee arrived crossed her beautiful face. "He's doing well, considering. I'm waiting for the day he meets his match. That man needs a woman."

Beauregard Jackson was a panty-soakingly handsome man. There was something about him and his southern accent that made him irresistible. Ethan reputedly had charm as well but it oozed from Beauregard.

"I'm sure he says you need a man."

"Sometimes," she concurred. "Others, he wishes me on one so I could bring them down."

Bailey merely smiled. In truth, she wasn't sure what to say. While she finished her scone, Anabelle Lee drank and gazed about. The woman turned heads for sure. However, this was the only time Bailey had seen her this at ease. The previous times their paths had crossed, she'd been much more intense. Many might not understand that, but those who lived the lives they did would.

"I'm not interrupting your plans, am I?"

Bailey shook her head. "Not at all. I had a layover, decided to stretch my legs and eat some real food." She finished her tea. "I'm going to walk through the gardens. Would you care to join me?"

"Sure thing." Her drawl came more pronounced this time.

So they walked and enjoyed their time in the gardens. Before departing, Bailey swung through the gardens' gift shop. She meandered through and got a few knick-knacks then progressed to the counter.

"Good day."

"Hi," she replied, reaching in her pack for money.

"Visiting?"

"I am. This place came highly recommended. I must say it was worth it."

The lady bent and withdrew a bag from beneath her counter. She placed Bailey's purchases inside. "Anything else?"

Bailey looked around. "No thank you."

"Very well."

Once she'd paid, Bailey and Anabelle Lee headed to the door. Two kids barreled into them before running on, their harried father following. "So sorry," he called as he passed them.

Anabelle Lee shook her head. "That's why I have no wish to have children."

Bailey readjusted her backpack. "No desire to chase after them?"

"Not a single one. I am not mother material." They stopped at the street. "What about you?" Together they headed for the Tube station.

"Never gave it much thought. Guess I'm ambivalent on it. No pressing need to add to the population but not dead set against it either." A shrug. "If it happens, it happens."

"So no man you can't wait to start a family with?"

Images of Ivan flashed, surprising her such that she tripped. "No," she said after righting herself.

Anabelle Lee stared at her and deadpanned, "Yeah, right, hon. Mighty convenient trip if that were actually the case."

"Things happen."

"I agree, they do." She halted at the entrance. "If he's your heart, I would say don't let him get away."

Bailey shoved a hand in her pocket. "I'd heard so many say you're a bitch."

A flash of perfect white teeth. "Make no mistake, I am. However, Ethan has always spoken so highly of you. I think he was in awe of you—is, *is* in awe of you." There was a hint of pain in her words. And desperation.

"That I doubt, but I'm glad his words were kind." She faced the redhead. "I know I'm not on your team but if I can be of assistance, let me know."

The pain spread to her blue eyes—only lasting briefly—but it had been there.

"Thank you." Her words sounded heartfelt. True.

"If my contacts come up with anything I'll let you know."

"Thank you again. Travel safe and luck with your job." A smile—albeit somewhat forced—made an appearance before Anabelle Lee departed along with it.

"Same to you," she whispered, hurrying along on her own way.

Bailey kept to herself on the Tube, remaining vigilant. Since she'd added her purchases to her dark green backpack she wondered if she would be stopped and checked. However, once back at the airport nothing changed, they waved her through easily. It didn't take long to get back through the airport's checkpoint and to her gate.

She bought a book, a Coke and a large bag of salted peanuts, then sat and waited for her flight to board. Never once did she check her phone. Unlike some, she wasn't addicted to it.

The flight from London to Cairo fell into the uneventful category. How Bailey preferred her flights to be. So she slept.

It wasn't a deep sleep. One because she only fully rested when she was at one of her homes. And two, a man named Ivan Vinokourov occupied her thoughts. Regardless, the sleep she'd gotten was enough in her estimation.

When the captain announced their impending landing, she followed instructions given by the flight attendants. She took in the skyline as they circled closer. A beautiful city really—not her favorite place in the world, but one she enjoyed visiting.

She disembarked and took her time going through customs, giving off all appearances of a woman not on a tight deadline.

Which I am.

Passport stamped, she made her way to collect her bag. Once at her hotel—and she'd checked for bugs out of habit—she sat on the edge of the bed and turned on her phone.

One message from McNeal. She opened it to read.

Hope you had safe travels.

She gave a short chuckle before sending back her one-word reply.

Claro.

Bailey went to the table and withdrew her purchased items from her pack, including the folded thick paper that had been slipped into her pocket by the father of those two children in the gift shop at Chelsea Physic Garden—what she'd needed from

London. That sat off to her right as she went through the rest of her items.

Most likely this would get messy.

Chapter Eight

Rubbing his eyes, Ivan leaned back in his chair. The slight creak of leather was the only other sound aside from his groan of frustration. The past two weeks had been more stressful than he cared to admit.

He was surviving on three hours of sleep a night. Work had consumed him, as well as it was proving to be his only respite from thoughts of Bailey. No, he wasn't sitting around pining for her, but he did miss her.

And I'm concerned for her.

This job had gotten more stressful than he liked it to be. *I understand the desire to have results but I don't — won't — risk the lives of those who will be using these things.*

He sat forward and opened his eyes. His computer's screensaver distracted him for a moment. Fractals had always intrigued him.

"Get back to it, Ivan."

He drank from the white mug beside his computer, the watercolor abstract design fading as the drink cooled. With another sigh, he hit a key on his keyboard and the multi-hued fractals vanished, replaced by boxes of equations and notes.

Ivan closed the window relating to electrogravitics. He was good — damn good — in that field, but it wasn't his only one. He had many interests. *Not to mention projects, so I should quit daydreaming and procrastinating and get back to work.*

Right now, he closed all the windows except the one dealing with dark matter and got to work.

"What are you still doing here, Doctor?"

Ivan glanced up, startled. "Chrissy? What do you mean what am I still doing here?"

"It's ten at night." Her tone was one of reprimand.

Seriously? He peered at his watch and was again amazed. She hadn't been lying about the time. He rubbed the nape of his neck then pivoted his chair so he could see her head on.

"So what are you doing here, Chrissy?"

"Finished up some work on the electrogravitics for use in the personal pack. Was on my way out when I saw your vehicle still in the lot. Came to check and see if I could be of any help."

He rubbed his temple as she carried on about him staying too long in the labs or his office and not taking time for himself. Ivan grunted and held up a hand. "I don't think that's necessary. As you pontificated, it is ten at night. You should go home and get some rest."

She laughed and shook her head. "Coming from you? My hours may be long but you still put in so many more than I do." She leveled a finger in his direction. "You need to eat something at least."

He could use some food, not having eaten since eight in the morning. "You win. I will take a break and eat if you head home for the night."

"You positive you don't need any assistance?"

He stood. "Absolutely. I won't be far behind you. Do you need me to walk you out?"

She went to the door and grinned at him over her shoulder. "I'm sure I will be fine. See you tomorrow, Doc."

"Goodnight, Chrissy. Thanks for the hard work."

"I do love my job." One final wave and she was gone.

Ivan put files on his tablet and powered down his computer. Cell phone in hand, he checked. Eight missed calls—seven from Howland and one from his mother.

He made his way home, stopping off at a restaurant on the way to grab some food. Carrying the bag, he took the stairs two at a time to his door. Once in his place, he fixed himself a plate, eating bites between changing his clothes.

Finally comfortable in a pair of shorts, he swiped his plate and sat in time to catch the eleven o'clock news. As it wound down, he picked up his phone and scrolled through to the number he sought.

It was after six in the morning for her and he had no fear of waking her. He pressed the call button and leaned back, propping his feet up on his coffee table.

"Hello?" The warm Russian voice made him smile.

"Hi, Mama." He also spoke Russian.

"Ivan. It is so good to hear your voice. You haven't called in so long. How are you? More importantly, when are you coming home?"

"Good to hear yours as well, Mama. I'm sorry it's been crazy getting this lab up and running. Long days, short nights. How are you?"

She harrumphed. "You work too much. Probably forgetting to eat."

He looked sheepishly at the plate he'd cleaned moments prior to calling his mother. "I do eat."

"You need a woman in your life. She would make sure you ate and slept."

"Actually, I do have a woman in my life."

Silence.

"You still there, Mama?"

"Where did you meet her?"

He debated how to answer that question. There would be nothing gained by telling her he'd been kidnapped and forced to work on some things for people the world would look upon as terrorists. He drank the rest of his beer.

"I was in Madagascar."

"So you can go to Madagascar but you can't come home and see your mother? Or the rest of your family?"

He pinched the bridge of his nose and groaned. "I wasn't there on vacation, Mama. I was there working."

"Not such you didn't have the time to find a woman."

Not like I was out looking for one. "She was working as well. It was a chance meeting."

"But it's something serious."

How like his mother not to make it a question but a statement. "I'd like to think so."

"Good, bring her here. I want to meet her."

Bailey and his mother. "She's very busy as well, so—"

"I don't want your excuses, Ivan," she snapped. "Bring her so I can meet her. We will have a party and it will be like a reunion because my son has been away for far too long."

"I can't just grab her and go, Mama. Besides, she's not here right now. She's off on business and I'm not sure when she will be back."

"Do you not talk? Is this just about sex?"

"Okay, not talking to you about my sex life."

"So it is about sex."

"Enough, Mama. It's not just about sex. She travels a lot with her job and doesn't always know when she will be back. But— But I will ask her if she will come with me to St Petersburg when I see her next."

"See you do. What does she do?"

"I'm not letting you get all her information from me, Mama. You can ask her yourself when you meet her."

"Good."

Ivan rolled his eyes and let his mother continue talking. She had to fill him in on all the family drama. And in their home, it wasn't something that was lacking. Only after he had heard about aunts, uncles, cousins and even the neighbors did she let him off the phone.

He put his dish in the sink then went to his bedroom. After brushing his teeth, he crawled into his bed, closed his eyes with a groan, and succumbed to the exhaustion wearing on him. He had to get some sleep for this was about to start all over for him again. If he wasn't rested, he might miss something, and that wasn't a chance he was willing to take.

* * * *

Ivan slept heavily and woke when his alarm went off. Slapping a hand on it, he muttered some unpleasantries in Russian before rolling off the bed and stumbling to the bathroom.

I said rested, not well rested.

He reached in the shower and turned on the water. As it heated up, he stripped out of his shorts, rolled his shoulders, then stepped in. He braced his hands along the wall and allowed the heat to seep into him and loosen up his tight muscles.

The water ran down his skin, slowly waking him up. He tipped his head into the spray then stepped back to pick up his soap and cloth. Ivan got out of the shower about fifteen minutes later, more awake and less stiff.

Wearing just his towel, he made himself some breakfast and stared out of the window overlooking the busy street below. He could hear the vendors hawking their wares, children laughing and more.

He watched a woman accept a flower from the man with her with a smile and a kiss. Then she placed it in her hair. Bailey had had a flower in her hair the day he had found her again.

Bailey. He turned from the window.

How is she doing? What is she doing? Is she going to kill someone else?

He hadn't quite figured out how he felt about what she did for a living. She wasn't a mercenary. She was a killer. But one could argue they were all sanctioned kills. *Right?* All he knew was what she'd told him and that hadn't been much at all. Bailey was pretty close-lipped about what she did.

Regardless, I hope you're safe where you are, Bailey. Come back soon.

* * * *

Coffee in hand, Bailey gazed around the street. People went about their daily business without paying her any attention. She'd been here for a few days now and on each one, she took her morning meal at this location.

Across the café was the man she had to get. He looked a lot like his picture—it hadn't been hard to recognize him. For a man who wanted to be in hiding, he didn't appear like he was avoiding the general public.

Perhaps he's confident no one knows he is here. She wasn't stupid—he might appear without a care but she wasn't green enough not to see the men who were around him, blending in as best they could. *Ex-members of Unit 777, I'd bet anything, except for the white man closest to him – I would say ex-spec ops from America for him.* Unit 777 was Egypt's Special Forces group.

They were good, real good. She was better. He had six of them around him. This man, Theodore Ramsey, had no intention of going anywhere without his consent. *All plans have a wrench in them. I will be your wrench, Theodore.*

She sipped slowly and smiled at some antics the children nearby were doing. Two minutes before she knew he would leave, Bailey finished her drink and made her way out to the street, looking as if she was minding her own business. In truth, she was—just her business had to do with the man seated at the corner table.

Why this man was wanted, she didn't have a clue. That wasn't her business or concern. What was is that her boss had told her to bring him back to the States. Alive. So she would. Or die trying.

She walked away, down the route he took, and stepped into an alley. Then she looped back around to the building across the street from the café, making her way to the roof. Once there, she withdrew her scope and watched. Knowing his pattern for every day of the week was important. The men with him were good and they varied but everyone had a pattern.

While they had and utilized seven different routes for coming and going from this location, she would learn them all. Then take him.

Kevin had said fast but obviously if he'd sent her in he didn't want this to be a smash and grab operation. Still, she wasn't positive why he had sent her as opposed to, say, Anabelle Lee. There were other operatives who would be better.

Maybe he suspects a leak somewhere. I don't know.

She readjusted and continued her vigilant observation. Sure enough, he finished his drink, wiped the corners of his mouth with the white linen cloth then rose to his feet. The white man went with him while the other six trailed a bit farther behind.

He and the one who'd left with him didn't converse. She ran her gaze over the muscle. He packed some heat. She'd say two in shoulder holsters. SIGs or Glocks. And he also had a backup on his right ankle. A revolver of some sort. Perhaps a .38 special.

The one thing Theodore did every other day was go into a small door and vanish for a good hour. This was what she was looking at. Not even the one man was allowed in with him. While she didn't know what went on in there, she had a pretty good idea, having seen the women that came out in the evenings.

Perhaps her best bet would be there. *Damn it. Why can't I just sight down my scope and do my job? I hate all this damn planning for this kind of thing. I much prefer my kind of planning. Or waiting.*

Sure enough, he vanished in and came out one hour and ten minutes later. Just like clockwork. Bailey let them go, deciding instead to figure out a bit more about that little place. She went to the alley that led to the back of that row of buildings and sought the entrance. When she found it, she looked at the lock then continued on her way without slowing. She would come back tonight.

She wore black and made her way through the shadows to the door. A minor wait and she'd picked it, allowing herself entrance. When the smell hit her nose, she scowled but continued on. *Nothing like the smell of old sex and sweat to get the juices flowing.* Avoiding the ones who worked there, she familiarized herself with the layout. It was actually the office that held the most promise in her mind. From the closet in there, she could make it to the laundry next door and get him out that way.

Bailey counted the steps from the room closest to the front door to the office and figured out how long that would take. Any of the other rooms, it would be less. There was always the chance of running into someone but from what she observed here, it was more about keeping out of the way of those there to utilize the service. All points that worked in her favor. If she did run into people in the halls, they would just seem like another drugged, happy couple. She could dispatch the one person in the office if necessary.

The laundry was closed but this establishment remained open all day. No surprise really. It was, after all, a brothel and men came when they could. She snuck into the closet and did some calculating. It would all be ready in two days.

As cautiously as she had snuck in, she left, just not through the same door. She made her exit via the roof. Five streets over, she caught a taxi back to her hotel.

Taking a seat in the lobby, she withdrew her phone then placed a call.

"How are things?" Kevin McNeal's greeting was gruff.

"You know how I feel about doing this. It's not my area but I've got it figured out. Will be going down in two days. I may or may not be out of touch for twenty-four with him before we call for pickup. It all depends on how swiftly they learn he's gone."

"They?"

"He's got seven that I've seen around him. Ex-spec ops. American and Unit 777."

Kevin muttered under his breath and Bailey waited. It was her policy not to ask questions. She went in and did her job but she had to be honest with herself. This was making her wonder a bit more about who this Theodore Ramsey was.

"As soon as you can make it possible, Bailey. One day would be better than two."

While it was rare for her, it wasn't unheard of—a flash of annoyance spurted through her. "You wanted it done faster then perhaps you should have sent someone here who did retrievals. Not me. I'm not upping my timetable because you want it done faster. I am checking and double-checking my exit routes. Again, this isn't just me I have to get but this man as well. This isn't my area of superiority. You know this—why are you acting like I do these all the time?"

"You did this with Dr Vinokourov."

"I rescued him. This man doesn't look like he wants to be rescued. I'm assuming this is a man you want. I don't care to know the details but you should not expect me to do this like someone who does it often. You wanted him sooner, should have sent anyone else. I'm doing this my way. Back off." She ended the call and stood.

After several deep breaths to calm down, Bailey strode to the elevator and rode it up to her floor. In her room, she packed her bags. Correction. Bag—by the time she had finished it was all in one. It wasn't a lot nor was it heavy and she took it back downstairs and got directions on where to go to mail it home.

Once it was on its way back to her place in Southern California, she returned to her room and stared over the items she'd not packed away.

"What the hell was I thinking? Extracting a man I know nothing about to take him back to the US with this little bit of stuff. This is going to be fun," she stated sarcastically.

She spent her night in preparation for the next day. She grabbed around three hours of sleep before she shoved the stuff she was taking into her pockets. One final eyeball sweep of the room then she exited and made her way to the counter where she checked out.

"We hope you enjoyed your stay."

Bailey nodded. "I did, thank you." She signed her bill and walked away with a wave. Outside in the late morning, she gazed around Cairo. She flagged down a taxi and hopped into the back seat when it stopped. "The Egyptian Museum, please."

The driver nodded and she reclined as they entered the flow of traffic. Bailey paid him at the museum and got out. She meandered for a while then walked inside the building and took her time enjoying the displays.

Once the nightlife began, she melded into that as she made her way back to the place she needed to be for tomorrow. She snuck in the same way as before and got to work setting everything up.

* * * *

She heard loud voices and she froze in the office, debating on where she needed to hide—out here or in the closet. If they found her in there it would totally compromise what she had planned. *On the other hand, if I'm caught and killed it's really a moot point.*

They grew louder and she made out three different male voices. The group spoke Arabic and she stepped into the closet, leaving it cracked open as she sought her hiding spot in the small dark space.

The trio entered the room. Two in jeans and shirts, one red and one blue, and the third wore a linen suit. Suit Wearer closed the door behind him and went to pour everyone a drink.

Bailey watched, frozen in her spot. She wouldn't move until these men were gone. She took it all in. The knowledge took a minute to formulate but it did and she realized the man with the blue shirt was familiar.

He's one of the six who guarded Theodore.

Was there a plot against that man from those who were tasked with protecting him?

She listened to them discuss wives and girlfriends. Even mistresses. Blue Shirt drained his drink and wiped the back of his hand across his mouth.

"So, his women will be here tomorrow?"

Red Shirt withdrew a large knife and began cleaning his nails. "We said they would. They have always been here for him."

Blue Shirt shrugged. "I had to check." He paused and stared in her direction. Cool calculation appeared in his brown gaze. He drew his sidearm—an IMI 9 Jericho pistol—and tapped it against his thigh before making his way toward the closet door.

Bailey's breathing slowed as she remained still. He was good, he'd felt her gaze and that something was off. The other two watched him with a look of suspicion on their faces.

"Come out or I fill you full of holes," Blue Shirt ordered, his voice brisk and no-nonsense.

The other two pulled their weapons as well. Bailey refused to move and kept her heart rate slow and even, breathing so shallow it was barely there.

"What is it?" Suit asked.

"I thought I heard something," Blue Shirt responded. He grasped the door handle.

"No one is in here," Red Shirt spoke. "You have to come in through the front and get past the two guards out there to get back here. You worry too much."

Blue Shirt shot him a look of condemnation. "No such thing as worrying too much. The truth is, you don't worry enough."

"Look, I can't have you firing off your pistol in here. It will create panic and bring police."

After a long look at the door, Blue Shirt acquiesced and backed away. "Fine." He sat where he could stare in her direction. "Let's get the details worked out. I want him in room five this time. He's not been in there for a while and it's more centrally located."

And the talk continued. Bailey held her position for two hours as they talked things out. She took notice of everything, when they wrote things down instead of talking. Blue Shirt was still unsure about the space she was in and she knew tomorrow wasn't going to be easy. Finally, the men left and she waited even longer before she slowly unfurled from her place.

Working out the kinks in her neck, she finished setting up for tomorrow then crept out to look at the papers where they'd written things on. Running a pencil over the sheet, she smiled when she could finally read the indentations.

Theodore would be in room eight, not five, and he would be arriving at the same time for his three women to be there. Bailey crept down to room eight and slipped inside. She ignored the people on the bed — she wasn't here to be a voyeur, she was here to get a job accomplished. It didn't take her long to get set up in there, hiding where she needed to be, in the snug closet where the extra sheets were kept, and ensuring she'd not be discovered. Resting against the wall, she closed her eyes and did her best to tune out the voices coming from the bed. *It's going to be a long night.*

Chapter Nine

The incessant ringing of his phone woke him. Ivan rolled over with a frustrated groan. He didn't want to be disturbed. He wanted to be left alone so he could go back to the remarkably vivid dream of him and Bailey.

"Hello?" he barked into his phone once he'd managed to locate it.

"Did I wake you?"

"Yes." His brain didn't comprehend who was on the other end. "Ruined a perfect dream."

"A woman?"

Bailey. "Yes. Who is this?"

"McNeal."

Ivan pushed up and ran a hand down his face. "What do you want?" He blinked against the sunlight streaming in through his bedroom window, bathing him in its glow.

"You at work. When can you get here?"

He looked at his clock and flopped back with a grunt. "Can't I take a sick day?"

"No. I already told Howland you were going to be late but I can't stay all day. One hour." *Click.* He was gone.

Ivan dropped his phone. "Sure," he muttered. "I live to serve your every whim." He lay there and listened to his breathing. This sucked. His dream with Bailey had been so realistic.

I smelled her skin, could taste it beneath my tongue as I licked along her toned muscled. Starting at the collarbone, I worked my way down as she squirmed beneath me, trying to get me inside her. The rasp of her nails along my back, biting deep when I ignored her pleas.

"Do I get to continue that? No, of course not. I get to talk to a man that I could do just fine without speaking to." He pushed up on his elbows and scanned his room. His sheet covered him but there was no denying the tent caused by his hard cock.

"What you do to me, Bailey Hyde. What you do to me."

With a final grunt of frustration, he climbed from the bed and headed to his shower. Once he stood under the warm spray, he finally turned his attention to his relentless hard-on. It wasn't going anywhere without a little assistance.

He grasped himself and began to stroke. This wasn't about prolonging his release, or building it up for a more intense ending. He wanted to come—his dream had been potent enough to leave him lingering over the precipice long enough.

Ivan tightened his grip as he worked his penis. He tugged on his balls with his other hand and alternated the pressure on his cock. Eyes closed, he conjured up the image of Bailey. Their first time. Against the wall. Hard and fast. It hadn't been making love. It had been fucking, plain and simple. Raw. Pure. Honest.

The echoes of her cries filled his head. The way she'd clenched her pussy around him as he'd thrust within her. The way she'd reacted to his touch. All of it combined.

Ivan growled low as he came hard. Thick streams of his cum shot from him as he leaned upon the tile. "Bailey," he said, struggling for breath.

He allowed the water to stream over him for a few moments until he had regained his breath. There was just something about that woman that he couldn't explain. He wanted to see her again. Hold her. Fuck her. Kiss her. Fuck her. Go to sleep with her in his arms then wake that same way.

"Christ," he muttered, washing his body. "I'm turning into a sentimental old fucker." He shook his head. "I just never realized after Jaydee that anyone would be even close to getting under my skin."

Leaving off his commentary, he finished getting ready for work then grabbed something to eat on his way out of the door. He checked in at work before making his way to his office. Opening the door, he frowned at the sight. Kevin had made himself at home behind his desk.

Ivan was extremely territorial when it came to things he considered his. His desk would fall under that category. "Get out of my seat."

"Morning to you, too, sunshine." McNeal thumped the pencil eraser on the top a few times before he slowly left the leather chair.

Ivan walked to his seat and sat down. "Something you needed, McNeal?"

"How are things going here for you?"

He rocked back. "That's why you called me in? That's something you could have asked me over the phone. I am hard pressed to believe you have the unmitigated gall to wake me, call me in just to ask me something like that. So let's cut the spy agency shit, all the smoke and mirrors, and get to the crux of what it is you truly want."

Kevin sat across from him. "Wake up on the wrong side of bed?"

"Late night and no sex."

His lips twitched. "Sorry to hear that."

"What do you want? Since you called me in, I do have things I could be doing."

"I want to know how things are going here for you. Truly. No, before you get pissy, that's not all I wanted to know but it is one of the questions I had for you."

"Things are fine." *Be better if Bailey were here.* "I get to let my imagination run wild. Why?"

"What do you think about Howland?"

Ivan hesitated. "Howland's my boss. I don't think about her any more than that. What's going on?"

McNeal's expression sobered and he leaned forward. "We've been worried about a mole within this department."

"I'm assuming you don't feel it's me if you're letting me know about this."

"Not you. Howland."

He controlled the shock in both expression and voice. "Wouldn't know. Don't interact much with her."

"You've not seen anything out of the ordinary?"

"This is a brand new lab. Lots of things are out of the ordinary. We're sitting beneath a farm that local workers come to daily. This facility goes ten stories below the ground and we're working on things that some may label science fiction. So yes, I see lots of things which are." Ivan shifted in his seat. "I don't, as I stated, deal much with Howland. I don't have time for bureaucratic crap, so I avoid it. She keeps to herself for the most part, or at least out of my way."

"So nothing with your assistants?"

"Nope. Nothing that I would say screamed suspicious." He lifted his shoulders. "But, again, when I'm in the lab or looking over files, I'm in my own world. I missed seven calls from Howland and one from my mother last night while I was sitting here working."

"She after you about the bracelet thingy?"

"Yes. How did—?" He shook his head. "Never mind."

"I follow what you're doing down here. We got you for a reason, Ivan. I told you that. And we're glad you're working on some of the things you had been asked to do for the other guys."

"Right, now it's just my conscious that is questioning why is Theta Corps better than the others?"

Kevin crossed his arms. "We aren't terrorists."

"No offense, but you are to some."

"Are you having a problem working here and with what we do?"

"Honestly, I'm not sure. I love working with all this equipment and having an endless budget at my disposal. But do I truly know what you're using this stuff for? What is the purpose of getting this dark matter to create a stable version of a wormhole? It gives power and that can be dangerous."

"We are the good guys, you know."

His smile wasn't as ready as it usually came. "That's what everyone says."

"But does everyone mean it?"

"I'm sure they do, McNeal. People will say anything to get the results they are after." He leaned forward. "Now, what else did you want to ask me?"

"How are things with you and Bailey?"

"What is it any business of yours?"

"Because she's like one of my own."

Okay, he was intrigued. "Meaning?"

Kevin McNeal cleared his throat and readjusted in his chair. "I've known her since she was born but she's been in my life since she was six."

"What about her parents?"

"Murdered before her eyes."

Ivan drummed his fingers along the edge of the desk. "And she came to be with you, how?"

"I knew her mother."

"She have any siblings?" Lord, he wanted to talk to her about this, not McNeal.

"Nope, an only child." The man cracked his knuckles and leaned forward. "So, how are things between the two of you?"

"They were fine before she left. Has she said anything?"

McNeal smiled hugely. "Son, that woman don't talk about much, surely you've noticed."

"Yes but with the two of you being so close I thought she may have said something to you about it."

"She treats me as her boss."

"How did you let her get into that line of work? You were there to point her in a different direction but you stood there and are okay with her killing people?"

"The world isn't perfect and we all have to play to our advantages. Bailey is perfect for it and that's just how it is. Most people would have been a wreck about that but not her, she never shed a single tear. When I got to her side, she just stood there, blood on her face. I looked in her eyes and I saw the fire. The burn. The need. So I gave her the opportunity to do just that."

"You turned her into a killer." Disgust filled his tone. "You took advantage of a young girl and molded her into what you wanted. What you needed. This had nothing to do with what she needed. She needed her parents not to be killed. And how did you manage to get to her side so fast if you weren't watching her parents die?"

Kevin didn't respond, just held his gaze. Ivan made a sound of frustration.

"You should be ashamed. Does she know you did this?"

A smile, unpleasant this time, crossed his face. "That's not what I'm here to talk about."

Ivan's stomach churned with distaste.

* * * *

Bailey stirred slightly when the door opened again, using the noise from the hinges to mask any noise she might make. She ignored the couple who came in. Luckily for her—or maybe it wasn't—they didn't change the sheets often.

Since this wasn't who she was after, she settled back. If he were on schedule—and this whore was keeping to hers—he would be the next on in the room with his three prostitutes. Doing her best to ignore the noises, she focused on what she had to do.

Big difference when I do my job, I only need to have an escape plan for myself. I hope this works.

Eventually the noises—faked by the female in her estimation—subsided and the woman waited, her robe around her, for the man to get dressed.

After they had departed, two more women entered. They began stripping the bed. When they came to the closet space, Bailey barely breathed. Her camouflage was exceptional and unless they bent closely to stare at the bottom shelf, she was not concerned about being discovered.

They left after they had finished their job, dirty linen in hand. Incense burned, erasing the scent of sex best it could. This time when the door opened, in came Theodore Ramsey and the whores. He had his arm around two and the third trailed behind. The age of the last one had Bailey curling her lip in disgust. *Bastard, that girl can't be more than eleven. Why the hell did McNeal want me to bring him back alive? He should die.*

Anger grew in her gut as the man she was after instructed the women to undress. The older women snapped at the girl and when everyone's attention was on the child, Bailey moved.

She drugged with the correct amount of the potent concoction to knock him out for a day. Then she used a lesser dose on the women before they could scream. The little girl stared at her with wide eyes. Bailey didn't even try to break their falls—she kept her gaze on the girl and put a finger to her lips.

A slow nod finally came.

"Get dressed," she whispered in Arabic.

The child did as ordered and Bailey got ready to go. Yet, she couldn't help continually gazing over to the small girl. Nor could she ignore the fear in her big brown eyes.

Damn it!

No way in hell she could leave her here. *I can't save everyone.* Perhaps she couldn't, but she could save this girl.

She cursed McNeal again and checked her watch briefly before crouching before her. "I will take you out of here and you can have a better life. You have to do as I say and be quiet." Another check of her watch — her precious window was closing rapidly. "Or you can stay here. Decide quickly."

One blink. "I want to go. I cannot go home, my father will send me back here."

Another man who deserved to die. "Very well. Stay behind me. Stay close. And be quiet."

Eyes that were too old for the body they were in remained solemn as the girl nodded.

Bailey hefted Theodore and made it look as if she was assisting him. There wasn't much eye contact in a place like this. A fact that made her job a bit easier. Thankfully, the bastard didn't weigh a lot. With luck, they made it through to the office. The one man there she dispatched with a knife through the neck.

It took a while, especially with the girl, but she made it through to the laundry and the next hiding place before erasing signs of their escape through the office. The dead man she put in the office and she propped open the rear door slightly to lay a false trail. Then she returned next door.

"Stay here. I will be right back." Reversing, she paused. "He won't bother you. You're safe."

Bailey searched through the laundry until she found more suitable attire for the girl, some for Theodore and a blanket. Then she returned.

"Here, put these on. We have to stay here for a while. In the dark. You can't be afraid."

"I am not afraid."

"Good. Here's a blanket so you don't get cold while you sleep."

Bailey was slightly shocked when the girl did so without complaint or comment. Before the first people arrived, she transferred a still-out Theodore and the girl to a large laundry hamper before slipping on the uniform. She kept her head down, her long hair shoved up under her cap, and wheeled them out into the back of the waiting truck.

She saw some of the men tasked with watching over Theodore out back. They hardly glanced at her, the movement of the laundry service familiar.

Once she was in traffic and positive no one was following her, she pulled into a parking lot. Hopping out, she went to the back and opened it. Stripping off the uniform, she unburied the girl first then Theodore. He remained unconscious.

I don't need him waking up yet. Not until I get this child somewhere away from him.

She held out her hand to the child once she'd adjusted the man on her shoulder. Bailey got him to the van she'd left there the day before. She tossed him in the back and locked it before helping…

"What *is* your name?"

"Safa."

Cruel irony for a child to be named something that means innocent and her having to have gone through what she has.

"Let's get you some food and to somewhere safe."

In the van and driving through the streets of Cairo, Bailey withdrew her phone. She glanced over at the child riding shotgun beside her, face drawn and tired.

"Bailey Hyde, what are you doing calling?"

"Salihah, I need help."

"Anything."

Salihah worked for Theta Corps as well and lived in Cairo. She had been taking a chance expecting her to be there but with the girl, she'd not had a choice.

"Are you in Cairo?"

"Yes." A slight pause. "Are you?"

"I am. I have a girl here who needs help. I can't take her with me to the US but I found her being used as a whore. She's not older than twelve, if even that. I need you to take her and do what's necessary to make sure she doesn't ever have to go back to that life."

"Meet me at the Great Pyramid of Giza."

"Thanks." She disconnected the call.

Bailey headed that way, stopping to get some food for the child. As Safa ate, Bailey leaned against the hood of the van, staring out at the pyramid. *Damn, that thing is impressive.*

"Hey, stranger."

Bailey turned to see Salihah striding up, her thick black hair drawn back in a ponytail.

She smiled and hugged her friend. "Thanks for coming."

"What's going on?"

"Long story but I found her"—she jerked her head in Safa's direction—"being used as a whore. Her father sends her there."

Salihah muttered some words that Bailey agreed with wholeheartedly. "What do you want me to do with her?"

Bailey shrugged. "I hadn't thought that far, just asked her if she'd like to leave. I don't have a passport for her and I'm on a time crunch. She needs to be somewhere where she can have a childhood." She beckoned to Safa. "I want her with people who will do that."

"I can arrange that for you. I'll get her out of Egypt."

"Thanks, Salihah." She faced Safa. "This is Salihah. She will get you somewhere safe. Where you can run

123

and play with other kids. It won't be here in Egypt. But you will be loved and well cared for."

Safa ducked her head before nodding. "But not with you?"

"No, not with me. I can't take you with me any farther than this. You'll be fine, you're strong." Why did this suck so much? "Salihah will give you a number to reach me, any time day or night. Okay? You need me, you call. I will find a way to get to you, no matter what."

Those damn eyes ripped into her, all the way to her soul. "Thank you," Safa said, hugging her tightly. "Thank you for saving me."

Bailey met Salihah's gaze and saw understanding in her friend's expression. "You'd better go." She unwrapped thin arms from her neck. "Goodbye, Safa." Bailey also hugged and said farewell to Salihah.

The child stuck her hand in Salihah's and waved before they walked off and climbed in a Mercedes. Bailey stood there until the vehicle had disappeared from her sight. Ignoring the pain in her gut, she climbed into her van and got on her own way. She still had a job to complete. And it had to do with the man who still lay unconscious in the back of the van.

* * * *

Bailey stared at the man seated in the wheelchair before her. Theodore Ramsey. He sat there, glaring at her, hatred pouring from his blue eyes.

"I don't want any shit from you, I had a hell of a time getting your ass out of that brothel and I'm not one who likes getting people. Not alive, anyway. So, you and I are going to the airline. You will sit there and be good."

He shook his head and muttered behind the swath of duct tape she had over his mouth.

She smiled at him. "See, you're under the impression I was asking you if you'd be good." Her smile vanished. "I wasn't. I'm telling you." Bailey held up a small vial and shook it. "You see, what we have in here is yellow jasmine juice. I won't bore you with the details on how I got it here, or how I put it back to this form from how I received it. Point is, it's poisonous. I could kill you within ten minutes if I gave you a high enough dose. Problem is, I am under orders to get you back to the States alive. So, can't kill you."

His expression paled and his eyes widened more.

"But, I will use enough to drug you. Make you weak, have languor. Slow your cardiac rate, drooping eyelids and more. Enough that you won't be able to argue or make a sound because it also brings with it a loss of articulation."

She showed him a plastic spoon and poured the contents from her tiny vial in there. He gasped when she ripped off his tape and used the opportunity to shove the spoon in his mouth. The tape went back on so he couldn't spit it out.

"You're glaring like you're refusing to swallow. It doesn't matter, it's working already. You may as well give in so I can enjoy the flight."

Once it had taken effect, she untied him, pushed him out to the street, and hailed a taxi. She kept a close eye on him through the airport to their gate. Because he was in a wheelchair, they got to board early and she put him in the seat by the window before settling herself in. It was going to be a long flight back to the US.

Chapter Ten

Another late night. Ivan stumbled to his apartment a few minutes before the witching hour. As usual, he hadn't eaten anything since early in the morning and he was hungry. His plan was food then bed. He even had the day off tomorrow — or was that now today — and he intended on doing nothing but sleeping.

He reheated some leftovers and ate standing over the sink, unsure whether if he sat he would remain awake. This wasn't the most comfortable way he could enjoy a meal but, currently, it was the smartest.

Death by borscht. He snorted and shook his head. *I must be exhausted if this is what my sense of humor has amounted to.*

Ivan placed his dish and silverware in the sink. Turning off lights as he went, he made his way to his bedroom and stripped nude. After taking care of his nightly ritual, he dragged his tired body back to his bed and flopped forward, groaning as the soft mattress surrounded him. He closed his eyes and nothing else mattered.

* * * *

It wasn't the phone this time that woke him—it was the pounding on the door. The task of opening his eyelids was such it took him a few tries before he managed to be successful.

I am going to kill whoever is at my door if the place isn't on fire. Why do they only knock when I'm trying my best to be comatose?

With a huge lurch, he got out of bed and rooted for a pair of sweats to pull on. Once those were in place, he slowly made his way to the door and opened it.

"What?" he snapped, eyes shut as he rubbed them.

"I'm sorry, were you busy?"

That voice. He dropped his arm and opened his eyes to spy Bailey standing there, holding a bag and a tray with two coffees in it.

"Bailey?" He blinked a few times, partially wondering if this was yet another cruel dream where he would wake up alone.

"Ivan."

"God, woman, I missed you."

He cupped her face and kissed her. Her tongue met his and they tangled as he tried to get closer.

She drew back. "Hot beverages here."

Ivan pulled her into his place and shoved the door shut behind her. Taking the drinks from her, he placed them on his counter as, in his periphery, he watched her do the same with the bag.

This time when he reached for her, she met him halfway. Their lips connected and he moaned at the taste of her, once again sliding along his tongue, seeping into him. He dragged his hands down her back to her hips, holding her close. His cock, rock hard, dug into her.

He wanted nothing more than to bury himself deep within her. Again, she moved away.

"I woke you, didn't I?"

"I don't care," he uttered.

"No. You were sleeping. Go back to sleep."

"I haven't seen you in weeks, Bailey. You want me to go back to sleep?"

She took two more steps back and began unbuttoning her green shirt. "I could go for some shut-eye myself."

He was mesmerized by the dark skin that was exposed each time she undid another button. She tugged her hem free from her white jean shorts and kept on until her shirt hung open and he could see her black bra.

Ivan grabbed himself through the sweats, outlining his cock. "You think I can sleep with this?"

The tip of her tongue snuck out and a siren's grin lifted her lips. "I can take care of that for you." She approached him and sank to her knees in front of him. "That would be my pleasure."

She leaned forward and nuzzled his dick, simultaneously moving his hand away. "My definite pleasure."

Her words were soft but he heard them clearly.

Bailey gripped the sides of his sweats and tugged. The material fell easily and his cock sprang out, long and hard.

"Perfect," she said, her warm breath fanning along the sensitive head.

He ground his jaw and held still as she took her time. Her tongue dabbed out and licked along the shaft, as if she were tasting ice cream, or a lollipop. Fast licks. Slow ones. Some with the flat of her tongue and others with just the tip.

Ivan was ready to come already and she hadn't even taken him in her mouth. Her hands, she kept on his thighs as she inched closer to him. He stared down at her — she wasn't focused on anything other than his cock.

Her right hand curved around the shaft and he groaned. She moved it while her tongue continued to shower attention upon the large head. She swiped it along the rim and underneath, all the while working her hand, alternating the pressure she used.

Just when he thought he had himself under a bit more control, she opened her mouth and drew him in.

"Fuck!"

She bobbed her head taking in more and more with each move. He closed his eyes and locked his knees when she played with his balls as well. The touch, the pressure and the knowledge it was her catapulted him along a fast track to coming.

Bailey began circling his dick with her tongue while she continued to work his length. He squirmed when she flicked her tongue over the ridge between the shaft and the head.

"Bailey," he called out.

She didn't respond in any way other than what she was doing. Pleasuring him. Her moans and sighs spurred him on even more. She loved what she was doing and that heightened his own experience.

When she positioned one hand so she could massage his perineum, his legs shook. He couldn't hold out much longer.

She must have known, for she tightened her lips around him and sucked without pause until he shot his cum into her throat. She swallowed it all then proceeded to lap at his cock until he reached down and lifted her off the floor.

"Christ, woman, I think you almost killed me."

"You would have gone with a smile on your face," she countered.

"Hell yes I would have." He kissed her.

* * * *

Bailey still slept when he woke. He rolled to his side and stared at the woman slumbering beside him. A quick glance at the clock had it past noon. He didn't care—he did not intend to leave his apartment for the entire day.

He couldn't see any new scars on her and she didn't act as though she had been injured. Bailey lay sleeping on her back, one hand beneath the pillow beside her and the other across her stomach.

"You're staring at me." Her voice was soft and sleepy.

"I can't help it. You're beautiful."

She gave a slight chuckle. "I think you need more sleep."

"Not going to change your beauty." He sat at the side of the bed and looked for his sweats before recalling they were in the living room.

She finally opened her eyes and looked at him. "Why are you up?"

"I was hungry. Want me to fix something for you as well?"

"Please."

He almost missed it. The flash of concern on her face—it was there then gone so quickly, but with the intensity he'd been watching her, he'd caught it.

"What's wrong, Bailey?"

She began to shake her head and he captured her chin.

"Don't lie to me and say nothing. Tell me. Did your mission not go well?"

"It went. It was successful. I guess" —she sighed— "I was thinking of someone."

"Who?"

"Safa."

He lay back on the bed but used the headboard to prop himself up. "Who is Safa?" Ivan wanted her to open up to him, wanted her to feel she could share with him anything and everything. Deep in his soul he knew she was the one for him, no matter that they were so opposite. "Bailey?"

"A young girl I found in a whorehouse." She sat up, using the sheet to keep her covered.

"Like, eighteen young?"

"No. Between ten to twelve would be my guess."

Anger coursed through his veins. "What the fuck was she doing there?"

"Her father was pimping her out. I took her."

Bailey looked at him and he thought about what McNeal had said about her losing her parents right in front of her.

"You did the right thing." He brushed some hair back from her face. "Where is she now?"

"I don't know. I called in a friend and told her to make sure Safa is put in a place where she will be loved. She won't be in Egypt anymore, but I don't know where she is."

"You want to know." *So she was in Egypt.*

She nodded. "I need to make sure she's okay." She shoved a hand through her hair. "I don't know why, I just need to."

"Because you care about her."

"I hardly know her. Had she not wanted to come with me, I would have left her there."

He frowned. "Really?"

Bailey stared off at something only she could see. "Yes. I was in the middle of a mission."

"You were at a whorehouse to kill someone?"

"It wasn't that, I was there for another retrieval. I don't know why McNeal sent me on it. But he did and I was there."

Ivan had his suspicions but kept them to himself. He drew her closer to him and kissed the top of her head. "So call your friend and find out where she is. Go see for yourself that she's doing fine."

"I ripped her from her family and put her with strangers. How will she be fine?"

"Because any guy who sells his daughter isn't a father. That fucker isn't even a real man. You know you saved her life. Someone would have been too rough with her or gotten her pregnant. You did the right thing, Bailey."

"Maybe."

She sounded so despondent he wasn't sure what else to say. So he held her. After a short time, he planted another kiss on her head. "Let's get something to eat. And you can tell me about the rest of your trip."

Bailey slipped on one of Ivan's shirts. His scent surrounded her and she felt her soul settle. Why this man? She didn't know.

"I went to Egypt and brought back someone to the US. Then I came back here."

Ivan paused in grabbing a pair of workout pants and looked over his shoulder at her. "That's it?"

"I don't know anything about him or why he was wanted. McNeal said it was important and I went."

He pulled on the pants with a shake of his head. "I don't know how you do it."

"Do what?"

"What they ask of you. Do you ever know more about the person you are sent to kill?" When she raised an eyebrow he amended, "Or retrieve?"

"No."

"Why not?"

"Because I do my job."

He grunted and tugged on a shirt. "I see." Ivan left the room.

Bailey didn't understand but she didn't linger either. She followed him out, the bottom of his shirt brushing the tops of her thighs. The food she'd arrived with was now cold but he had a microwave and so he put it in there.

"You don't approve of what I do."

"I don't want to get into that right now. Tell me more about Egypt."

"Not much to tell. I wasn't there for a sightseeing tour. I did go to the museum and I saw Giza."

"But didn't run into any trouble?"

"Not really. Like I said, Safa was unexpected but she wasn't actually a problem."

He put two glasses down and strode over to her. "Go away with me."

"What?"

"Come away with me. Take a vacation. We can go see and make sure Safa is okay then we can be somewhere where we're not working for Theta Corps. You're just you and I'm just me." His hands cupped her face as he stared in her eyes. "What do you say?"

Sounds wonderful. "I'd say you had an idea of where you wanted to go."

"Russia."

She stared for a moment. "You want to go home. And what…introduce me to your mother?"

"Yes."

His response came so quick, it shocked her and she wasn't sure how to respond. The beeping from the microwave pulled him away and she utilized the moment to try to recover.

Why does he want to take me home to his mother? I didn't realize he felt this way. Then again, maybe he wants to merely take a trip and I will be like a friend who's traveling along with him. Nothing romantic about it.

She gazed back in his direction. Nothing romantic. Did she truly believe that?

Ivan put the food on their plates and looked at her. "You seem surprised by that." He carried the items to the table. "Why are you surprised?"

"Why do you want to introduce me to your mother?"

"Because you're my girlfriend. It's what couples do."

Standing behind the chair at the table, she gripped her fingers into the smooth wood. Girlfriend? "Couples?"

His laughter was rich and deep, oddly comforting given the panic that was setting into her.

The tall Russian walked over to her, turned her so they were face to face, and placed his hands on her waist. "Baby, did you really think I took a job in the middle of this country and got this apartment to see you because we were just friends? I could have had a lab built in Russia and been close to family. I chose here because I chose you. And I was hoping this place was one you came back to often. So yes, I think of you as my girlfriend and us as a couple." A quick brush of lips. "Got it?"

She swallowed. "Yes."

His grin would have melted all her clothes off were she wearing much more than her panties and his shirt. As it was, her nipples beaded and drew tight and longing rose within her. Food was appearing less and less important by the heartbeat.

"Excellent." Another kiss and he was back on his side of the table. "Let's eat."

She sat and stared down at the reheated French toast. Picking up the fork and knife, she paused at his laughter.

"What's funny?"

"You seem really confused there, Bailey. Why is that?"

"I don't know." She cut into the food. "Guess I didn't know you thought that way about me...or us."

He leaned forward. "Don't you?"

"I think so. I've never had someone pursue me like you are doing, Ivan. I'm not sure what to make of it."

"Is it bad? I mean, are you thinking I'm stalking you?"

Now it was her turn to laugh. "No. You knew what I did for a living and came. I don't think you'd be dumb enough to stalk someone who kills."

He chewed his food and took a drink. "So you're okay with being my girlfriend."

"Yes, Doctor. I am."

He settled back in his chair. "So, about the trip. Tell me what your thoughts are on it."

"I could use a vacation so yes. I would love to go with you."

His smile was immediate and perfect. She shifted in the chair. *Damn him for doing what he does to me.*

After they had finished eating, she washed the dishes while he made a phone call. She assumed it was to his mother but since he spoke Russian, she wasn't positive. They finished about the same time and he had a weary expression on his face.

"Everything okay?"

"My mother can be exhausting. I hope you're ready for parties. She plans on throwing 'a few'. Those would be her words."

"I don't party much but sure, I'm game. As long as this isn't something where you leave me to fend for myself."

He prowled toward her. "And here I thought you were used to working alone."

"Not against mothers. They are something else entirely." A slight shrug. "I don't have much experience with them."

He sobered. "Do you want to talk about it?"

She lifted an eyebrow. "It? What's *it*?"

"You not having much experience with mothers."

"No." She waved off his question. "I do not."

For a moment, she thought he was going to push the subject further but he let it go. Instead, he swept her up in his arms and carried her back to the bedroom.

"What are you doing?"

"I thought we should figure out when we're going so we can get tickets. And tell our bosses."

Casting a look around, she cleared her throat. "So, then, we're doing what exactly in your bedroom?"

"I have a calendar in here. Somewhere," he muttered, tossing her on the bed. "You should help me look for it."

She squealed when he lifted her shirt. "I don't believe you'll find it there."

"No, but there's something I want under here." He nipped the top of her thigh and pressed a kiss to her belly button. "Most definitely want."

She began to stop him but when his mouth covered her pussy, she stopped. They could plan the trip later.

* * * *

It wasn't until late afternoon that they finally left the bedroom and went to figure out their trip. While he called to get time off, she placed her own call.

"Strange, Bailey, for you to be calling me."

She sat on the couch and stared at her hand. "I'm taking some time off, McNeal."

With his silence, she could picture his expression. Both eyebrows raised, leaned back in his chair and lips pursed as he tried to find his words.

"You need some time? Take a day, sure."

"No. You don't understand. I'm taking about a month off or so. Getting away."

Keyboard typing came through to her ear. "You know I could just deny this request."

"And I could quit. Both things we know aren't going to happen. Stop being a prick, McNeal. I've never taken a vacation, I need one."

"This have something to do with bringing Theodore Ramsey back to the States?"

"Why would it? I don't even know why you want him. You sent me to do a retrieval and I did. Just for future reference, I despise doing them. Don't send me on any more."

"He's reviving the terrorist group The Watchers. I told you about the targets — this is the man behind it all. But he was hiding out of the country and he knows most of the players from previous interactions with Theta Corps."

"I fail to see how this is relevant."

"I'm telling you more about why we wanted him."

She shook her head. "I didn't ask."

"Bailey. You are needed."

"I'm confused. Are you saying I can't go because I may be needed to kill a man you just had me bring to you alive instead of killing him there?"

Ivan looked at her, confusion on his face. She didn't have time to explain it to him and she wasn't sure she even understood. She broke eye contact and waited for her answer.

"No, we needed him alive. Hopefully he will be able to tell us more about what the group has planned."

"All of which I fail to see how it pertains to me and my vacation."

McNeal coughed. "What if I don't want you to take all this time off?"

"Then that's your problem. I wasn't asking. Ivan and I are taking time. You and the rest of Theta Corps will leave us alone."

"You're going, aren't you?" The statement was resigned.

"I will call you when we're back."

"Do you have an idea when that will be?"

"Years, McNeal. I've gone years without a vacation. Don't push me on this."

"I'm only asking so I know to worry if you're not back by a specific time."

"Would it make you feel better if I say I will call you once a week on Sundays? And give you an update?"

"Yes."

"You would?"

Another surprise for her. She had been being facetious and hadn't expected him to want that. Ivan's smile was gentle and contained a bit of knowing in it, as if he had just gotten a revelation.

"I would. That is acceptable. You two have fun." The call ended.

She stared at her phone, looking for an answer she knew wasn't there but that she hoped to locate anyway. *What was that about?*

"I'm good on this end and he said so were you. So figure out when you want to go then tell me where so I know how to pack."

Ivan knelt before her and slid her to the edge of the sofa. "Thank you for coming with me."

Bailey leaned forward and pressed their lips together. "Thanks for inviting me. Now tell me what I can do to help."

He nipped her lower lip and winked. "I have a few ideas."

She'd just bet he did.

Chapter Eleven

St Petersburg, Russia

Crisp air flowed around them and Ivan held out a hand to Bailey, assisting her from the taxi. He stared up at his childhood home and smiled. This felt right, being back again at the good-sized two story house.

"Very nice," Bailey said beside him. She took her hand from his and grabbed her bag.

"Thanks. Can't wait to take you on a tour."

The front door opened and his mother burst through.

"Ivan! I can't believe you're actually here," she cried in Russian.

He hurried to meet her at the bottom of the steps and hugged her. It had been a long time since he'd seen her — close to three years.

"I've missed you, Mama."

She kissed him and stood back to look at him. The tears in her eyes were daggers to his heart. He'd been a terrible son, not coming home for so long. She looked the same, her thick brown hair still without any gray and her blue eyes sharp as a hawk's.

"It is good to see you, Ivan." She brushed at the tears and patted his cheek before she smiled. "Introduce me to her."

Ivan turned and found Bailey waiting patiently by their luggage. Just looking at that woman made his heart skip a beat. She had her hair loose and it fell free around her face, moving slightly in the breeze. Her navy knitted pants and Bordeaux mock turtleneck combined with the boots she wore highlighted her natural good looks. Her expression was serene as he beckoned her forward.

She moved with the grace he was used to seeing from her. When she reached his side, he took her hand. "Mama," he said. "I'd like for you to meet Bailey Hyde. Bailey, this is my mama, Aksana Vinokourov."

"Nice to meet you, Mrs Vinokourov." She held out her hand and shook his mother's.

"Please, no need to call me that. You are with Ivan, I am either Aksana or Mama," she replied in English.

Ivan stared at his mother, eyes wide, before swallowing hard and putting his attention on Bailey. If she was shocked, she didn't let it show. The smile remained in place and she nodded slowly.

"Let's get you inside and settled. Then we can catch up. Unless you'd like some more rest."

"Actually, I would love to lie down for a bit," Bailey chimed in. "I didn't sleep much on the plane."

His mother gestured Bailey forward and said, "I understand. Come along, Ivan, bring the bags."

Ivan dutifully followed and trailed his mother and his girlfriend inside his ancestral home. They both had rooms on the second floor, separate but within close proximity. Bailey didn't make any questioning looks over that, just gave his mother a smile.

"This is beautiful, thank you so much for your hospitality."

His mother patted Bailey's hand. "You are friend of Ivan. We see you after you rest. Explore anywhere."

"Thank you, ma'am." Bailey gave him a small nod before she closed the door on them.

His mother walked off down the hall. "Come, Ivan." This time she spoke Russian.

They went back downstairs and sat in the large living room. There was tea, coffee and pastries. He settled in with a drink in one hand and a plate of sweets in the other.

"She's not Jaydee."

The statement shocked him such, he nearly dropped his drink. It still wobbled in his hand.

"No, she's not. Jaydee is married with children. Why would you think it was going to be her?"

"You sounded so happy when you said you were bringing a girlfriend."

He tilted his head to the side. "I am happy. With Bailey."

"Are you still in love with Jaydee?"

He took a drink of his coffee. Was he? "No."

"You didn't answer immediately. I think maybe you are not sure."

"Whether I am or not, doesn't matter. Like I said, she's married and they have triplets."

"What does this one do?" She smoothed her dress and sipped her tea. Ever the lady, his mother.

"We work for the same organization."

"So she is a scientist like you? Did you meet in your lab?" A frown. "Are you her boss and taking advantage of that position with her?"

"Calm down. She's not a scientist. We don't even work in the same department. Our business is large so not everyone works together. So, no, I'm not her boss and I'm definitely not taking advantage of her." *I don't know if anyone could take advantage of her. Except perhaps...* Nope, he wasn't going there right now.

She ate a little bit, dabbed the corners of her mouth then said, "You have nothing in common then? At least with Jaydee you were both scientists. So what does she do?"

And it got a little tricky. He couldn't very well tell her she killed people. "She acquires things for them."

"Is that why she travels so much? She's off getting these items?"

"Yes."

"What was she acquiring in Madagascar when the two of you met?"

Me. He shook his head. "I don't ask, she doesn't talk a lot about her job. Neither do I. You know I work in top secret stuff so it's just easier not to discuss work."

"I can understand that." She stood and lifted the tray. "I am so glad you're back home, Ivan. I can see you're also tired, so get some rest. We'll catch up later."

"I'm not tired," he protested.

"Then you can come with me and tell me what else you've been up to, but I have to start tonight's meal."

"I'd love to help."

* * * *

Two hours later, Ivan was out walking around on the property. He couldn't describe how wonderful it felt to be home. He loved his country and the place where he'd grown up.

His mother still had a good chunk of land with the house and so he walked around it, taking his time and allowing the feeling of home to settle in him. He leaned against a tree to readjust his shoe and looked up to find Bailey standing there.

"Hey."

She smiled and walked toward him. "Hi."

"Did you get some rest?"

"I did, thank you." She gazed about. "You have a very beautiful home, Ivan. Thank you for inviting me."

He crooked his finger at her. "I'm glad you agreed to come."

She slowly approached him and slipped her arms around his waist prior to resting her head against his chest. "I haven't been to Russia in a long time. And then it wasn't even to St Petersburg."

He drew back and stared down at her. "Where were you?"

"Arkhangel'sk."

Her accent was near perfect. "Archangel? What the hell were you doing there?"

She stepped free of his touch. "My job. I've also been to Moscow but I don't tend to get sent there. All I recall is that it's a beautiful city at night. I had more time in Moscow and saw a few things, also beautiful."

"You never cease to amaze me, Bailey."

She gazed up at the sky. "Why is that?"

He shook his head. "You just do. Come walk with me. Let me show you my home."

She slid her hand into his. "Okay."

They walked toward the back end of the property.

"Tell me where else you have houses."

"No houses, only apartments."

He filed that away. "Okay, so where are they? Other than Chile."

"I also have ones in Paris and Brisbane."

"What about the United States?"

"Chicago and one in Southern California."

"Any others?"

"Five isn't enough for you?"

"Is it enough for you?" he countered.

"Yes, if it wasn't I would have more."

"Where do you stay more often than not?"

"Santiago. But I move around. Depends on where my mission was and my condition after plays into my decision of where to stay as well."

Ivan didn't respond, he just tightened his hold on her hand. Bailey Hyde was a unique woman. He wasn't entirely sure why she did what she did, nor had he figured out her thought process yet. It was a journey he was looking forward to, however.

* * * *

"You're where?" McNeal didn't sound pleased.

"St Petersburg." Bailey sat on the stone bench in Ivan's mother's garden and watched the birds fight for the food in the feeders. Some played in the stone basin that made up a bath.

"I'm guessing this isn't the one in Florida."

"Well, when they stamped my passport it said Russia but I suppose they could have been wrong."

"Why are you in Russia?"

"Does it matter, McNeal? I'm on my vacation and am calling you as I said I would. Be happy with that."

"I'd be happier if you weren't with him."

"Luckily for both of us, we don't answer to you about our relationships. Is that all?"

"Got somewhere to be?"

"Actually yes, he's taking me sightseeing, I'm just waiting for him to bring the car around."

"You're sounding domesticated."

"And you still sound like an ass. What's your problem with Ivan, McNeal? This is your fault, you know. You're the one who sent me on that first retrieval to begin with. Had you allowed me to keep to my normal job, I wouldn't have met him. So I guess I should be thanking you. Bye." She hung up and chuckled as she envisioned his expression.

"Ready?" Ivan asked from behind her.

"I am." She stood and slid her phone into her pocket. "Where are you taking me?"

"I thought we'd go to one of the parks today. Sosnovka. And the Summer Garden."

"Let's go." She double-checked to make sure her passport sat in another pocket then went around the bench and walked beside Ivan. "I've heard about the marble sculptures in the Summer Garden. Can't wait to see them in person."

"Who was on the phone?" He draped an arm around her shoulder.

"McNeal."

"And he wanted?"

"Me not to be in St Petersburg."

Ivan slowed and halted her. "He has a problem with me?"

"Knowing McNeal, yes. He has a problem with most people. So I told him we didn't answer to him and thanked him for allowing us to meet."

"You didn't."

"Actually I did. It wasn't a lie. Had he not sent me, I wouldn't have met you." She wasn't sure how she liked that knowledge. "Let's go."

"And you're okay with that?"

She cocked her head to the side. "With what? It's fact. That's all there is to it. Nothing to feel one way or the other about." *Despite what my heart may be saying.*

"Things are so simple for you, aren't they, Bailey?"

"I like simple."

They began walking again. She ogled him in her periphery. Ivan was a man you didn't see then look away from. He drew your eye. Or rather, he drew hers. Repeatedly.

Today his chinos fitted his lower body in a way that made her think of things best suited to being behind closed doors instead of heading to a public area. His black shirt offset his blond hair and ice-blue eyes spectacularly.

During the ride to Sosnovka, Ivan kept her entertained with tales of his childhood.

"Where's your father?"

He shifted gears and sighed. "He ran off with some young woman when I was five. I was the only child so it's just Mama and myself."

"I'm sorry."

"Nothing to be sorry about. I barely knew him. He was always gone. With his whores, from what Mama says."

She listened to his intonation and discovered no bitterness. Just an acceptance of how things had been.

"But you have a big family? How does that work?"

"Mama came from a family of thirteen, so I have lots of aunts and uncles, cousins and the like. When I was younger, she kept me away from them for a good while. She didn't want to have the sympathetic looks for having lost her husband."

"How'd she lose him if he was the one who left?"

"The shame of not keeping her husband. Some were judgmental."

She grunted. Large families were apparently complicated.

"What?"

"Seems to me if they were her family they should have been supportive because he didn't honor his vows. Not blaming her."

Ivan's smile warmed her. "I agree. Unfortunately, there are always some who feel it is the woman's job to keep the man happy and satisfied at home so he won't look elsewhere. Then again, some feel men have the right to look elsewhere despite being married."

She angled herself to stare at him. "And what is your stance on such a thing?"

"Well, a woman who keeps her man satisfied is a definite plus, and you know it's not too shabby to be able to go out and—" He burst into laughter. "Sorry, but your facial expression is priceless. I couldn't resist."

She crossed her arms and glared. "You know you're going to pay for that."

His grin was pure sin. "I do hope so. Will there be ropes?" He parked the car in the lot and shut it off."

Bailey smirked. "I've never had to tie a man to keep him in my bed. Don't plan on starting now. If you need to be tied up then you don't want to be there with me." She climbed out before shutting the door with her hip.

Ivan was at her side in seconds. He crowded her against the side, nibbling along her neckline. "I will stay in your bed willingly. Any time. Just say the word."

"Humph. You still didn't say where you stood on that."

He took her arm. "Baby, I'm all man but I will treat the one I'm with like she's a queen and deserves the moon. To be disrespectful to a woman is not my way. Never has been nor will it ever be."

She pushed up on her toes and kissed him. "Good answer."

Lacing their fingers, she led him toward the front entrance. Sosnovka was beautiful and she had a lovely time. It was huge, covering two hundred and forty hectares. She needed so much more time there. After they'd visited there he took her, as promised, to the Summer Garden and she spent her time checking out the marble statues.

"You like art," he said as she moved from one statue on to the next one.

"I love it. Even though the statues out here are the replicas, it doesn't matter. I especially enjoyed some of the remaining fountains depicting scenes from Aesop's Fables."

"Do you collect art?"

"I do, paintings." She moved on to another Venetian sculpture.

"What type of paintings?"

"Landscape, mostly. I find it calming to have nature scenes around me."

"Why don't you have a place in the country if you enjoy it so much?"

"Easier to hide in a city. When I'm done with Theta Corps, I plan on having something with acreage. Not sure where. Haven't figured out if I want mountains or ocean. Or just open fields or a thick forest surrounding me."

"When are you finishing with Theta Corps?"

"I don't know, when it no longer works for me. Haven't really thought about it."

"I see."

Bailey knew he had more inquisitions but she didn't want to play twenty questions right now. So she didn't encourage more about that. "What's your favorite thing to do here?"

They sat on a bench and she watched people as they wandered by.

"I haven't been in a while, but I really enjoy the Scarlet Sails celebration."

"Scarlet Sails?"

"It's amazing, held during the White Nights Festival. The water show is incredible. There's also fireworks and concerts. But the ships all have the red sails. Beneath the fireworks exploding above, it's one hell of a view." He kissed her temple. "It's also one huge draw, gets big stars and entertainers as well."

"I'll put it on my wish list."

"I'd love to go to it with you." He stood and drew her up with him. "Let's go. I want you to myself tonight. Tomorrow we have a party with everyone."

"And you don't want to share?"

"Not tonight."

His words created a swell of desire. She smiled and leaned her head against his arm. "Sounds fine to me."

Ivan took her out to a lovely restaurant for a romantic dinner then back to his home. His mother had made herself scarce and they didn't even run into her. After changing from her dress into pants and a shirt, they went out for another walk and Ivan laid out a blanket for them to share as they gazed up at the brilliant stars.

He held her in his arms as if she was the most precious of possessions. For once, Bailey allowed herself to truly relax. Not to be listening for someone sneaking up on her from behind or potentially stepping on her as she lay in wait for her target. There was none of that, just her and Ivan. Together.

Chapter Twelve

Laughter filled the air and Ivan smiled as he stood beside his uncle Roman as the man expertly worked the grill.

"You are staying for a while this time?" The question came in Russian.

"A while, we're not sure yet for how long. We have to go visit a friend of Bailey's as well and see how she is doing."

His uncle grunted and flipped the meats. "She is a special woman, this Bailey."

Ivan nodded. "I know."

"You two are nothing alike. Polar opposites."

"Is that a bad thing?"

"It is what it is. Opposites can be a good thing in a relationship, but it can also make it hard."

"Are you and Aunt Lidia so similar?"

"God no. Me? I like working with my hands and don't mind being dirty. You know your aunt. The opposite. She would sit on silk all day if she could and be waited on hand and foot."

"She is kind of a snob like that." He glanced over to the woman they discussed. Even now, she sat on a special chair with an extra cushion and a top to keep her out of the sunlight for fear it may cause a wrinkle or two.

"Bailey's not like that."

"No, I can see that. She's barefoot playing with the kids." He smacked Ivan on the back. "Still doesn't negate the fact there is something about her. She would be fine putting herself off to the side. And there's an edge about her. You, Ivan, are an open book. Always have been."

"What?"

"Yes. You wear your emotions on your sleeve. When you said that Jaydee was married, we all knew how much it hurt you. You've always been that way. You show how you are feeling. No, it doesn't make you less of a man. It makes you you. But with this one, I just can't read her. Even Jaydee we understood, not so much Bailey."

"Stop trying to figure her out, Uncle. She's not in trouble with the law so you don't need to investigate her."

"Already did."

Ivan wasn't sure what to say. He hadn't a single clue what would come up when someone typed in Bailey's name. They 'worked' for a place officially called Belmore that had interests across the board and numerous subsidiary companies. Interests that could cover everyone who worked at Theta Corps without announcing to the world it was a headquarters and cover for a place that carried out clandestine operations. But the actual label of what was beside her, or her job position, Ivan didn't have a clue. Ivan's was a company called Futuro. But if it were traced it back, Belmore would be the parent company.

"Then you know."

"I know she carries herself like someone who was in the military. Or still is. But her record doesn't state that. So is she in a black op?"

"She's had a hard life, Uncle. Lost her parents when she was young in a senseless murder. She tends to be a bit on edge. Don't bother her about this."

"That explains it." He worked the grill. "I like her, Ivan. She makes you smile. And you're protecting her. That's a good sign as well." He put some hamburgers on a plate. "Has my sister asked you when you're giving her a grandbaby to spoil? She's the only one of us who doesn't have any."

Shit! "No, Mama hasn't said anything about that and I don't need you talking like that around Bailey either. Don't scare her off."

Roman laughed loudly. "I bet that woman isn't afraid of much."

For the most part, Ivan would agree, but it didn't mean he wanted them harping on at her about children. He'd seen the brief panic in her eyes when he'd mentioned girlfriend. *Somehow I think mentioning mother may just be a bit much.*

"I would just prefer to not find out, thanks."

"I give you my word but I can't speak for the other twelve."

Ivan groaned and dropped his head forward as his uncle shouted out that the food was ready. The noise swell increased as everyone approached the grill and formed a line. Ivan smacked his uncle on the back and went to join Bailey in line.

"Hey," he said, smiling at his cousins.

"Hi."

"You looked like you were having fun out there."

"I was. Been a while since I've played soccer and they're good."

He tugged her back against his chest, needing the contact. "They like you."

"Perhaps," she said non-committally.

"I know these things. They do."

Around him the Russian conversation grew and he almost told them to speak English. Bailey put her hand on his arm and shook her head.

"What?"

"This is their party, Ivan. They don't have to struggle to remember to speak English just because I'm here. I don't mind."

"It's not polite."

"They speak English when they talk to me. That's polite enough. Don't make it an issue, I'm fine."

They got their food and joined the long table set up. Ivan sat on one side of her and Mavra, another aunt, sat on the other side of Bailey.

"How long have the two of you been going out?" Kiryl, an uncle, posed the question.

"Not too long yet. But I've known her for nearly a year."

"Your mother says you two met in Madagascar. Bailey, what were you doing there?"

She drank some of her punch. "I was retrieving an item my boss asked me to pick up for him."

"And met him there?"

"Yes. It was at a dinner. He was there with some others and we brushed into one another." She finished fixing her hamburger how she wanted it.

Chuckles rippled along as the older ones winked and nodded.

"So love at first sight?" Mavra this time.

"No," Ivan said simultaneously with Bailey. They shared a look and he was grateful she was taking this without getting upset. Her eyes twinkled with merriment.

"Did you know Jaydee?" Margosha, his youngest cousin, queried. "He brought her here many times."

The table fell silent and Ivan wanted to go back in time to make sure that question never got asked.

Bailey, the epitome of calm and grace, merely smiled. "No. I've never had the pleasure of meeting her. I heard a lot of wonderful things about her, though."

"Ivan loves her."

"Margosha, enough," Roman admonished. He glanced at them with a sheepish smile. "She is young."

"She's a wonderful child," Bailey said before eating some more.

After a few moments of uneasy silence, the chatter picked up again. Not as loud as it had been, but loud. He watched her but Bailey didn't seem the least bit put out by the circumstances. She chatted and laughed with those around her. She also didn't pull away from the press of his leg against hers.

"Can I get you any more?" he asked, standing.

"Oh, goodness no. I saw the desserts over there and have to save room for some of that." She smiled at Roman. "The burgers were delicious, thank you."

Margosha hopped over to Bailey. "I'm getting cake. You come?"

She slid back her chair and grinned. "A girl after my own heart. Yes, let's get some dessert."

Bailey kept the smile on her face as she looked over the vast array of sweets. "How do you pick just one?

They all look so good," she said conspiratorially to Margosha. "I want them all."

"Me too."

As she worked with the girl, she did her best to ignore the pain in her heart. She couldn't blame Margosha. She'd only said what she knew to be the truth—Ivan loved Jaydee.

Man's holding one hell of a torch for her because I know the kids are a few years old. Now wasn't the time to think about such a revelation. She had to get through this first. Not that it was a hardship. Ivan's family was wonderful and she truly was enjoying herself.

With three small samples on her plate, she and Margosha returned to the table. Ivan had gotten her a cup of coffee and it waited for her as well.

"Thank you," she said.

"Are you okay?" he whispered the words in her ear.

"Of course. Why wouldn't I be?"

Ivan held her gaze and gave her a soft smile. He wiped the pad of his thumb along her lower lip. "You know why. We'll talk about it later."

"Sure." *No thanks. I don't need to be reminded again of who I'm not.* She picked up her fork and cut off a piece of the white cake with lemon frosting. It melted in her mouth and she couldn't stop the groan from slipping free. "Oh God, this is so good."

They spent the rest of the day playing games, talking and eating more than she could ever need to eat. No one left until after the night meal—also huge and filling—had been devoured and everything cleaned up.

Bailey hugged and shook hands with everyone as they left. They all made Ivan promise to bring her by their place for a meal before they left. She just smiled and tried to remember who was who—her brain was on overload.

Finally, the house was quiet, Aksana had retired to her room and Bailey stood in the front room, staring out over the lawn. The night lights cast a mystical glow about the benches, and plants sporadically dotted the area.

Ivan slipped his arms around her waist and rested his chin on the top of her head. "So, what do you think?"

"I think your family is fun and very loving." She squeezed his hand. "Thank you for allowing me the opportunity to meet them."

"About what Margosha said in regards to Jaydee."

She stiffened but didn't pull away. "I don't need an explanation, Ivan. In fact, I would prefer the matter be dropped entirely."

"I need to explain—"

"No, you don't." She turned in his arms and placed her palms on his chest. "You feel how you feel. I can't change that and no explanation will either. *You* don't owe me one."

He covered her hands with his larger ones, the calluses comforting in a way. His thumbs skimmed the backs of her fingers in abstract patterns.

"I don't want any confusion about this lingering."

She weighed her words carefully. Removing her hands from beneath his, she took a step back. "If you insist. Speak your piece."

He snagged her wrist before leading her to the midnight blue loveseat. Their knees touched when they sat.

"Do you know Jaydee?"

An unpleasantness filled her gut. *Could I actually be jealous of that woman? Is that possible? Or feasible? What reason could I have to be?*

"No," she said. "I've never met her." She took a breath and calmed herself. "Like I said earlier, I've heard wonderful things about her, however."

His smile was akin to a dagger being stuck in her heart, slowly. "Jaydee and I have known each other for years. Since she was twelve and I was fourteen."

"So you were childhood sweethearts."

"No. I mean, I was wanting. She never once saw me in that light. There wasn't emotion like that between us. We were friends. That's it."

Yet you loved, or love, her. "Okay, thanks for explaining."

He took her hand with a harsh chuckle. "I'm not done."

She was a bit taken aback by the amount of ferocity in his voice. Ivan was normally even keeled, from what she knew. "Thought you were finished."

"I love Jaydee, that's true. I always will. But I am not *in* love with her. I had believed myself in love with her. Even after she married I wondered if I would be able to truly let her go. Then you came into my life."

She stared at him, silent, waiting for him to continue.

Ivan lifted her and settled her upon his lap. "You changed my life since you walked — sashayed — into that room wearing the sexy-as-fuck red and black pin-up couture dress. Seeing you in it gave me a dick that could have punched a hole in the wall of the house. It's not something I can quantify but —"

Bailey placed her hand over his mouth. "Stop, Ivan. I felt it too. Feel it too."

His actions were slow and deliberate as he moved her hand away.

"There's no one in this world quite like you, Bailey Hyde."

She wrapped her arms around his neck and rubbed against his cock. "There's not supposed to be."

"I really want to—" He sighed. "We need to learn more about one another."

"Isn't that learning more if you know what makes me scream in passion or come hard around your cock?"

"Baby. I have every intention of learning *all* the things that make you scream. And purr. Moan. Beg." He stood, keeping her at his waist. "Right now, we talk."

"Being naked and sweaty with limbs entwined is a form of communication."

"Very true." He gripped her ass and walked through the house.

"So no more talking?"

He frowned at her. "More talking."

She groaned and turned to track his movements around the room. When he ducked into the bathroom, she walked to the window and peered out. Ivan's room overlooked the backyard. The moonlight sparkled off the fountain's spray, as if someone stood at the base, tossing up handfuls of diamonds, both white and colored.

"Come here, Bailey."

She rotated away from the serene image to find Ivan standing beside his bed, clothes from earlier gone and replaced by a pair of dark workout pants. Doing as ordered, Bailey strolled over to him, taking in the bottle beside the bed. Opaque and unlabeled, she couldn't identify it.

"What's going on?"

"Talking. You naked. And a massage." He gestured to the bed. "Deal?"

"Absolutely." She made short work of her attire, gloated internally a bit about his reaction to her, then climbed on the bed. On all fours, ass in his direction, she peered at him. "Where do you want me?" She dragged her tongue along her lower lip. "And how?"

Ivan's throat worked fast. His pupils dilated and there wasn't any way she could miss his erection, creating a tent in his pants.

"Stomach." His word was graveled and rough, sending pulses from her clit out through her entire being.

"Okay." She lowered her upper body to the coverlet. "Here okay? Or want me a different direction?"

He muttered something in Russian before he caressed her ass with his palm then pressed on the small of her back. "This is fine."

She melted down and sighed. "Very well."

The mattress dipped as he joined her. He straddled her ass and she moaned when he leaned forward and put his hands on her back.

"You told me you speak a few languages."

She grunted her acknowledgment. His touch disappeared only to be replaced by a cool liquid. The air filled with a heady, woodsy scent with hints of floral.

"How many and which ones?" Ivan touched her again, rubbing, stroking, even petting her skin as he spread the oil across her body. It heated as he created some friction between it and her. "Bailey, talk to me."

"Your hands are like magic and you want me to think?"

"And converse."

"Just don't stop touching."

"No plans to do that. Now, answer my question."

Bailey had to think hard about what he'd asked. "Languages."

"Uh-hmmm."

His touch was utterly blissful and she closed her eyes, allowing the pleasure to take center stage.

"English and Spanish."

"I got that already." An amused chuckle accompanied his statement. "What else?"

"I speak...oh God, yeah right there...passable Arabic, not fluent but I can make it without being taken advantage of."

"Is that all?"

She rolled her shoulders and burrowed deeper into the mattress. "No."

"What else?"

"German." She moaned throatily as his strong and talented fingers worked out the kinks and tightness in her lower back. "Portuguese. Italian. French."

"You" — he kissed her spine — "are an" — another kiss — "amazing woman."

"Hmm."

He moved his hands lower as he slid over her ass and down her legs. Bailey couldn't help it, she tuned out everything but the experience. He might have longed to talk while this happened but he was too good, the encounter too drugging for her to continue any hope of concentration.

Chapter Thirteen

Ivan readjusted the woman on his chest. Bailey settled back into him instantly. He loved how she allowed her body to meld into his. Were he to prognosticate about their future, he had them married with a few children running underfoot. A girl who looked like Bailey with those expressive gold eyes. Four kids would be perfect. A large family so the house was full of laughter and life.

"Four kids, what?"

He tipped his head and found those golden eyes watching him. As usual, they created this incredible wealth of emotion within him. Something about her.

"I thought you were asleep." *And I didn't think I spoke out loud.* He wasn't ready to tell her what he'd been envisioning.

"Mention of four kids kind of punctured my slumber."

News he would address later. He kissed her instead. "Go back to sleep."

"Won't your mother be less than pleased to learn I spent the night in your room?"

"I moved us to yours early this morning."

Confusion leeched into her expression. "You moved me and I didn't wake?"

He didn't even try to contain the smirk. "I wore you out."

"Sound proud of that."

Ivan waggled his brows and grinned. "Fuck yeah." He untangled their bodies and climbed from the bed. "Took me a long time, so to know you were too exhausted to wake up is a prideful bit of knowledge."

She stretched, the sheet dipping to expose the tops of her breasts. His cock stirred again at the sight.

"Isn't pride a sin?"

"So is gluttony." He tugged on the sheet, exposing her nakedness. "Something you are more than welcome to accuse me of. I am a glutton when it comes to you." He lifted her foot to kiss her ankle. "Go back to sleep. I'll be back in a bit."

"Okay." Bailey closed her eyes and he drew the coverings over her, ignoring the lust pounding through him with every pump of his heart.

Ivan grabbed his clothes, put them on and quietly departed. In his rooms he showered and put on clean clothes then left, clean-shaven.

His mother was in the kitchen as he had figured she would be.

"Good morning, Mama."

She smiled at him from where she stood at the counter chopping vegetables. "Morning. Where's Bailey?"

He shrugged. "Still in her room?"

"Do you really think she is the one for you? Roman told me he spoke to you about her."

Ivan experienced a bolt of anger. He didn't appreciate people meddling in his life. Glass in hand, he opened the fridge for some juice.

"Nope, I don't."

The chopping halted. "You don't think she is?" His mother's question was drenched with confusion.

"No. I don't think it." He closed the refrigerator and stared at the woman who had given him life. "I know it."

"You two have nothing in common." She picked up the knife only to immediately drop it. "She will only break your heart. I married an outsider. Your father didn't understand anything about our ways, our customs. He wanted the money. She will be the same."

"She is nothing like *him*."

"So she's not interested in your money? What you inherit when I'm gone? I find that hard to believe. You make a lot and will get even more."

Her derision got his back up. "She has homes throughout the world. Money isn't an issue with her. I think she makes more than I do."

Can't assume it's cheap to kill who she's sent after.

"I don't think that matters."

"Mama, I love you and I'm sorry for what that bastard did to you but it doesn't mean everyone who isn't one of us will hurt either of us."

She scoffed. "You need a good Russian girl."

He drank his juice and walked to the sink. "Tell you what. I will do my best to give you half-Russian grandchildren."

"What about her parents?"

"Thought you talked to Uncle Roman?"

"I did."

"Then you know."

She picked up her knife again. "Wasn't sure if that was true."

"I have no reason to lie to you or Uncle Roman." He went to the door, kissing her cheek on the way. "She's what you see, Mama. A lovely woman who has my heart." Ivan left.

He jogged out the front to grab the paper. On the way down the steps to where the paper lay, he slowed and took in the sounds of morning life in St Petersburg. It wasn't rife with the noise of living downtown for they had some property, but some noise still reached them.

A beautiful place to either visit or live. Ivan swiped the paper and made his way back inside.

"Do you want breakfast?" she called from the kitchen.

"I can make it, Mama. Don't worry."

"It will be ready in twenty minutes."

He sighed. "Yes, Mama." There was no point in arguing with her on it.

"Tell Bailey to get up as well."

"On my way."

Ivan took the stairs two at a time, the paper left behind on the entry table. At Bailey's door, he opened it and stepped inside quietly. The room was bright, courtesy of the sun streaming through the window.

"Bailey?" He checked the bathroom, which was also empty.

He stood in her room, hands on hips. The bed was made. Lips pursed, he went to the window and peered out. There. Out in the front yard.

He crossed his arms and leaned against the sill. She was doing some kind of martial art. One he couldn't name. It wasn't a world he was part of.

Whatever it is, she's sexy and graceful while doing it.

Ivan made his way down to the porch. He could feel the intensity of her workout concentration. Taking a seat, he observed her, her fluidity, and he noted how there were no wasted movements.

Poignant. The word he would use to describe the image.

"Need something?"

Bailey's question shook him free of the focus that had surrounded him.

"Breakfast," he said. "Time to come eat."

She stopped and put a hand against her throat. "I'll be right there, just need to shower."

He pushed to his feet. "Want me to wash your back?"

Her smile brightened her face and, in turn, his day. "Your mother's awake, right?"

"Yes."

"And she's seen you already?"

"Yes."

"Then no. You don't need to show up as if you'd just gotten out of the shower. Especially when that's how I'll look."

He approached and kissed her. "Water conservation?"

She chuckled. "Nope. I'll see you in the kitchen." Bailey trotted into the house and disappeared. "Give me ten," she called behind her.

"Damn," he muttered playfully.

True to her word, Bailey showed up ten minutes later. Ivan paused in carrying the fruit to the table. She had dressed for a day of being a tourist, comfortable and functional. Her hair was drawn back from her face by a braided gold hair accessory. He noticed it when she turned to speak with his mother.

Breakfast was lighthearted but even so he watched his mother, unwilling to allow her to be rude or mean to Bailey. They cleaned up and Bailey waited out by the car for him. He watched her pull out a phone.

"Are you gone all day?" His mother spoke Russian, as she tended to do when Bailey wasn't around.

"Most. Why? Did you require my assistance with something?"

"I wanted you to accompany me somewhere this morning."

He had plans. With a smile to hide his disappointment, he nodded. "Let me talk to Bailey."

"Thank you."

When Ivan walked out, Bailey was still on the phone, but she hung up and faced him.

"What's wrong?"

He admired her intuitiveness. "My mother needs my help this morning." Ivan reached for her. "I'm sorry, I know we had plans."

"She's your mother. Go help her. I'm capable of exploring on my own."

"Are you sure? Want me to drop you somewhere?"

"No, I'm good. I'll walk for a bit then grab a taxi." She kissed the corner of his mouth. "See you later."

Bailey walked toward the street and with a wave over her shoulder, vanished from view. Ivan shoved his hands into his jean pockets and rocked back on his heels. Expelling a large sigh, he returned inside and tried to figure her out.

She didn't get upset nor did she try to insert herself in his business. He'd said his mother needed him and she took it as such without question.

Back in the house, he prepared to call for his mother but shut his mouth when she walked into view, purse in hand.

"Come on."

"Where are we going?"

"I need you to come with me. Where's Bailey?"

"Went exploring. Why?"

"If she was staying here, I didn't wish to lock her out."

"Don't worry, I'm guessing she'll be gone most of the day."

"Okay."

Ivan assisted his mother into the car then slipped behind the wheel. "Where to?"

* * * *

Bailey gazed around The Hermitage, amazed by the art available to her. She currently stood in the Winter Palace and was witness to the collections in the building.

Her phone vibrated against her thigh and she pulled it from her pocket. Kevin McNeal.

"Did I miss my check-in?"

"Hello to you as well." His dry tone had her smiling.

"What do you need?"

"Perhaps I wanted to say hi."

"I'm trying to enjoy my day, McNeal. What do you need?"

He sighed. "When are you going to be done with this vacation of yours?"

"Not for a while. Why?"

"I want you back at work."

She stepped back and moved to the next item hanging on the wall. "Why? It's not like I live close even if I'm working. Do you have something which needs to be attended to?"

"Yes."

"Luckily you have others to send. I like being on vacation. I should have gone on one a long time ago."

"Bailey, you're needed here."

She cocked her head to the side. "Why?"

"Can't you just take my word on it?"

"I could, but no."

"Christ, woman, can you ever make things easy?"

"I do. I am a very simple person, McNeal. You know this. I don't do well with complications. In fact, I avoid them. With extreme prejudice."

"So what's with the nerd scientist?"

Bailey located a bench and sat, bracing her free hand behind her. "I am not beholden to you in such a way I'm required to answer that. Surely you know this?"

"I'm your boss but I was—" He hemmed, hawed, and cleared his throat. "Where are you going after you leave St Petersburg?"

"Don't know."

"What do you mean you don't know?"

"Exactly what I said, and what is your reason for keeping tabs on me?"

"It's not hard for me to track a cell, Bailey." He had a point there.

"If you're following my progress, why do I need to call and update you?"

"A cell phone doesn't tell me *how* you are, Bailey." There was some slight chastisement in his tone this time.

"I'm sure there is more than desire on your part to know how I am doing as a reason for this call. How about you let me in on it so I can get back to what I was doing."

"I need you to do something for me."

She tracked an extremely pregnant woman who waddled from piece to piece, hands upon the small of her back. Bailey thought of her discussion with Anabelle Lee.

"I'm sure you do. What is it?"

Did she want a baby? There was no biological clock raging inside her, demanding it. She liked her life how it was.

"Bailey." McNeal sounded exasperated and she realized she'd gotten lost in her own thoughts, tuning him out.

"Repeat that."

A groan of frustration this time. "I know my request is a bit unorthodox but I need you to do it."

I should have paid attention. "Say it again, I want to make sure I have it all."

"I need you to go to the coordinates I'll provide."

She sat up, curiosity piqued. This wasn't anything she'd expected. Bailey paused and narrowed her eyes. "I won't do any more retrievals."

"You're on vacation, I merely need you to check on a person for me."

"A person." She rubbed her eye. "A very vague statement."

"I need you to do you and not ask questions."

More frustration but this time with a hint of desperation was how she would label it.

"This is not my typical job. 'Check on' is open for a variety of interpretations. Look at and make sure there is life. Meet and discuss to assess well-being. Plus plenty more. I will need more than 'check on' if you require me to do this."

"I could order you."

"Doesn't change the fact you would still need to explain what you mean by 'check on' in greater depth."

His muttered cursing came then a loud thump. Bailey rose and walked to another painting, activating her hands-free then placing both hands and her phone back in her pockets. Whatever this was to be and whoever this person was, it was important and heartily personal to McNeal. Given he was one of the few she honestly respected, she wouldn't push his answer, allowing him to speak in his own time.

"Her name is Lynn."

She continued walking. "Okay."

"Theta Corps rescued her from a situation, one I wouldn't wish on my worst enemy." He paused and drummed his fingers on something solid.

His desk perhaps. He could be in his office.

"Want me to see how she's doing or if she needs something else?"

"Yes. I rescued her from the hell she'd been in. It's been a year but I believe if she sees me, she may regress from what small progress she has made."

"Is she alone? Will someone be a problem I will need to consider when I go?"

"She was in a facility for battered and abused women."

Immediately Bailey shook her head as if he were before her in person. "No. I will not go to a shelter to check on a woman."

"I said *was*. Last check she was in a place similar to a halfway house."

She furrowed her brow. "You're not telling me something. What's the catch?"

"It's a TC facility."

It was one of Theta Corps'? "Then you have access. Why exactly do you need me?"

He cleared his throat and Bailey made her way to the entrance.

"You have no wish for others to know you're checking on her. Or you only get clinical answers."

"I'm sending the coordinates. As soon as you can, Bailey."

There wasn't a please nor did she expect one. McNeal could come off as a hard ass or one who cared only for results but she knew he truly cared about his people. This woman must have hit a nerve with him for him to do things this way.

She departed and headed to flag down a taxi. "I will keep you informed." Bailey touched the device in her ear, severing communication.

After hooking up with a cab and getting back to the house, she tried the door. It was locked so she settled on the top step and grabbed her phone. She opened the message from McNeal. Nothing but the coordinates. She typed in the latitude and longitude then waited for the destination to appear. Gazing around, she left the covered steps and went to sit on the sun-warmed bench.

Sharing her attention between her phone and the driveway, she ignored the road when the location appeared. Adast, France. Bailey memorized the address and closed it down to open a screen to search flights.

Time lost all meaning as she figured out the rest of her vacation. When a shadow fell across her, she paused to peek up. Ivan stood there, arms crossed and a sexy half-grin on his face.

"Have you been waiting long?" He bent and kissed her lightly on the cheek.

"Don't rightly recall. Got lost taking care of some business that required my attention."

He crouched before her. "Business?"

She gave him a wry grin. "Want to stop over in France?" Unsure of his reaction, she found herself holding her breath.

"Spend some nights there with you? Are you talking Paris where I'd get to dine and walk along the Champs-Élysées with you? I'm in."

"Not Paris, although we can stop there too. It's a vacation, after all."

"Put me down as game."

She was touched he didn't ask too many questions right then, for she didn't have the answers. "I'll get tickets."

"I want to know—on the plane—why you need to go there. I know it isn't Safa."

"You know that how?"

"A hunch."

She dragged a finger along his torso. "Are scientists allowed to have hunches?"

"This one is."

"Good to know."

He winked. "Come on, we have a few things to do yet."

"I thought a vacation was supposed to be relaxing."

"I will make it up to you. Promise."

She stared at his jean-clad crotch and licked her lips. "Good. I'll look forward to that. Come on, I don't want your mother to look out here and see me jumping your bones in her front yard."

He helped her up and chucked her beneath the chin. "For the record. I'd be all for it. Front yard, backyard. Side of the house."

She laughed and looped her arm through his. "You're insatiable."

"When it comes to you, yes I am."

Bailey pocketed her phone and leaned her head against his arm as they strolled back inside. She might be unsure of what awaited her in France, but she couldn't argue with the company she was keeping.

Chapter Fourteen

Adast, France

Ivan stepped from the bus and glanced around. This town, more of a village, was small and quaint. A calm aura hovered over the area.

Bailey brushed by him, her fingers grazing the small of his back. He peered at her, taking in all he could about her. The brief and tantalizing flash of skin exposed when she bent forward to pick up her bag, courtesy of her leather shirt riding up. The curves of her body, ones he enjoyed thoroughly. The way her outfit molded to her.

There were some people who couldn't wear leather, for it never looked right. Bailey Hyde wore the hell out of it.

She'd crashed on the flight and he hadn't had the heart to wake her to learn more about this impromptu side stop. Once they'd checked in to their room, that was a situation he would rectify.

The inn was in line with the rest of the buildings, well kept and older in appearance. He listened to her speaking flawless French as they checked in. Once in their room, he placed his bag beside hers on the bed and turned to look at her.

"Are you okay?"

Her head popped up and she gave him a slight smile. "Sure. Why do you ask?"

"Because—and don't take this the wrong way, please—you, well, you seem nervous."

She skimmed her hands down the smooth leather of her pants. "I am."

He walked to stand before her, settled his hands upon her shoulders and waited for her to make eye contact again. "I've seen the things you do, Bailey. How can you be nervous? What's going on here?"

"That's just it," she hedged. "I'm not sure."

His curiosity grew. "You're not sure? Then why are we here?"

"McNeal called me and asked me to come here, a few buildings away, so I could check on a woman named Lynn."

He waited. "And what is she doing here?"

"Recovering, I suppose. I'm not sure. All I know is she was rescued by Theta Corps and he's been keeping an eye on her. She has to be special enough for him not to want the top of Theta checking in on him and wondering why he's watching this one. That and he says he is afraid if he comes, he will set her recovery back."

Christ. What happened to her? "So you don't know anything about her then."

"I was texted coordinates and while we were on the bus from the airport, he sent me her photo so I would know what she looked like."

Ivan went to the window and stared out over the small village, or commune, as it was also known.

Outside, people talked and laughed with one another as they carried on with their daily activities.

On one hand, he was ecstatic Bailey was opening up to him enough to trust him with this obviously personal information. On the other, he wondered what she would be walking into.

"Is it safe?"

"It's a Theta Corps facility."

He pivoted around to face her. "Here? What's the purpose of this one?"

She shrugged. "I don't know. Until McNeal told me, I'd not even known this one existed. Personally, I suspect there are many like this around the world."

"So when do you go talk to her?"

"Tomorrow."

"Would you like me to come with you?"

Her smile was kind. "Thank you but no. From how McNeal worded it, I think she's afraid of men."

"Okay, I'll head over to the Col du Tourmalet and get in some running while you take care of what you have to do."

"Thank you for understanding." She walked toward him, wrapping her arms around him when she reached him.

"I'm a nice guy, Bailey. Just don't let it get out." He settled a hand along the curve of her spine and held her tight to him. "So what do we do tonight?"

She nipped at him through his shirt. "Whatever we want to do. Care to go exploring with me?"

"I'd love to explore you."

She laughed. "Not what I said."

"Are you sure?" he teased. "I'm positive that's what I heard fall from your lips."

"Nope. But if you explore with me now, I'll let you explore me later."

"You do hold all the cards." He squeezed her ass and ground against her. "If you want to explore, we'd better get going."

After a lengthy kiss, they left the room and walked outside into the crisp, clean air. She tucked her hand into his.

"There's a small café in Saint-Savin that's about a kilometer from here. We could walk there and take a look around if you'd like." Bailey watched him while waiting for a response.

"Sounds perfect."

They began their way along the road, not rushing, just taking their time. The scenery was incredible and jaw-dropping.

"I could retire in a place like this. Small, where you know your neighbors. What do you think, Bailey?"

"It is beautiful, I'll give you that. France has tons of places that you can't even begin to describe the majesty of until you see it in person. I've always loved this country."

"Is that why you have a place here?"

"I have a place in Paris because I spent part of my childhood in France. I love coming back to visit."

"Who'd you spend it with? McNeal said you lost your parents."

A ripple of energy moved through her and Ivan realized what he'd just stated. *Shit.*

"You and McNeal seem to talk about me quite a bit." There was an edge to her tone.

"I'm sure he didn't mean anything bad by it."

"That man doesn't need you to make excuses for him. Did he tell you or did you ask first?"

Ivan wasn't sure this was going to end well. "I asked him about your parents."

"To what end?"

"I wanted to know."

He watched her as they continued walking. Her body was tense and unwelcoming. After a few steps, that look fell away and she was relaxed. Or so she showed to the world—he could still feel anger within her.

"Perhaps you should ask me something if you wish to know."

Somehow, he didn't think she knew a lot about her childhood. "You're right, and I'm sorry. I will ask you in the future."

"Thank you."

Ivan waited to see if she would say any more about it. When she didn't, he gave himself a mental smack. Bailey didn't hold onto things for long. She faced them, dealt with them and moved on.

Saint-Savin was also breathtaking. The open square in the center had the café they'd be visiting, a fountain, some *colombage* houses and a few other things. On one side of the square was a belvedere that overlooked the valley below the village.

Ivan followed her to the abbey-church, the Abbey of Saint-Savin—a monastery that has stood since the tenth century. As they toured it, looking at the carvings on the outside walls that dated from the Romanesque origins of the church as well as the inside, the rare sixteenth-century organ and a tabernacle, he realized how deep her love of history went.

Bailey absorbed all she saw. Bliss was etched into her features as they continued. He didn't rush her, allowing her to pick her pace. There was also a look at the treasury and the *salle capitulaire*.

For a while, they also meandered along the terraces behind the church and took in the lovely views across the valley. Once they'd finished all the exploring they wanted to do, they went back through town and stopped at the café to eat.

Their leisurely stroll back to their room in Adast was quiet and intimate. It was a day of exploration he wouldn't soon forget.

After a shared shower, they curled up in bed and true to her word, she let him explore her. As much as he wanted.

* * * *

Bailey slowly exited the room. Ivan had departed an hour ago to get to the Col du Tourmalet and she'd taken a long shower as she'd tried to figure out what she was going to say to this person.

She'd dressed comfortably and had her hair pulled away from her face. She walked to the place the coordinates identified. A bookstore. She snorted. *Isn't that how they do it in the movies? The secret lab and stuff is hiding in a bookstore?*

She entered, noting she was the only one in view, and walked up to the counter where a middle-aged man sat working on cleaning books. He looked at her and smiled.

"Can I help you?" he asked in French.

"I hope so. I'm here to see Lynn."

His expression hardly changed. "Hand on the counter, please."

There was a very small space where this could be accomplished given how cluttered with books it was. She complied and he glanced to his left where she noticed a small screen. What it contained, she couldn't say.

"Very well, Ms Hyde. Proceed to the back left corner and you'll be given access."

Following his instruction, she made her way there, still noting there was not another person around. She waited until a corner shelf moved, offering her a look into a well-lit corridor.

Here goes nothing. She stepped through, not moving until the wall behind her was replaced. She couldn't hear the music from the shop anymore. One direction to go, since she wasn't sure how to open it up again.

She proceeded down the hall and around a corner before it dropped five steps. An armed guard stood there. He nodded.

"Ms Hyde. If you will continue on, Dr Treymous will meet with you."

"Thank you."

She remained alert, despite this having been reported as a Theta Corps place. She hadn't been there before and didn't know what to expect. The hall spilled into an open area and she saw one woman moving along the colorless tile. Her black hair was vibrant against her pale skin.

"Ms Hyde. I'm Dr Treymous." She didn't offer her hand and neither did Bailey.

"I'd like to see Lynn now." Bailey lifted an eyebrow when the doctor grimaced. "Is there a problem?"

"No, it's just that, well, can I ask the nature of your visit?"

"Private."

She made a sour expression. "Of course it is. I'll take you to her. She may or may not talk to you. And she may attack you if she feels threatened. Would you like for me to post a guard in there for you?"

"No, that won't be necessary."

"Right," she muttered. "This way."

Bailey trailed her across the open space and down another hall. She could feel the slight decline, like in the previous hallway. This time, however, it wasn't just a corridor. Now they passed doors with tiny squares for light.

This is like a maximum security prison. Who do they have in here?

The doctor stopped. "Here you are." She knocked on the door. "Lynn, I'm coming in." She unlocked and opened it. "There is someone here to see you, Lynn."

Bailey adjusted so she could look in the room. It shocked her, what she saw. It wasn't just walls. This gave off the projection one was outside in a wide-open field on a clear day, and warm sun shining down.

"I have to lock you in with her." She gave Bailey a button. "Panic button."

Lynn watched her carefully, suspicion and something else in her blue eyes.

"Thanks but we'll be fine. Lynn, might I come in and speak with you for a moment or two?"

A slight shrug, which Bailey took to mean she could.

Dr Treymous waited until Bailey had entered, then she closed the door and locked it. An ominous sound.

Bailey kept her gaze upon Lynn, who watched her in return. There was no hiding the fear in that stare and for that reason, she remained where she was instead of approaching.

"You have a lovely room. I like how you make it as if you're outside, no walls, no boundaries. Free."

No response from Lynn. The woman looked about twenty but Bailey couldn't be sure. Using the corner to assist her, Bailey slid down until she sat on the floor.

"I'll just stay over here. I'm not here to hurt you, Lynn. I just need to know how you're doing. And see if there is anything I can do for you."

"What do you care?" she snapped. Her voice was a lot deeper than Bailey had assumed it would be.

"Me? I don't actually. I was asked to come here by someone you know."

Her entire body leaned forward slightly. "You don't care?"

"I don't know you. I know you were rescued a while ago but I haven't read your file."

"Who wanted you to come?"

"A man named Kevin. Do you remember him?"

Her fingers dug into the pillow she held. "Yes. He saved me. I never saw him again."

"He's the one who asked me to come here."

"Why would you do that for him?"

"Because he asked it of me."

"Are you his wife?"

"No."

"Girlfriend?"

"Nope."

"Have you slept with him?"

"Not once."

"But you'd come here to check on me because —"

"He asked me to. No other reason."

"So you do his bidding. I'll never do another's bidding." Venom coated her words.

"I'm doing a favor for him."

"Are you friends?"

"I respect him."

"So he can't come here himself?"

"Do you want him to come see you? He told me he didn't want to remind you of what he removed you from." She shifted on the floor. "If you want him here, I will tell him."

"I want to see him."

"I will tell him as soon as I leave here. I can't promise he'll come, but I will let him know."

"Sure you will," she muttered.

"Is there something I can do for you while I am here?"

"No. No one can." She waved a hand around. "They keep me here, thinking I'm dangerous. They even gave you that button to call the ones with the sleep medicine, if I happen to scare you."

"The one you heard me tell her I won't need because we'll be fine?"

"You're foolish to think I'm a good person."

You're an angry person. "I don't know you to make that judgment call."

"You're not like the others who come here."

"What others?"

"The ones with the coats and masks."

Something wasn't right here. "What do these people want?"

"To run tests. Always with the tests."

"How often do they come?"

"Once a month." She put down a blue pillow and picked up a yellow one. "Always the same time." Her grip tightened. "They take away the happiness."

"The happiness?"

Lynn rose and walked toward her. Bailey didn't move, she wasn't worried. This woman wasn't violent unless she felt threatened. This she knew just from being with her a short time. The stiller Bailey was, the more relaxed Lynn was.

"Do you know what it's like to have them take away the sun?" She looked up. "Make it dark and gloomy? Monsters come at night. I don't like the dark." Her blue eyes met Bailey's. "Why do they want to take away the light?"

"I don't know, Lynn. But it's something I will look into."

Her eyes grew wild. "No. No!" she screamed over and over again. Bailey watched her closely for any signs of an impending attack.

"Don't say anything or they'll hear you!" Lynn backed away until the bed was behind her, and she curled up in a small ball, rocking with her pillow, muttering.

Bailey pushed to her feet and had just stepped away from the door when it burst open. Two men rushed in and Lynn screamed again. Louder. More fearful.

"Stop!" Bailey ordered, shifting so she was in front of them. "What do you think you're doing?" Above her, the sun vanished, replaced by dark rolling clouds.

"Get out of the way, she was attacking you. We need to sedate her."

"You need to leave this room so I can finish my talk with her. There was no attack. She screamed. And you're frightening her."

"You don't know what she can do," one protested.

She narrowed her gaze. "And you don't know what I can do. Get out." Her voice was low and dangerous.

They shared a look then left. Bailey turned back to Lynn, noting that the sun had been put back. Her eyes were wide and Bailey smiled at her, hating the tears that streamed down her face.

"I'm sorry about that. Are you okay?"

"Dark. Dark. Always to put me in the dark. Why? I don't like the dark. I'm good. Just leave me in the light. The light is good. Not the dark. Dark. Dark. Dark is bad."

Bailey touched her ear and called McNeal.

"Have you gone to see her?" he asked the moment he picked up.

"I'm with her now. She wants you to come and, McNeal, I think you should as soon as possible." She hung up and approached the bed. The rocking continued and Bailey reached out slowly to the young woman and touched her leg.

She jumped, startled, but didn't strike out.

"The dark is gone, Lynn. You're back in the light. It's okay."

Frightened eyes flashed up and the relief that poured through her was obvious to Bailey.

"I know you're scared, Lynn, and you have every right to be. I don't know what you went through but I know this. He's on his way to you. He'll be here. I have to go. I'll be back tomorrow to see you before I leave the country."

The fear receded and the anger took over. "I don't give a damn what you do."

"I know you don't. Nevertheless I'll see you tomorrow."

Bailey went to the door and knocked. She didn't look back as she left. Dr Treymous waited for her.

"I saw she spoke to you, what did you talk about?"

"Wasn't much more than muttering about the dark from her. The men scared her when they burst in."

"We feared for you."

I bet you did. "They were just doing their job. I understand. I will be back tomorrow to see if I can get some more from her. Thank you for your time, Doctor."

"I'll walk you out. I hope you let them know we're taking excellent care of those who stay here."

"I'll make sure the appropriate people know precisely what you are doing here, don't worry."

They reached another door and the doctor typed in a number on the panel. Silently the door swung open and Bailey found herself in another part of the bookstore. She walked toward the curtained area then stepped back into the main part, behind the old man at the counter.

"I do hope you found what you needed," he said without looking at her.

"I hope so as well. See you tomorrow, and thank you for all your help." She smiled at the other patrons in the store and made her way outside.

Bailey didn't look back at the store, just headed for her room, needing to digest all this and aware McNeal would be calling back.

Chapter Fifteen

Ivan wiped the sweat from his brow and thanked the man who'd been kind enough to give him a return ride to Adast. His lungs burned and his legs were no stronger than a piece of hay in a hurricane. The run up and down had so been worth it.

The scenery was stunning. The passing cyclists had been friendly and had called out encouraging words to him as he had moved along. He'd gone up as far as he could, then grabbed a ride from a kind couple to the top and had stood there snapping some pictures on his phone. Then he'd gotten a ride back to the place he'd caught the vehicle up and had begun to run back down.

He walked to the door of their room and turned the knob, pushing inside. Bailey was across the room by the window, hands on hips, but she angled her head to look at him when he entered. Her grin was more of a brief flash than anything.

"I don't know, I'm only reporting what I saw and dealt with personally. Like I told you there, you need to get over here. I'll stop by tomorrow and see her again but there's something going on, in my opinion, there. You're welcome." She touched her ear. "How was your run?"

"It was awesome and totally kicked my ass. Who were you talking to? Is everything okay? How'd your visit go?"

"McNeal. I suppose. And it was, hmm, interesting to say the least."

He kicked the door closed behind him. "Interesting good or interesting bad?" He removed his shirt and slung it over his shoulder.

"I'm not sure. My instincts say bad but I don't know enough of the situation to judge."

"Bullshit."

He could see his statement had startled her. She cocked her head at him and hooked her thumbs in the waistband of her pants.

"What?"

"Bullshit. Your gut is trustworthy. If it says the situation is bad, then it is. Why do you doubt yourself?"

"It's not that simple."

"Really?" He strode toward her. "Why not?"

"She's not all there and I don't know if it was an act or not."

"Seems to me for a woman who assesses situations all the time, you would know when you can and can't trust yourself. There are some things which can't be faked, you know that."

"I do. Maybe I just don't want to think anything could be wrong."

"So what are you going to do?" He walked to the bathroom and turned on the shower.

"I'm going back to see her again tomorrow and I let McNeal know what I saw."

He peeked over one shoulder and noticed she'd followed him to the doorway. The worry and stress were blatant on her face. "Come here."

She listened and soon stood before him.

"Do you want to do something about her right now?"

"You willing to help?"

"In a heartbeat."

"It could be your death or loss of your job."

He captured her chin and put his mouth over hers, lightly. "You don't go off half-cocked, Bailey. If you feel strongly enough to go now, I'll help you."

"Thank you," she said, curling her arms around his neck. "I want to see her tomorrow and see if it's just that I didn't know what I was getting into. The orderlies have to be fixed for sure. They are scaring her and I don't like that."

"But not tonight?"

"They know I'll be back tomorrow and I am going to assume they will let me see her in good shape."

"Okay then."

He gripped the hem of her shirt and lifted. She stepped away from him to help out, arms over her head. He dropped it on the floor and hooked his finger through the blue of her bra, drawing his fingertip along the material.

"Lose the clothing."

She didn't argue, just bent and went to work on her shoes. He shucked off his remaining articles as well and soon the two of them were standing together under the heated spray. Bailey stared up at him, the water slicking her hair down against her head.

He trailed the back of his hand down her skin. Her eyes burned with a fire he had never imagined any woman would look at him with, much less the one who shared the shower with him now. "Bailey," he murmured, leaning in to kiss her.

She opened beneath him, her tongue slipping against his as she pushed it into his mouth. He groaned and lowered his hands to grip her ass. She ran her hands over his back, working the muscles and digging in slightly with her trimmed nails. His cock hardened between them and he almost froze when she curled a hand around it.

"Shhh," she whispered before pressing her lips tighter to his.

The kiss grew heated and she stroked his erection as their tongues swirled around one another. The water helped her hand to glide easily on him. Ivan released her ass and put one hand on her breast while he dipped the other between her legs.

He positioned two fingers inside her wet pussy and worked them as she kept him teetering on the edge. Their moans combined growing louder as their pace became more frantic.

She came around his fingers, coating them with her thick cream, and he reveled in the way her velvet walls clutched at him, desperate to keep him buried deep inside her. It was a feeling he desperately craved to experience again with his cock in her body. Fingers out, he took her hand away and lifted her up so he could slide into her pussy.

"Oh, shit," she moaned.

The warm heat cocooned him and he was at a loss for words. Heaven. Bliss. Perfection.

In and out he stroked, her cries filling his ear as he moved. Soft. Hard. Shallow and deep. With each thrust, he felt their connection deepen, enrich and grow. Her lithe body trembled around him as she orgasmed once more.

Ivan knew he wasn't going to last much longer. A few more strokes and he pulled out of her body to come on her belly.

It was the hardest thing he'd ever done and he hadn't been sure he'd be able to. He longed to come within her, covering her with his seed. Getting her pregnant.

Those words gave him pause. *Am I insane?* A baby was a whole new level of commitment. It didn't matter how much he thought they belonged together, a child changed everything. Was he ready to bring one into his life?

I thought of four children with her already. Why is this shocking me now? Because then he hadn't almost shot his load inside her.

"Ivan?" Her voice was sated and her expression mimicked that.

"Yes?"

"You look lost in thought."

She had no idea. "I'm good. I think you drained me."

"Up for a nap?"

He wiped a hand over his face, ridding it of the water there. "With you? I'm always ready for bed."

Her tongue snuck out as she lifted his semi-hard cock in her hand. "Let's see what we can do about getting him back to full strength." She brushed her wet hair out of the way and dropped to her knees before him.

Any protest he would have said vanished like the mist after a rain when the sun beats down again when her mouth closed over him.

* * * *

The bookstore still played the same music. Bailey walked in with a smile affixed firmly on her face. The man barely glanced at her but when she arrived in the corner, the door popped open so she knew he had been paying some sort of attention to her.

She made the walk and paused by Lynn's door, waiting for someone to open it so she could enter. Dr Treymous arrived shortly after. The woman appeared a bit more harried than usual.

"Good morning, Ms Hyde."

"Doctor. Thank you for allowing me to see her again."

"Yes, yes. Just please keep in mind she didn't have the most restful of nights."

"I will." She gestured to the door. "I'd like to see her now."

"Right, sure thing."

After fumbling for a moment, the doctor managed to open the door. Bailey looked up the first thing, grateful to see it was the sun image this time.

I have to make sure to remember and ask Ivan about this technology, see if he knows more about it.

"Here's a panic button, you know, just in case."

"Thank you, but this time, I don't want to see anyone in here unless I press this. Do I make myself clear?"

The doctor's jaw was set and she swallowed a few times before she reluctantly nodded. Bailey smiled and stepped inside, drawing the door shut behind her.

"Good morning, Lynn."

The young woman sat against the far wall as if she could hug the openness the image depicted. She slowly turned and stared at Bailey. Her eyes were haunted and she had large circles beneath them.

"You're back."

"I am. And I brought you something." She held up the bag she'd been carrying. "Are you hungry? I brought you a croissant and some pastries. Thought you might want something different to eat."

Her tongue peeked out before she shrank back and shook her head. "I'm not allowed."

"Really? They didn't tell me that. So I am sure we're good. May I join you?" Bailey walked in that direction as if she'd been given a green light. Still, she kept herself on the opposite wall, not wanting to push her too much.

Lowering her body down, Bailey smiled as she looked around. "This is much nicer here than where I sat yesterday. Okay, so this is all for you." She slid the bag over then leaned back.

Lynn took it and opened it. The rich, heady scents left the bag and filled the room. Lynn ripped the bag so it became a plate and focused on the items within.

"Thank you." The words were so soft, Bailey almost missed them.

"You are welcome. I didn't know what you liked that's why there are a few smaller samples."

No words were exchanged while Lynn ate. Even the ones she didn't like as much, she still ate. Then the croissant was all that remained and Lynn looked up at her.

"Did you want this back?"

"Me?" She shook her head. "I ate while they were putting this together for you. Eat, then we will go for a walk."

"It's not my time to walk in the hall yet."

"We're not walking in the hall." She had a hunch about the technology in this room and if she were right, which she believed she was, Bailey had every intention of letting Lynn walk farther and in a much nicer place than a sterile hallway. The moment Lynn bit into the croissant, Bailey rose and walked to the door. She knocked then waited.

Dr Treymous opened the door and peered in. She frowned. "What's she eating?"

"A croissant from the bakery by where I'm staying. I need to talk to you, outside for a moment."

The woman backed up and Bailey stepped from the room.

"She's on a strict diet, and that shouldn't have been given to her."

Arms crossed, Bailey arched an eyebrow. "It's my understanding she's here to recover, not because she needs strict dietary restrictions."

"It's… We… Fine. What did you need?"

"That stuff in her room that makes it look sunny."

"The Imager?"

"If that's what you call it. I'm guessing you have a larger room with one in it. So people can feel as if they are in a certain place or not. You can't just parade a bunch of different people out into a small village such as this. This is what I want. I want use of it with Lynn. We'll take a walk in the warm sun and feel the breeze on our faces. Just walks in the sterile hall aren't good for her. She needs to be where she feels the most comfortable. I want it ready in five minutes."

Dr Treymous desperately looked as if she wanted to argue but she gave a forced smile and said, "Sure. I'll come back to get you then."

"Perfect." She went back in the room to find Lynn back on her bed, holding a pillow. "Ready for a walk?"

"I don't need to go on one."

"I think you do. Come on. Bring your shoes if you wish. They'll be back for us in a few minutes."

True to her word, Dr Treymous returned within five and opened the door. Bailey waved Lynn forward and brought up the rear. It wasn't difficult to notice how the woman shrank from the men who also walked near but she didn't offer up any resistance.

"Here you are." Dr Treymous typed in a code and a large panel slid back into the wall, offering them the view of a large, sunny field.

"Go ahead, Lynn," Bailey said. "I'll be right there."

Like a deer stepping out into a meadow, uncertain, nervous, Lynn walked in.

"We'll be out when she's done and not a moment sooner."

The smile was more akin to a baring of teeth. "As you wish."

Bailey walked through and the door closed behind her. She walked up to Lynn who stood still, arms out to her sides and head tipped up to the sun. Bailey could smell the crisp air, feel the sun and the gentle breeze. Even the grass beneath her feet appeared real enough. And to Lynn it was.

"Ready to walk?"

Lynn glanced at her, and it was the first bit of hope Bailey'd seen in her eyes. "Yes please."

"Lead the way." She gestured with her hand.

* * * *

"I know about the Imager." Ivan accepted his drink from the airline attendant with a nod of thanks. "You say they have one there?"

"I've never heard of it. But I'm wondering why, with the ability it offers, don't people who go out into the field get one? It could make them shelter and all that, right?" She took her own drink and bag of peanuts. "Thank you, ma'am."

The woman moved on.

"Not with the power it needs to run it. I'm guessing most times when you go out you're on something like you did for me. Can't be carrying around some generators to keep it up. Plus I'm not sure about the real world applications. It works in a building because things can be kept constant, but out there you will have animals and such that could cross through the hologram and potentially dissolve it. I know a few of the guys working on making it smaller and I could ask if you'd like."

"I'm just curious."

He sipped his drink. "So, did it help her?"

"I think it didn't hurt. She looked happy out there with me. We were there for four hours while she walked and just enjoyed life."

"Still have that bad gut feeling?" He ate some pretzels.

"I do. They tried to get on me for bringing her the croissant and pastries. I don't get it—she's there to recover and get better. Who cares what she eats?"

"Perhaps she is allergic?"

"Then she should have come with that argument. She just said it wasn't allowed." Bailey sipped some of her Coke. "Then again, this woman's exercise is walking in the hall."

"I thought she had an Imager in her room?"

"It shows the image but I didn't feel the breeze or sun. It's so real you can almost create it in your mind but it wasn't like when we went into the large room and the breeze was blowing our hair and I could feel the warmth from above sure as if I stood outside in person on a sunny day."

He stroked his chin, fingers moving along the short scruff he had on his jaw. A jaw she wanted to kiss. "Interesting," he commented. "Sounds like they've found a way to manipulate the program to give them what they want."

"At one time when the door opened the entire image changed. It went dark and stormy. Freaked her out too."

"I'm sorry I can't be more help, Bailey. I just don't know that much about it and what they do to make it work."

"It's all right. I was just curious."

"Have you talked again to McNeal?"

"He'll be there tonight. I don't think he's pleased with what he heard. I told him it's more like a prison or a looney bin than anything. I just don't comprehend how they are assuming treating her like that will help her recover."

"You've done what you can."

"Guess I have." She wished she could have done more. "Okay, now, where were we in my kicking your ass?"

He laughed and dropped a kiss on the top of her head. "I've never known someone to be so competitive about Hangman before."

"Stop stalling and get the notebook. I was winning."

He did as ordered and she settled in to see if she could figure this out. Most people on the flight had their heads in their electronics. It wasn't her style so she'd asked him if he would play with her. Turned out Ivan enjoyed the game as well. Her problem now was figuring out all those big scientific words he liked to use. But it passed the time and she was enjoying herself, for as they played they talked about other stuff and grew closer.

Chapter Sixteen

Seattle-Tacoma Airport, Seattle, Washington

"The Space Needle is something I'd like to see. You know, if we have time." Ivan carried their bags to the rental desk and waited as she filled out the paperwork to get their vehicle.

"You'll see it shortly as we drive. But if you mean go to it and see it, then sure, we can do that as well."

She thanked the woman at the desk and the two of them walked to the door to get their transport. When she stopped beside a Chrysler 300, he nodded in approval. She opened the trunk and he put their luggage in the dark, carpeted space.

Not much later, they were on I-5 heading north, gliding in and out of traffic with ease.

"Anything else you want to do while we're here?" Her question came over the low music playing.

"How long are we here for?"

"I have us booked for four nights. Not sure how much more time off I'll have after that and I want a few days back in Chile before I am officially back on the clock. But I have no problem extending your stay and changing your ticket if you wish to hang around here longer."

"Do I get to rest with you in Chile?"

"Absolutely."

He winked at her. "Then I'm good with four nights here." Ivan took her hand and laced their fingers together before brushing a kiss along the back. "What else is there to do here?"

"Lots of things. They'll have a guide in the hotel which may give you some ideas."

"Of that I have no doubt," he said.

Banter remained light between them as they neared their hotel. He took in the view of the Seattle Marriott Waterfront as they pulled into the parking lot. *Very nice.* They checked in and settled in their room. Bailey went to shower and Ivan stared out of the window and took in the Olympic Mountains and Mount Rainier beyond the expanse of Elliott Bay.

"I'm in Seattle. Jaydee isn't that far away."

He sat on the edge of the king-sized bed and stared at the phone in his hand. *Am I ready to do this? Face her again? She was one of my best friends and I've never even seen her children.*

How would Bailey feel about this? He wasn't sure, but Seattle was a hell of a lot closer to Oregon than Chile was. He pulled up his contact list and stared at her name. A short burst of unamused laughter left him. He still didn't have her down with her married name. She was still Jaydee Amos there.

Time to move on.

He glanced at the bathroom door then pressed the call button, exhaling a few times while it rang.

"Hello?" a man answered. It was Giovanni, Ivan recognized his voice.

"May I speak to Jaydee please?"

"Sure, hang on."

It didn't take long for her to get on the line. "This is Jaydee."

"Hello, darling," he said in Russian.

"Ivan. I haven't heard from you in so long." She spoke Russian as well. "How are you doing?"

"I know and I'm sorry, Jaydee. It's been hectic for me. I'm in Seattle and realize I may not be this close to you for a long time again. Do you have any availability to meet me so I can see you, meet the kids and catch up?"

"Can you come here for a day? Two of the kids are sick so I don't really want to drag them around if I can help it."

"Yes. I can." If he had to rent another car, he would do so. "Let me look over my schedule and see what works best for me then I'll call you back. Should I call your cell phone or this one?"

"Either gets to me, so your decision."

Of course it was. "I'll call you back shortly, Jaydee. Good to talk to you."

"And to you, Ivan." She hung up and he stared at the phone again.

"Jaydee," he muttered.

A noise behind him had him turning. Bailey stood there, absolutely adorable in a pair of flowered pants and a white camisole. Her hair sat piled on her head in haphazard fashion. He smiled, only to realize she wasn't. "What's wrong?"

"Nothing. Why would you think something is wrong?"

"You're not smiling."

"Sorry. Didn't realize I was supposed to when I step out and hear you sighing a woman's name that you love."

He tossed his phone on the bed and went to stand before Bailey. "Could this mean that you, Ms Bailey Hyde, are jealous?"

"Anything is possible, I suppose."

"Are you going to tell me?"

"Nope. Are you going to need the car?"

"Wait, what?"

"The car. I'm assuming you'll be going to see her." She walked around him and sat in the chair by the window, placing one foot on the seat so she could drape her arm over her knee. "That's fine, I can make do with public transportation."

"Slow down, Bailey."

"Slow down? I'm sitting in a chair. How am I going fast?"

"Back up to where I asked you if you were jealous."

"To what end? I told you I wasn't going to tell you. There's no point. I don't own you, you're more than free to go see your friends."

"I'm not ready to move past that yet." He approached her and crouched before the chair she occupied.

"Okay, then hang out there, let me know when you do move past it."

"You know, you could just say you're jealous."

She allowed her leg to slide from the chair to the floor. "Is that what you want? Me to say I'm jealous?"

Was that what he wanted? "Yes. No. Hell, I don't know. I want to make sure you know why I called her."

"I don't want to know. Ivan, it's not my business. I know some women, most probably, would be pissed and raging against this entire thing. I'm not like them. You're a grown man. One who makes his own choices. Bottom line is, I trust you. You've already explained your past with her and told me where you stand now. Why would I think anything else? I'm not that insecure I need constant petting and praise just because you mentioned another woman. You're with me or you're not, and you said you were. That's all I needed to know."

"You did say that before. I'm sorry, I guess I'm still not used to how you think."

"I don't have the time to walk around with a chip on my shoulder ready to fight anyone who looks at my man."

He grinned and leaned closer. "Your man?"

"Figure of speech."

"I don't think so, I think it's much more telling than that."

"You would, it strokes your ego."

He tapped himself on the end of the nose. "You got it, baby."

"So then we can move on from the jealous thing?"

"Sure." He ran a hand up the outside of her legs. "Although one day you'll tell me you were jealous."

"Don't hold your breath on that. You wear your emotions out for people to see, Ivan. I admire that about you. You don't care it may make you look like a weaker male. It doesn't, but you don't seem to give a damn. I don't do that. I'm contained for the most part."

"Yes, I know. People will always form an opinion based on something or another. I don't care what they think of me. I don't need to beat my chest to tell people I'm an alpha male. Nor do I need to be an asshole. I'm confident where I am and with who I am."

"I can see that."

"Good, now, I want you to come with me to meet Jaydee and her children."

Her hesitation told him more than her words had. She was jealous but she didn't want to admit it, nor focus on it.

"Are you sure she'd like me to be there?"

"I'll let her know we're on vacation together. Maybe we could check out a day early and spend time down there."

Her eyes narrowed slightly. "Exactly where is down there?"

"Oregon. They live in the Cascades."

"So you've been there since she's gotten married?"

"No, but she's had that house long before and I've been there."

"As long as she and her husband are okay with it then sure, we can do that. After all, you took a side trip for me."

"You'll have fun." He pushed to his feet. "I'll call her back. Oh, one thing, though... Jaydee is not like a lot of other people. She doesn't have tons of social niceties. She's blunt and straightforward."

"Okay." Bailey rose and stared out of the window. "I'm going to read a bit while you talk to her."

Ivan let it go and retrieved his phone. Calling her back, he watched Bailey draw a romantic suspense from her bag and curl back up in the chair. It didn't take her long to get lost back in the story and he knew for all intents and purposes, he was alone in the room.

"When are you coming?" The question came in Russian.

"I am wondering if you mind if I bring my girlfriend with me? We've been on vacation and I'd like you to meet her."

"We have plenty of room. Will you wish to share a room or be separate?"

"Sharing is fine. And will three days from now work?"

"That won't be a problem. We'll be here. And Ivan?"

"Yes?"

"It will be wonderful to see you again."

"You too, my friend, you too. It's been far too long."

"I concur. I will see you then, in a few days." She ended the call.

For the second time in less than an hour, Ivan tossed his phone on the bed. Bailey didn't move, just continued to read. He strode to her and tapped her lightly on the knee.

Those damnable gold eyes got him every time. "Yes?"

"All's set for three days from now."

"Wonderful. Are you hungry? We could order in."

"I like that idea. I'll get the menu."

* * * *

Bailey watched Safa as she ran around the backyard of the home she now lived in. She'd put on much-needed weight and had a smile on her face, which was brilliant.

"How's she doing?" Bailey asked Martha, the woman who had taken her into her home and life. Martha had been a missionary years ago and spoke fluent Arabic. She'd also worked with Theta Corps in the past, for what she hadn't a clue, but the woman was a good home for Safa. Bailey was pleased with the choice her friend had made when deciding where to put Safa.

"Remarkably well considering what she went through. Kids are amazingly resilient. A few nightmares here and there but" — she waved her hand — "look at her."

"No questions about her family back in Egypt?"

"Not a one. Hopefully she'll be ready for school next year, I'm inclined to believe she will be. We're working on her English now and she's a quick study."

"Salihah said you were thinking of legally adopting her?"

"Yes, we've already started the process. Since she's declared an orphan, I don't foresee any bumps."

"Thank you, Martha."

The woman hugged her. "Sweetie, there is no need to thank me. This child has brought such joy to my life. Now, I'm going to get some cookies and something hot to drink for all of us. I'll call you when it's time to come in."

Bailey slowly approached the swing set Safa was on.

"Hello, Safa." She spoke Arabic and sat in the swing beside her.

"Hello."

"How are you doing?"

She slowed the swing and stopped, her toes digging into the soft sand. "I remember you."

Bailey smiled. "Are you enjoying it here?"

She nodded, her large brown eyes wide. "You took me from that place."

"I did. I just came to make sure you were okay and to give you something."

"A present?"

"Sort of." She reached into her pocket and withdrew a card. "This is my number. I know Salihah gave you the information but I also wanted to. If you ever need me, call any of those numbers and I will come for you."

She took the card and stared at it. "Anywhere?"

"Any time, any place. This one is to my cell phone. This one is a way you can always get a message to me."

"Thank you."

"You're welcome."

Martha called to them.

"I think the cookies are ready. I don't know about you but I could go for some."

Her eyes brightened. "Me too." She bounded off the swing, shoving the card into her pocket. "Race you." Safa took off running and Bailey set off after her.

"You're just too fast for me," she panted at the porch. "I'm exhausted."

Safa laughed and bolted up the steps only to disappear inside. Bailey followed at a more leisurely pace and smiled in return at Martha.

"You're so good with children," the woman said. "Do you have any of your own?"

"No, ma'am."

"Nieces? Nephews?"

"No, ma'am."

"Well, you'll be a great mother someday." She poured tea and slid over a plate of cookies. "Help yourself."

Bailey accepted the tea and took two chocolate chip cookies as Safa had hers with her milk. She stayed a few hours, playing with the girl and talking to Martha. Both stood on the front step waving as she drove away, her unease about the situation settled. After parking the car at the hotel she made her way to Pike

Place to meet Ivan before they returned to their room for the night.

"So, how is she doing?"

"Settling in wonderfully. Martha is adopting her."

"So you feel better then?" He stopped to smell some of the flowers at a vendor. Ivan paid for a mixed bouquet and handed them to her. "For you."

"Thank you. I do. I mean, in my heart I knew that Salihah wouldn't send her to a bad place but to be able to see her happy with my own eyes is something totally different."

"You are a woman of many faces, Bailey. I love learning them." He draped his arm around her shoulders and tucked her close to him.

They meandered through the market, sampling, purchasing and just having a wonderful time. They indulged in a lovely dinner at a small shop where they could watch others who had come to experience Pike Place. The evening was lovely as they walked back to their room.

In the room, he tossed a deck of cards at her. "Let's play."

Eyebrows up, she cocked her head to the side. "What are we playing?"

He flopped on the bed. "What game do you suck at?"

She chucked the cards back at him. "What kind of question is that?"

"A legitimate one. I want to know what I can win at."

"Gin."

"You suck at gin?"

"Not saying, just that we're playing it."

"Strip gin?"

She climbed up on the bed, laughing. "Is that all you think about?"

"You naked? All? Not all but a good portion of my day, yes."

"Shuffle and deal." She sat cross-legged.

"Are you sure you don't want to go out to a casino?"

"I'd rather be here with you than out there."

He leaned close and kissed her, hard and passionate, then returned to his side. "Me too." He cracked his neck and rolled his shoulders. "Now, prepare to get your ass kicked at gin."

She snorted. He shuffled and began to deal. Bailey put her hand over his, halting him.

"What?"

"Is this something you can count cards in?"

He blinked. "Why are you asking me?"

"I'm assuming you can count cards."

He waggled his eyebrows and she smacked his shoulder.

"Don't."

"Hey, you picked the game. I'm just doing as I'm told."

"So if I said we're playing this game with you naked..."

He put down the deck and ripped off his shirt, then began shrugging out of his pants. Bailey licked her lips while he stripped down to his birthday suit. His cock grabbed her attention and refused to release it. As she stared, it grew fully erect.

"If you plan on playing gin, you'd better look at your cards. After you strip off your clothing."

"I never said I would be naked. I asked if we were playing it with you naked."

"So you did. Let's play then."

He stretched out on his side and she shifted on the bedspread. Damn him for lying there and looking so tempting.

Play. Oh, she wanted to play with him all right.

Ivan reached for the stack of cards and placed it close to his groin then flipped over the first in the discard pile.

"I dealt, you get to go first."

She stared at her hand and swallowed. This wasn't going to be easy. Bailey rearranged her cards then leaned forward to pick a card. Her knuckles brushed his cock and it jerked, distracting her. She flashed her gaze up to Ivan whose glacier-blue eyes were dark with desire. His cock held too much pull for her and she returned her stare to it. Large, long, thick and what she wanted. She dropped her cards and crawled over to him then took him in her mouth.

"Fuck! Bailey, I thought we were supposed to be playing cards."

"Want me to stop?" she asked, the question muffled a bit by the fact he was in her mouth.

"Hell no. I want you out of your pants. Put your pussy on my face, baby. I want to eat you."

"Busy," she said as she moved her head up and down his shaft, her saliva wetting it, allowing for easier motion.

He tugged on her pants and they slid down to her knees. One leg at a time, he removed them and her underwear. Then he lifted her and moved her so her pussy was right above his mouth. She whimpered when his tongue slipped up the lips the first time.

"Fuck yeah," he muttered before he thrust his tongue deep.

Bailey's moan vibrated along his cock and she knew this night wasn't going to have anything to do with cards.

Chapter Seventeen

Cascade Mountains

Ivan steered them up the drive and he smiled at the sight of the large A-frame house sitting against the incredible backdrop of the Cascade Mountain range. He surreptitiously observed Bailey. Nothing showed on her face to let him know if she was even the slightest bit nervous.

It wasn't every day a woman got to meet the one he'd loved before her and had shared a bed with. He thought over Bailey's words in the hotel about how she wasn't like others and how she looked at the situation. She trusted him. And he her. Time to let it go and move on. Just have fun with his friend.

He parked them near the top of the drive by the walkway leading up to the front door. "Ready?"

"As I'll ever be, I reckon. Let's go."

He got out. Bailey met him at the hood, and together they traversed the nice stepping stone walk to the porch. He noticed the American flag flying on one side of the steps and slightly lower and on the other side flew the Navy flag.

"Her husband served in the Navy, so did she for a while."

"No longer?"

"I honestly don't know about him. She's out." He walked up the steps and pressed the doorbell.

Less than a minute later, it swung open and he found himself standing before Giovanni. The man ran his gaze over both of them then smiled.

"Ivan, good to see you." He offered his hand.

Not the man he remembered from before. That Gio had had a chip on his shoulder and had been seconds away from beating the shit out of him for daring to offer marriage to Jaydee. This one seemed relaxed. Calm. Happy.

Taking the hand, he shook it. "And you." He slid an arm around Bailey and said, "This is Bailey Hyde. Bailey, Giovanni Cassano."

"Come on in. Honey," he hollered. "Ivan is here. It is nice to meet you, Ms Hyde."

They entered and the door was shut behind them.

"Bailey, please."

Even though the man was married, Ivan wanted to snarl when Gio took her hand and shook it. *How long does he plan on holding it?*

Jaydee walked into view and Ivan realized just how much he had missed her. Her grin was wide and welcoming. He brushed by Giovanni and went to her.

"It's so good to see you again, Jaydee," he whispered in her ear as they shared a hug.

"You too, Ivan. It's been far too long." Her grip was solid and true. "I have missed you."

He kissed her cheek and stepped back. "I agree. Look at you. You're beautiful. I like your hair short like this. You look so happy, Jay, I am so glad." It took him a moment to recall they'd been speaking Russian and made sure to switch to English. "I want you to meet Bailey. Bailey, this is Jaydee."

"Nice to meet you," Bailey said without offering her hand.

"And you." Jaydee didn't make an offer either. "Please come and sit in the living room. I have some refreshments waiting. We can talk before the trio wake up from their nap."

Ivan squeezed Bailey's hand then followed. He stopped by a picture on the wall depicting an image he'd not thought about for a long time.

"Jaydee? Is this what I think it is?"

She stopped at his side. "The shot of us when we made it back from our flight. They had one and my father found it. He had it sent to me for Christmas last year. He took out the flashing lights of the police who were there."

He chuckled. "Look at us." They were scrawny teens.

"You seem a bit green."

"Can you blame me? You'd just stolen a chopper and taken it out for a test flight. Of course I'm green. I was petrified."

She shook her head in playful disdain. "I was a perfect pilot. I don't know what you had a problem with. There wasn't any reason to assume I wouldn't be able to fly it. Besides, no one made you come along."

"You dared me. Besides, I wasn't about to let you go up there alone. It's not all green, though, that suit I'm wearing wasn't a good look on me." He crossed his arms.

Her laughter was so familiar it made him join in. "You always did find excuses."

"Humph. I don't think so, it was the facts."

"You never were much of a daredevil."

"Because I respect the laws of gravity and all those other rules you wanted to break."

"So much is available if you're willing to try."

"As was obvious by my joining you, I was willing. Doesn't mean I wasn't scared shitless. Besides, I can't just ignore such things."

"You could," she countered. "You just chose not to."

"Sorry, doll. I don't have your ability. You always were better than I was."

In true Jaydee fashion, she just shrugged it off. She wasn't impressed, she knew it was fact. He was smart as hell but this woman, with how she processed stuff, put him to shame.

Jaydee shook his arm. "You do. You didn't do that bad in the chopper. I still think you should have come base jumping with me. I believe you would have enjoyed it."

"Careening to my death at that speed? No thank you."

"You always did have a flair for the dramatics."

He nudged her. "So I did. Now, tell me how you're doing?"

"I am finding motherhood to be an acceptable state. I love my children and my nephew and niece."

He shook his head. "Wait, Lexy? She has children?"

"No, Gio's other brother Enzo has two with his wife, Halyn."

"I was about to wonder how Lexy had wound up pregnant."

She turned her head and looked at him, deadpan. "Surely by now you know how that works with the sperm and egg?"

Ivan laughed, head back. It was good to be back with her. "I see you've not lost your sense of humor."

"Most think I don't have one."

"Most don't know you like I do, sweetie."

They continued catching up and talking about past exploits. Some with and some without Lexy along for the ride.

A child's whimper filtered down around them and he turned in time with Jaydee to see a dark-haired boy totter into view, one hand rubbing his eye as he moved.

Ivan watched Jaydee walk to him and pick him up in a smooth motion. The love on her face told Ivan she'd made the only choice she could have when she'd married Gio. He was the one who completed her.

With a glance at the couch, he saw Bailey and Gio talking amongst themselves quietly. He was ashamed to realize he'd totally forgotten about her while he reminisced with Jaydee about some of their adventures.

"Who is this?" he asked, walking toward mother and son.

"Dante. The middle one."

The child looked up at him and blinked. Then much like his mother had done to many who watched her, he looked away, dismissing Ivan without a thought.

"Down," Dante said, struggling. She complied and he made his way over to Gio, who swept him up easily.

Ivan returned his attention to Bailey and noticed she was continuing to carry on her conversation with Gio, not paying much attention to the boy who was on the man's lap.

"Tell me about her," Jaydee said.

"Bailey? She's special, Jaydee. Really special."

"You look happier than I remember seeing. Especially out of the lab. But it makes sense for her to be special for you moved to Chile for her."

"How do you know that?"

"I asked where you were and they said you'd gone there to start up a new lab."

"I could have just wanted to get away."

"Russia is where you would have gone, Ivan. I know you well enough to know that."

"Who'd you ask?"

"Gio's brother, Valentino."

"And he just told you?"

"I don't blurt stuff out. Besides, I asked. I believe he was so shocked I asked for his assistance he couldn't bring himself to say no."

"Why check on me?"

"You are my friend and I was concerned for you."

This was why he loved this woman. Right there. She didn't say it in a way to attempt to make him feel guilty for withdrawing and taking some time to himself, she just said why she'd asked and left it at that.

"Thanks for that, Jaydee."

Two more kids stumbled into the room and she grinned at him. "Come on, meet the other two. Michael and Cynzia."

As he went with Jaydee, he heard Gio tell Bailey, "That's how they are when together. They forget the world around them and that not everyone speaks Russian."

Bailey, bless her, responded, "They appear to have a wonderful friendship. That's precious to have in this world."

Ivan peered at Bailey. Dante had gone to her lap and was playing with her hair. He didn't blame the little man, Ivan loved the feel of it on his skin as well.

* * * *

Bailey stared at her reflection in the bathroom mirror. The evening had gone much better than she'd anticipated. Enzo, Halyn and their children had also come by for dinner. The house had been noisy and full of laughter.

This was the only place she'd been able to get some privacy. Splashing some water on her face, she dried her hands and face before leaving. Everyone was in the backyard enjoying the mild weather. The children ran and played while the adults drank and talked.

A deep breath then she stepped back out into the fray. A tall man stood in her way and she went to sidestep him.

"I was told you were here."

Bailey blinked and stared up at him. Valentino Cassano. The legend himself. Or one of them.

"You were looking for me?" *Why is he looking for me?*

"I was. Good to see you again, Bailey."

"And you, Valentino. Something I can do for you?"

"I'd like to talk to you, if you have a moment."

"Sure." They walked to a pair of chairs a bit to the side from the main group. "Something wrong?"

"Anabelle Lee said she saw you in London and said you'd mentioned feelers out for anything on Ethan."

She put one foot up in the seat with her and rested her chin on her knee. "I did. As of yet I haven't heard any more. There was a rumor of something in South America and last time I was in Chile I did some more digging with contacts."

"And?"

"I don't believe they knew where he was. Are you sure he's out of the country?"

Valentino shook his head, fist flexing. "I don't know shit. You know how it is when someone's been gone for a while."

She nodded. "I can put out more feelers if you—"

Laughter broke out and she looked over to see Jaydee, Ivan and another woman in the middle of it.

"Those three are amazing friends. I was shocked that Lexy and Jaydee were friends at the start. Add in Ivan and... Crazy things happen." He cleared his throat and turned his back on the joviality. "Please. I don't have much left to turn over. I know it's wearing on Anabelle Lee."

"He's her brother. It should be. Maybe they're moving him around?"

"We thought of that but part of me wonders if he's not being hidden right under our noses and we're looking past the forest for the trees."

Bailey knew he was concerned. This man didn't show emotion but there was no hiding it now. Still, it didn't detract from the man he was. She picked it up each time she saw him. The cool calculating end that would do whatever it took. She was the same way.

"I will ask again. I have some contacts here as well, I can tell them to keep an ear to the ground."

"Thank you."

* * * *

When she crawled into bed that night, her mind raced with the day's experiences.

"What did you think?" Ivan joined her and drew her into his chest.

"They are a loud, happy family." She wrapped her arms around his waist.

"Very much so. I saw you and Valentino talking. I didn't know you knew him that well."

She sniffed and rotated her ankle before closing her eyes. "I don't. He wanted to ask me for a favor."

Ivan stiffened. "What?"

"Does it matter?"

"What did he want?"

Apparently it did matter. She fought another yawn and was unsuccessful. "It had to do with a missing person."

"I thought you said you weren't doing any more retrievals."

Bailey pushed away from him and clicked on the light so she could see his face. It was drawn with anger.

She sat up against the headboard and canted her head to the side. "I'm sorry, is there a problem here?"

"There is if you're doing more work for him."

"I think we need to come to an understanding here. You don't get to tell me who I talk to, much less what work I accept or refuse. I fail to see what your problem with Valentino Cassano is. You brought me to a house I'd bet anything you used to fuck your ex-girlfriend in. I've been nothing but understanding about that you two have a past relationship and are still friends. However, that doesn't mean you have the right or the damn permission to begin judging who I talk to." Her words vibrated with anger.

"I do when I'm concerned."

"For what?" Her heart hurt further at the realization he hadn't denied fucking Jaydee here.

"He's one of the famous ones in Theta Corps."

"Oh my God. You're officially insane." She climbed out of bed and went to her bag.

"What are you doing, Bailey?"

She pulled on her pants and glared at him. "What does it look like? I'm leaving the room. I need to take a walk or something. Go somewhere where you're not."

"Don't be foolish, come back to bed."

Yeah right. "Listen, you Neanderthal. I don't get jealous a lot, I don't have time for it, but I don't tolerate behavior like this. Again, need we go back to you bringing me to a house where you fucked the woman living here? How she can do no wrong in your eyes and let's not forget how you wanted to marry her. I can deal with that but you are going to go all Tarzan on me because I speak to a fellow operative about something he asked to discuss with me? Hell no. Fuck you, and fuck your insane belief in what's equal."

Bailey pulled her sweatshirt on over her head. Her hands were shaking she was so pissed off. She sat on the chair and reached for her footwear.

Ivan got up and walked toward her. "Bailey, don't be like this."

"Right, I'm the one who's being a certain way." She finished tying her shoes and stood toe to toe with him. Even as angry as she was, it was hard to ignore the specimen before her. Ivan was just too damn hot.

Digging in her pocket for a hairband, she met his gaze and shook her head. "I can't believe this and yet, I should have known it was coming. It's okay that you do what you do but I can't even have a simple conversation with someone without you coming unhinged." She made a quick ponytail. "Find your own way home."

She turned her back on him and swung her bag onto her shoulder. He gripped her arm and stopped her.

"Don't do this."

Refusing to look at him, she shrugged. "I don't have a choice. I'm not going to explain myself to you while you attempt to judge my actions. Much less when you feel you have the right to do so."

"So instead of talking, you're just going to turn tail and run?"

She pulled free and went to the door. "Call it what you want. Goodbye, Ivan." It wasn't easy for her to do but she wasn't about to go down a road like this with a man. She walked down to the first floor and found Gio in the living room.

"Everything okay, Bailey?"

"I just have to go," she said. "Thank you so much for your hospitality. Please, thank your wife as well." Without a look back she went to the door and exited the large A-frame house.

In her vehicle, she sighed heavily before starting the engine and backing up and turning around. She drove away and made her way back up to Seattle, where she returned her car, changed her flight, then went to her gate to wait.

* * * *

Chicago, Illinois

Bailey rolled out of bed and ambled to the window. Peeling open the curtains, she stared out over the waters of Lake Michigan. She had endured a much shorter flight from Seattle to Chicago than it would have been to Chile.

She leaned her shoulder against the cool glass and closed her eyes. *Was I foolish to just walk away from Ivan? I could have stayed to talk about what happened.*

She shook her head and turned from the window, padding back to her bed. With a grunt, she flopped back down on her queen-sized mattress. There was no point in getting up right now. Exhaustion owned her body and she found no reason to fight it. She shuffled around until she was under the blankets.

Ivan.

She did her best to push him from her thoughts as she waited for the lurking sleep to claim her. It didn't work—he was in her dreams and when she woke, she was coming around her fingers as they thrust in and out of her pussy.

A leisurely shower and a nice brunch at her favorite place went a long way in making her feel all the more human. Her relaxing day took a turn for the worse when she opened the door to her apartment that evening, planning to get some dinner, only to find McNeal standing there. She blinked a few times when out from behind him peered none other than Lynn.

"Aren't you going to let us in?" His question was more of an order.

Bailey stepped back and allowed them in, wondering just how much his decision was going to affect her life from that moment forward.

Chapter Eighteen

Ivan sat at the end of the dock and dangled his feet in the water. Bailey had just left him. Packed her bag and left. His flight back to Chile didn't leave until this evening and right now, he wasn't sure he was going to be on it.

"Are you okay?"

Jaydee settled down beside him, her own feet slipping beneath the wet surface.

"Peachy."

"I've known you for a long time, Ivan. What can I do to help?"

"You've changed, Jaydee, you know that? Before you wouldn't have asked."

"That's not true. I always have cared for you and Lexy. It's the rest of the world I am learning to have cares for. And I don't believe it is pragmatic to discuss me when you are the one hurting."

"What makes you think I'm hurting?" He splashed his feet around.

"Because I'm not an idiot. And Bailey isn't here. Gio says she received a call that took her away."

"She's a busy woman." He ground his jaw and tried not to replay last night's events in his head *another* time.

"I'm sure she is. But all of us have ties to Theta Corps. Gio and I fly them places at times. You work for their research and development department. I'm not sure exactly what Bailey does, but she's part of them. Calls happen."

"Then why are you asking?"

"If that had been her reason for leaving you wouldn't be moping about as if you'd lost your best friend."

"I did lose my best friend, Jaydee." He looked at her. "I avoided you because I was a wimp and didn't want to face the fact I had lost you. Much less to the man who won you."

"We've always been friends, Ivan. Nothing will change that. And no matter what you were feeling, that is nothing compared to how this Bailey makes you feel. Why are you fighting it?"

"I'm not." He rested his head against the dock post. "I've accepted it. I'm in love with her. I want to be with her all the time."

"So what is her reason for leaving so abruptly?"

"I'm an ass."

"Of course you are." She lifted her legs and waved them about before submerging them again. "That's not new, nor does it tell me why she left."

"Bitch," he said playfully.

Jaydee's smile reminded him yet again how she'd managed to find herself and her place in this world. Something he'd not done yet.

"I was jealous of her talking to Valentino."

"To what end? Were you fearful she would try to seduce him?"

"Not at all. I didn't want him getting her into something that may put her in danger."

Jaydee looked at him. "Theta Corps."

He shrugged. "Like I said, I was an ass."

"What does she do?"

"She's an assassin."

"Like Valentino?"

"No, he does more than killing. That's her primary."

"Is she a cold person?"

"Not at all, quite the opposite. She has this knack for keeping the two separate. I don't know how she does it."

"And how did you meet her?"

Ivan told her the story of the adventure in Madagascar. Jaydee listened without more than a few interruptions.

"So her secondary is retrieval then?"

"According to her, I was the first one she'd done. Since then she's gone after one more. Some man they wanted back here in the States. I don't know who for, she doesn't tell me those things."

"You were thinking that Valentino was trying to recruit her for something else?"

"That's the problem, Jaydee. I wasn't thinking. Period."

"It happens."

They sat in silence for a while until Gio called down to her, informing her of a phone call.

"Go after her, Ivan. Don't let her get away. I saw how you looked when she's near. I know that look and the feeling it creates. It's the one Gio brings me. Trust me when I say it opens a whole new world to have that love in your life."

"I'm a scientist, not a fighter pilot."

"You are. Now, I will go see what this call is about then I'll take you to the airport so you can get home to her."

"Thanks, Jaydee."

"Lexy and I have discussed it. We think you need to be married like us." She hopped to her feet and walked away.

He followed at a much more leisurely pace. It didn't take him long to get his stuff in order and he was ready when she was. After a farewell to the children and Gio, the two of them piled into the convertible and drove away.

The ride up to Seattle was done in Russian with a lot of laughter. When she dropped him off, he gave her a big hug.

"I'm going to miss you."

"Don't be such a stranger this time. And bring her back. I like her."

"You got it. Drive safe, sweetie, and thanks for the ride." He shouldered his bag and jogged inside Sea-Tac.

Once he made it through to his gate, he pulled out his phone and dialed Bailey. The phone rang and rang without an answer. *This could mean two things. She's truly pissed at me or she honestly can't get to the phone.*

Ivan looked over notes on some of the projects they were working on in the lab as he waited for his flight to board. Once on the plane, he settled in and closed his eyes, wanting to catch some sleep before he had to change jets for the final leg of the journey home.

After some turbulence and delays, he found himself walking out of the airport in Santiago de Chile. He slid his shades on and waved for a cab. Directions given, he rested his head on the seat and closed his eyes. Sleep—he wanted and needed some sleep.

At his apartment, he took care of that most pressing need. Then he did some shopping and finally made his way to Bailey's place. He stood outside her door and knocked.

No answer.

"Bailey? Come on, open up." He knocked again. Still nothing.

He stood there and called her cellphone. He couldn't hear it ringing through the door.

"Maybe she's out on a job." Disappointed, he left her building and headed back through the crowd to his place.

He wanted to talk and make sure her anger with him for his stupidity didn't fester and grow. Ivan checked back twice more that day and called a few more times. Still nothing, either at her place or on the phone. And he grew frustrated. More and more with each passing moment.

Before he went to bed that night, he tried her phone, one last time.

"Hello?"

He blinked, honestly not having expected an answer. "Bailey?"

"What do you need, Ivan?"

"Where are you?" His heart beat steadier now that he was talking to her.

"In my place."

"I was there three times today and you never answered the door. I'm coming over so we can do this face to face."

"I'm not there."

"You just said you were at your place."

"And we both know I have more than one. Was there something you needed?"

"Yes, I wanted to apologize."

"Accepted." Loud noise erupted in the background. "I have to go. I'll see you when I get back there."

She was gone. Just like that. There one minute, gone the next.

Ivan drummed his fingers on the table and tried to figure out what he was going to do. His phone rang again. Answering quickly in the hopes it was Bailey, he never checked the caller ID.

"Yes?"

"Dr Vinokourov? This is Chrissy. There's been an interesting development. Could you come down here at your earliest convenience?"

"You're still there now? It's late, Chrissy."

"I know, but we've been working some long hours."

"I'll be right there." He hung up and went to change into something more suited for lab work rather than just his boxers.

* * * *

"You've been here for three days, McNeal. Don't you think you should be telling me what's going on? And what your plan is for Lynn?"

Lynn currently slept in the spare bedroom and Bailey sat out in the living room with her boss.

"I took her with me."

"That much, McNeal, is obvious even to me. You took her from the facility and brought her to my apartment. I'm sure there's a good reason for that somewhere and to tell you the truth, I'd really like to hear it."

"You know you'd told me that something was off to you there?"

She nodded and curled her legs under her on the sofa. "Yes. Something strange."

"You were right. The one who's running that place, Dr Treymous, has kind of decided that she had test subjects right there for her to work on."

Bailey leaned forward. "Test subjects?"

"Apparently, that woman is working on something to control humans."

"Control humans? That's vague. Control how? For what purpose?"

"I didn't get all the particulars but from what I saw, she's experimenting with a technique called optogenetics."

She shrugged. "You're going to have to explain what that is in non-smart-person talk."

"It's a technology which enables those in charge to control genetically modified neurons with a brief pulse of light."

"How were they genetically modifying them?"

"Each time she would 'freak out' and they medicated her, this woman was messing with her."

"I'm still not sure how she was doing this."

"Me either. I was hoping Ivan would be here so I could ask him."

"Why don't you call him?"

"You do it, he may be more inclined to answer you without asking a lot of other questions I don't know the answers to."

She reached for her cell and called him, leaving it on speaker.

"Hello?"

His warm voice washed over her and she wished that she was alone in her place to play with herself as she listened to him. Right now, however, she had to keep her focus and not let on how he made her feel. Especially not with McNeal in the room.

"Ivan? Bailey. I have a question for you."

"Hey, baby. Hang on a minute. I'll be right back, Chrissy. Keep that up." She heard a door close. "Okay, what can I do for you? Are you home yet?"

McNeal watched her with a curious expression but she ignored that. It was the 'baby' that had snagged his attention, she knew it.

"Nope, not there. What do you know about something called optogenetics, if anything?"

"Optogenetics? Using light to control the brain. You have genetically modified neurons, meaning it's coded — the gene inserted into the hippocampal neuron — for a light-sensitive protein. This is supposed to enable someone to use light to control the neurons. It's focused on the hippocampus because that's known to have a role in learning and memory. From what I remember, they wanted to be able to activate a memory on demand. This has also opened more insights into some brain disorders like schizophrenia, Parkinson's, anxiety, depression, et cetera."

Bailey and McNeal shared a look. "What would be the purpose of such a clinical application?"

"Depends on who is doing it. You could trigger memories that induce panic in someone, or ones that bring a calming memory. I suppose you could also trigger a mindless rage, depending on what you're training it for. Can I ask why you're curious? They claim there's no reason to worry about implanted memories or mind control but, given what Theta Corps has done with some things, I wouldn't agree with that. The right scientist and doctors could easily have that technology."

This isn't good. "You remember the woman I went to see in Adast?"

"Yes, Lynn."

"They've been doing something like that to her. Is there a cure?"

"That's not my area of expertise but I would be of the mind, if you weren't stimulating a portion of the neurons involved with the memory, she wouldn't be affected. Unless, of course, they had put in a wireless device they could activate from afar."

"Thanks, Ivan."

"Are we going to talk, Bailey?"

"Yes. Let me deal with this and I'll be back soon."

"Take care." He hung up.

"Do you think she's crazy enough to have been doing that?" Bailey slid her phone to the side and focused back on McNeal.

"You met her. Would you put it past her?"

"Not at all."

"Me either." He scratched the side of his neck. "I need to have her brain scanned to see if there is anything in there like a wireless device."

"You think she's going to go for that? Given what she's been going through in Adast and before?"

"I rescued her. I was supposed to have put her in a place where she would remain safe. Instead I put her with a sadistic woman who's been doing who knows what to her."

"You can't blame yourself. I don't think anyone at Theta knew what she was doing."

"They do now. I just sent a text to the head of the organization. If after we talk I ultimately hear back to let it go, I'll handle her on my own."

"What are you going to do with Lynn? You can't keep her with you at all times."

"Why not? I did you."

"I was much younger than that. She's in her twenties. She may not want a man around all the time." Bailey held up a hand. "And don't even think it. I'm not babysitting."

"I trust you to keep her safe, Bailey."

"I appreciate the confidence but that's not my concern. I don't stay in one place, McNeal. I travel. I have weapons and poisons in my possession. I can't watch her all the time. She's not staying here with me."

"She needs a good, strong female role model."

"There are plenty within Theta other than me."

"I want to do what's best for her, Bailey."

"I know you do and that's admirable. But what's best isn't pushing her off on me. I have enough crap in my own life to handle."

He crossed his arms over his chest. "Ivan?"

"This isn't about me. Why don't you get her a place near you? You can check on her and know she's safe."

"I travel."

"That wasn't a concern when you thought I would take her in. I travel as well."

"I can't put her just anywhere. If they have done something to her, I have to know what, and what will set it off."

"Have you tried asking her?"

"Asking her?"

"Who better to know than the woman herself?"

McNeal shook his head. "Have you *looked* at her, Bailey? She's small and scared. How would it be if I went to her and asked what they did to her?"

"I think it would be a sight better than trying to make assumptions. Ask her what she wants, allow her to be part of this decision-making process. A woman who's survived what she has can't be weak. She may not know or recognize her strength right now, but it's there. It's always been there."

McNeal got up and paced. Bailey readjusted in her seat to follow his progress. This was a side of him she'd not seen before and it more than confused her — it worried her. He ran his hands through his hair repeatedly and muttered under his breath as he continued to wear a path in her floor.

It dawned on her why it worried her so. His eyes. Dark circles were under them and they were red with exhaustion.

"Why don't you go get some sleep, McNeal? I'll stay up in case she wakes and needs anything. My bed is clean so make yourself at home."

"No, I should be up —"

"You should be sleeping so you're lucid and helpful to her. Go on, I got this. There's some things I have to do anyway."

"Are you sure?"

"Positive." She waved him on.

Ten minutes later, her place was silent and she went to her dining room table to make some more bullets. That activity kept her up until she heard the stirrings of Lynn in the spare room. Bailey had just finished putting everything away when the young woman walked out.

"Morning," she said.

Lynn wrung her hands in her shirt. "Good morning. Where's Kevin?"

"He's sleeping."

Her blue eyes snapped to the sofa then back to Bailey.

"Not there, I let him crash in my bed last night. I stayed out here."

"Oh." She stared at her feet. "Will you help me leave?"

Chapter Nineteen

Alarms blared and the fans sucked the smoke from the room. Ivan stood between Trick and Chrissy as they watched as the retardant shot from specific sites in the wall, near the dummy, dousing the flames.

"Looks like that one didn't go so well." He blew out an exasperated breath.

"Least we were just trying it on the dummy instead of one of us."

He couldn't argue that point at all. "I don't think we have to go back to square one. Looked as though it worked fine until it got to the powering down stage."

Chrissy laughed. "That would suck — manage to fly all that way then burn up as you're finished before you can strip if off. Kind of like re-entry for the space shuttle."

He chuckled as well. "Let's get back to it." He looked at Trick who had a slight smile on her face. More days than not he wished she would speak for he wanted to hear what she was thinking. She made eye contact and shrugged with a twinkle in her eyes.

"Some days all it takes is a good explosion to make us feel better."

The women walked off and he agreed with her assessment. It did make him feel better and yet at the same time he prayed it would work. There was something in the electrogravitics that didn't sit well when the wearer landed.

He made it to his office and sat at his desk. Pulling up a 3-D image of a B-2 Spirit, he watched it rotate on the screen.

Ivan picked up a pencil and tapped it against the edge of his desk as he thought. So obvious, it was right before him, he just had to see it. His phone rang and using the eraser, he pressed the speaker button.

"Dr Vinokourov," he said.

"Hello, Doctor."

He sat up straighter in his seat as that voice thrummed through him. Like a missing part of his heart and soul, it instantly revived him. Bailey.

"Hello, gorgeous. What are you doing?"

"Sitting in my apartment overlooking the market where you found me."

He didn't even attempt to stop the cheesy grin lifting his lips. She had returned. Had come back to him.

"How long have you been home?"

"About ten hours. I just woke up. I hear alarms, can you talk?"

His cock twitched as he pictured her fresh from sleep. Rumpled. Sexy as all get out. Sleepy eyes and full pouty lips that could and had delivered him to unmistakable heights of pleasure.

He lifted the receiver and spoke into that. "Just a slight mishap, don't worry, it's under control. I find it telling you called me when you first woke."

She gave a small bark of laughter. "I did. I promised I would call so we could talk. I know you're working right now but wanted to know if you could do dinner tonight?"

"I'll find a way to do just that. What time?"

"You tell me. My day is clear."

The alarms finally ceased. Through his window, he saw Chrissy talking animatedly with another lab assistant. Trick sat in her wheeled chair behind her row of computers, staring at the screens as she rolled between them.

"How about if I'm there by eight?"

"I'll have dinner ready."

Spinning his chair so the back was to the door, he rubbed his aching dick. "Are you okay?"

"Me? Sure."

That didn't sound too positive and he wanted to ask more but he could wait until tonight.

"I'll see you then."

"I'll be here. Have a good day."

"You too, Bailey."

"I plan on it."

She hung up and he sat there with a stupid grin on his face for about a minute. Dangling the handset between two fingers, he slowly pivoted back to the desk and put it back in its spot.

His computer screen snared his attention again and it hit him. "God, I'm such an idiot. I was right, it's so damn simple." He shoved back from the desk, heading out of the office. "Chrissy, meet me at Trick's station," he called out.

Soon the three of them sat facing one another.

"What'd you figure out?"

"It's so simple, I should have realized this before we even attempted the first one." He readjusted his arms on the back of the chair he straddled. "Now, think about the B-2. There are times when it lands that no one can touch it until the magnetic field's static build-up around it dissipates, or what can happen?"

Chrissy's eyes lit up. "It can kill you. So although the pack is still in powering down stage when they reach back to touch it, that's more than enough to set it off and explode the fuel cell."

He pointed at her. "Precisely."

"God, I can't believe we didn't realize that."

"We were thinking too grand, that it must be a huge problem, not something small and simple." Another glance to each of the women. "Now, suggestions on how we take care of this issue? How we contain the field until it's not going to harm the wearer?"

Trick rose and went to her bag. When she returned she had a tablet in her hand and she was using it. Ivan waited patiently and took it from her when she handed it over.

He stared at the diagram on the page before him. A low whistle escaped his teeth as he looked up. "Do you think this will work?"

Trick nodded.

"Do you have a prototype already or will we need to make one?"

Chrissy took the tablet from him. "There's a prototype. I've seen it at her house. I never knew that's what this was for."

"Amazing. Trick, can you send me all the specs?"

Another nod.

"How long have you been working on this?"

She wrote her answer on a piece of paper. *A while.*

Ivan took the tablet back from Chrissy and stared once more at the diagram. Two slim and long cylindrical tubes ran down, connected at the bottom by another. The static build-up was pulled in there and, from the looks of it, broken down.

He clicked on the notes and read. Impressive.

"What do you think?"

"I think Trick is one hell of a brilliant woman. She's using a combination of a natural static reducer with aluminum foil as well as having inside there a small humidifier to assist in neutralizing the static." He turned a page. "I want to see this compact humidifier, Trick." Ivan made sure he looked at her when he said that, then he lowered his head and continued to read.

"There's something else in here she refers to as Compound X, which assists as well. I think this is the smoking gun so to speak." He glanced at the woman who'd created this. "Do you have the prototype with you?"

Trick shook her head no and gave him an apologetic smile.

"That's okay, will you bring it tomorrow? So we can try to build another and not risk yours. I'd also like to see what this material is. From the compound it appears to be some type of rubber component but I don't know what it is." He handed Trick back her tablet. "You're going to be a rich woman if this works, Trick. And we'll take the appropriate precautions to ensure the patent is yours and not anyone else's."

They got back to work on setting things up for tomorrow. Ivan was hopeful—this could be just the thing needed to make this a success and able to be used out in the field. The rest of his day passed with incredible speed and before he knew it, seven o'clock had arrived.

He put stuff up and said goodnight to his co-workers as he made his way up and out of the building. Waving at a few of the farmers who were just leaving, he got on his bike and started toward his apartment.

Once there, he took a quick shower then put on some chinos and a black shirt. Shoes on, he locked up as he left. Ivan made one stop on his way to her place. At her building, he jogged up the stairs to her door. He wiped his palm on his thigh then knocked.

She opened the door and smiled at him. "Hey." She stepped back. "Come on in and make yourself at home. Food's almost ready."

He entered and inhaled deeply. The food and the scent that remained around her combined amazingly well. He faced her after she had shut the door and offered her the flowers.

"These are beautiful, Ivan. Thank you."

"It's my 'I'm sorry I was an ass' bouquet."

She rested her hand against his torso. "I could have stayed to talk it through. You're not the only one who could have made a better decision." She inhaled the scent and groaned. "Perfect."

He couldn't disagree. Her moan wound around him, especially his cock, and stroked it to a hard state.

"Am I allowed to kiss the cook?" he asked, capturing her shoulders with his hands.

She tilted her head. "Well, since you asked so nicely."

Ivan gathered her close and did just that. He took his time, allowing his tongue to rim her mouth, swiping along her lips before the seam where he pressed for entrance. She opened beneath his gentle push and her taste flooded him.

Bailey clenched his shirt in her hands, ignoring the flowers she still held. This was what she'd missed.

Him. His touch. His scent. How it felt to be in his arms.

He kissed her deeply. Held her like she meant the world to him. As if he'd missed her more than he could ever verbalize. In that moment, Bailey realized something. She might be an assassin who did her job with cool, calculating efficiency. But this man had the ability to strip all labels surrounding her other than *woman*. She wasn't working in a hard profession. She was all woman. Desirable. And from the way he had her bent back for his kiss, she would say his.

Ivan made her feel like a beautiful woman. Extremely feminine. No one had ever done that for her before. She clutched him harder, wanting nothing more than to crawl inside him.

As if he felt the change within her, he ended the kiss and lifted his head so they were staring at one another. "Are you okay?"

"I should put these in water."

"You should answer my question."

"I will be. It was a long stint in Chicago." She went to the kitchen and put the flowers in a vase after she'd filled it with water.

He sat at the kitchen table, his long legs out before him and watched her with those incredible glacier blue eyes. "Tell me about it."

"I... I—"

"Bailey?" He got to his feet and came to her side. Once he'd gathered her close, he pressed his lips to her temple. "Something's wrong. Talk to me." He led her to the couch and settled so she pretty much lay on him. "Am I wrong to assume this has something to do with Lynn and optogenetics?"

"McNeal showed up at my place with her in Chicago. He took her from that place. And he should have—that doc there was certifiable. A clean-up crew has gone in since and it's now under an entire new staff."

"That's good, right? Although I'm not sure why he showed up at your place." Danger lingered along his words.

"He wanted me to take her in and keep an eye on her while she recovered."

"You?"

"Not sure if I should be offended by your asking that but considering I did the same thing, I'll let it go. I told him I wasn't the right person to do this. I was gone too much and if she does want to hurt herself, I have weapons and poisons which she could eventually find and get her hands on."

"He removed her, why isn't he taking care of her?" He moved his hands up and down her back in a soothing motion.

"Thank you. That's what I asked him." She burrowed in closer, inhaling deeply and allowing his rich masculine scent to wash over her. "He said he had to get her out. And I understand that. He'd not been sleeping so I sent him to my room to do that and I stayed up. While he was out, Lynn came to me asking me to help her get away."

"Get away? From what? Or should I say who?"

"McNeal."

"Did you help her?"

"No. I was tempted to, though. Really tempted."

"Why didn't you?"

"How would she survive? I'm not about to let her go to live on the street. I told her she had to talk to McNeal. Their talk turned more into a shouting match."

"So she's not scared of him?"

"I think it's more scared *for* him. She's still under the impression that they will be coming after her and if he's discovered they will kill him."

He grunted. "I have a feeling McNeal will be a lot more difficult to kill than she may believe."

"He would be. Man's crazy deadly." She tapped a finger along his side. "But this woman is making him different. I don't know what it is with her. Or about her."

"How old is she?"

"Mid-twenties I would estimate. Why?"

"Is she his daughter?"

Bailey sat up, eyes wide. "I never thought about that. She may be."

"It would be a reason for him to be so protective. I'm guessing you all have rescued numerous people from situations like she was in. And if this one is the person who's making him different, there is a reason for it."

"Well, not just like that situation, it was" — she shuddered — "unspeakable."

"Does he have children?"

Bailey climbed off him and shuffled back to the kitchen. "I don't know. McNeal is my boss. Not a friend. We don't hang out or exchange Christmas cards. That's not our relationship."

Ivan joined her. "But he is close enough to you he wouldn't hesitate to ask you to look after a woman."

Is that jealousy I hear? "That's different. We have that kind of relationship. I trust him and respect him. He knows he can come to me about anything."

He rolled his eyes. "I don't understand you two but if it works then fine. My point is that she must be something more than the others if he's willing to go through what he did to get her out and bring her to you. It's obvious he thinks the world of your ability and he trusts you as well if he thinks you could keep her safe."

"I suppose. I never thought she may his blood."

"Will that change your mind about keeping her with you?"

"No. I'm still not the right person for that. I don't have that caring gene and she needs love and nurturing." She looked at Ivan when he laughed. "What's so funny?"

"The ridiculous notion that you don't have a caring gene, as you called it. Baby, I hate to break this to you, but you are very caring."

She pulled out the rice casserole. "I'm a woman who takes lives for a living."

"Yes. But that's your job. You, Bailey Hyde, are a warm, loving woman. If you weren't, why would you have checked on Lynn and told Kevin she needed to get out of there? Why would you have taken Safa with you and risked your easy escape to ensure the child was put in a much better situation? Then gone to visit her and check on her yourself?"

"That's different."

He snorted. "Nope. That's caring. You have a big heart in that chest of yours. No matter what you try to convince yourself of."

She withdrew the sheet of rolls and placed them on the bamboo trivet. "Children are different."

"Lynn isn't a child."

"She's younger than me."

"Okay," he conceded. "You win. We'll go with you're a cold, heartless bitch."

"Good," she said.

She wasn't sure what to make of his assessment. If she grew too soft, would she be able to continue her job? Bigger question, did she want to? Was she at the point in her life where she wanted to do something different?

How much sense did that make? She'd always done what she did. Bailey the homemaker didn't sound like her. What did assassins do when they finished their careers?

Why am I thinking about this? I do what I do and I make no apologies for it. I have no intentions of giving up my work.

Did she?

Chapter Twenty

She stood there, lost in her own thoughts. Ivan watched her as she worked whatever it was out in her head. He could practically see the wheels churning in her mind.

He'd missed her. Bailey and her crazy personality. Not crazy like she was psycho or anything but crazy in that she never failed to make him amazed. She was like Jaydee in a way—there were some things that just didn't matter. She didn't complicate things—she spoke her mind and was brutally honest.

He stared at the thin orange camisole strap that had slipped down her shoulder as she continued to stand there. Her white and orange sarong had him ready to unwrap her. She didn't have any shoes on and her nails were short and clean.

Bailey blinked and came to awareness. He smiled as she met his gaze.

"You okay over there?"

"Yes, I'm fine. Ready to eat?"

He was ready for something. "Sure, what can I do?"

They ate and he filled her in on how his work was going. Together they cleaned up and took a walk. Back at her place, she cut them each a piece of cake and they sat side by side on her sofa, plates in hand.

"Are you over whatever it was that was in Oregon?" She ate a bite of cake.

Ivan had known that the talk was coming, but that didn't mean he wanted to deal with it. He'd already acknowledged he'd been an ass. "Yes."

"I know this relationship is not the most common, given I'm gone a lot and you're extremely busy with your work, but I won't be in one where you think you can tell me crap like you tried to say there. I just won't put up with it, Ivan, and if you weren't you we wouldn't be having this conversation. I don't put up with it."

"But you are not breaking it off?"

"No. I meant what I told you before — whatever this is between us, I feel it too. And that is why I'm not calling it quits. But it can't happen again."

"I'm possessive. And I'm not going to be apologetic for being me."

"Not asking you to. Just that you realize what you're doing. How many women would have been okay with the situation in Oregon?"

"Not many. You know there's not anything between myself and Jaydee, Bailey. I told you that."

"Nothing but a long history. An intimate history. Such that when you first got there, I was sitting with her husband for fifteen minutes while the two of you conversed in Russian, as if you'd forgotten we were even in the room."

"She loves her husband and children."

"Not saying she doesn't. But when you come hard on me because I'm talking to a man who's not only her brother-in-law but a fellow Theta Corps member, I take exception."

"Understood." He finished his cake and set the plate aside. "I had blinders on to everything but you and him, looking all cozy together."

"Trust has to go both ways, Ivan."

"I know. I've apologized and while I can't promise I won't become a stupid male who's blinded by jealousy and does something you don't agree with, I will promise to try not to." He slid closer to her. "I do trust you, Bailey. On that, you have my word."

He took the fork from her and fed her the next bite. Her lips formed a lovely and tempting O as she drew the food off the utensil. He watched her chew and swallow before he kissed her.

She shuddered and he captured the plate before it fell. Without breaking their kiss, he fumbled around for the table and set the remaining cake there with the fork. He was pressing her into the couch and took advantage, deepening the kiss. Ivan cupped her breast in his hand. The nipple drew tight and poked his palm through her thin camisole.

Bailey widened her legs and slipped her hands beneath his shirt, skimming along his back. He ground against her, mimicking what he longed to do to her without a single shred of clothing between them.

"I want my dick in you, Bailey. I want you coming all over it as you scream in pleasure."

"Yes," she mumbled back, tugging up his shirt. "Off."

He obeyed, tossing it over the couch. She purred as she spread her fingers out and leaned forward to lick at his nipple. With the flat of her tongue, she lapped at him. One then the other, and goose bumps popped up all over his body. He encouraged her to lie against the armrest.

Reaching out, he lifted her left leg and hooked it over the back of couch. Her right she had around him. He took advantage of the access. Her sarong rode high and he could see a flash of her panties. He trailed his fingertips back along her smooth leg to her center.

"Silk," he muttered. "A thong?"

She shifted beneath him, attempting to come closer, whimpering when he pushed her back and held her there.

"My turn, Bailey."

White silk. Damp. He ran his fingers along her pussy, toying with the edge of the smooth material as she watched him, need blatant in her gaze.

"I've missed you."

"Ivan, please."

"No. I get to take my time. All these nights I've spent without you. My hand is a poor substitute for your pussy."

"So is mine," she admitted.

He tore his gaze from her panties and stared at her. "You've been playing with yourself, Bailey?"

"Nightly," she said, arching her hips, seeking more of his touch.

"I want to watch that sometime. Watch you playing with yourself. Watch you finger your clit and fuck yourself with your fingers. See them come out of you covered in your cream before you suck them clean." He slipped one below the elastic and touched one of her lips. She mewled and moved restlessly. "Will you let me watch you bring yourself pleasure?"

"Yes." Her response was more of a gasp than anything. "If you do the same."

"You've got a deal." He allowed his finger to sink into her pussy.

She cried out, softly, hips gyrating and her leg around him tightening.

"Show me your breasts."

She grasped the neckline of her shirt and tugged it down. Her white bra and the breasts it held were exposed. He used his free hand and dragged two fingers along the bra, freeing her breasts to his gaze. Dipping his head forward, he sucked a nipple in his mouth, swirled his tongue around it then bit lightly.

"Ivan!" Her cry was louder this time. He wanted her to scream until she lost her voice.

He pistoned his finger inside her as he shared his attention between her globes, ensuring to pluck and tweak the one not in his mouth. His cock dug insistently into his jeans, wanting out. Wanting her.

Her gaze, hooded. Her teeth captured her lower lip as he released her with a pop. They that begged for more attention. The way her shirt sat, they were offered up like a delicious temptation.

He trailed his hungry gaze over her. Rumpled. Her breasts were bared and wet from his administrations. The way her legs were spread bunched up her skirt, allowing him a direct view of where he had every intention of being. And soon.

Ivan turned and pressed a kiss to her inner thigh. She trembled. He did it again, his tongue lingering as he traced an abstract design upon her skin.

Bailey tightened her grip on his shoulders. "Ivan." Her cry was breathless.

"You are wearing a thong, aren't you?" He nipped her again.

Her chest heaved with each desperate attempt to breathe. He ran his finger to pull the material away from her pussy, careful not to disturb his other hand, which he held still, his digits buried within her.

Her body responded to his touch like a harp did to a harpist. Every touch creating a reaction, so raw, so pure. So real.

Ivan jerked once, hard, breaking the material of her thong so it was no longer in his way. He worked his wrist again, keeping her on edge.

He moved to the knot securing her sarong and untied it. Nearly impatient, he flung the soft cotton pieces back. Her pussy had a single strip of hair, leading him to where his fingers were buried. Where he wanted his cock to be.

Withdrawing his fingers, he brought them to his mouth and licked them clean, savoring her essence, before touching her right thigh.

"Why are you still dressed?"

"Shh. No questions. God, look at you. Laid out before me like you are. Do you know what you're doing to me?" He touched her clit, pinching it lightly.

She shuddered. "Th-thought you said no questions."

"To you. I can ask them." Another pinch.

"Ivan, please."

His cock screamed its agreement. Not moving back away more than he had to, he stood and kicked off his shoes. "Don't move. Stay just like that. No, play with your nipples for me."

He groaned as she did, her unpainted nails running over the beaded tips, plucking and rolling them. Pants undone, he shoved them down his legs, taking his boxers along the way. Her gaze riveted to his cock and he gripped it. The hunger in her eyes overflowed and he bent to grab a condom.

"Please." The word fell from her lips as a beg.

He ripped the packet and unrolled the sheath on his length then got back on the couch. One hand he positioned under her ass and he lifted her slightly as he guided himself into her.

Her gasp turned into a low purr of pleasure as he slid in slowly with one continuous thrust. *Damn, I missed this.*

Her tight pussy held him with the familiar warm heat no memory could ever properly recreate, nor compare to. She clenched and her muscles rippled. Ivan began to move. Bailey's entire body responded.

He pistoned and she rose to meet him, her hips undulating as she worked with him, in tandem to heighten their experience. Her breasts jiggled as he drove into her. Over and over.

Her leg went from the back of the sofa to his shoulder. Bailey released her nipples and grabbed at his wrists. He allowed it.

Back and forth he powered his hips.

In and out he sank, only to withdraw then do it all over again.

Harder. Faster. Deeper.

He couldn't get enough and needed more. Craved more.

Sweat trickled down his back and temples as he continued, desperate to prolong their pleasure and yet needing to explode.

Her cries. His grunts. Their passion. They crescendoed together, her pussy milking him as he thrust through his own orgasm and her thick cream coated him.

Expended, heart beating erratically and limbs trembling, Ivan stared at the woman watching him with burning passion in her gaze.

"Shit."

She smiled and reached up to touch his chin. "Well said. Are you up for more?"

"Fuck yeah." He readjusted so he could lift her while remaining buried in her. "Let's start over."

She winked. "I'm game."

And man, was she ever. Then again, so was he.

* * * *

Bailey sat at her table finishing her final stage of cleaning some of her pistols. The last two days had been idyllic to say the least. She and Ivan had spent all of their free time together. In bed.

Not only the bed. We've made good use of walls, tables, sofas and more.

He'd arrived a short time ago and had showered. She heard the water cut off and figured he was dressing. A soft chime filled the room and she glanced around.

"Ivan!"

"Yeah, babe?"

"Your phone is ringing."

"Answer it for me, I'll be right out."

She ensured there was no grease on her hand then did as he'd bidden. "Hello?"

"Hi? I am look for Ivan. This is his number, *da*?"

Bailey hid her distaste at hearing the female's thick, Russian-accented voice.

"Yes, this is his phone. He'll be here momentarily."

"Oh good. I am friend from Russia. He was just here visit me."

Bailey didn't recognize the voice and she was good at remembering them. "Nice. I'll get him."

Speak of the devil. He stepped into view, a smile on his handsome face. She held out his cell for him.

"Who is it?"

She lifted one shoulder. "Some Russian woman. She didn't give her name."

"My mother?"

"No, her voice I would recognize. Here."

He took it with a puzzled expression. Bailey returned to the table and cleaned up since she'd been finished with her project when the phone call came in. She did her best to ignore his timbre as he spoke to whoever that woman was.

Not like I understand Russian.

She grabbed the SIG, Walther and Kahr CW, carrying them to her mini armory and safe combo. Once they were in, she closed the door, ensured the lock had engaged then replaced the panel hiding it from view.

He continued to talk and she walked to her bedroom where she stripped then got in the shower. They were attending a *fútbol* game tonight. She was excited, not having been to one in a good long while.

Ivan sat on her bed when she strode back in, a towel wrapped around her midsection. He wasn't on his phone and she bit back her curiosity, opting to search for what she would be wearing tonight in her closet and chest of drawers.

"That was Kisa."

She found a nice three-quarter-sleeved blue and red shirt. "Should that name mean something to me?"

"My mother took me to meet her the day you weren't with us."

Of course she did. "Okay." She selected a pair of white premium painter's pants.

"I told her I wasn't interested in pursuing a relationship with her."

"Okay." She went to her dresser and dug for undergarments.

He appeared behind her, gripping her wrists. "Bailey."

"I didn't ask, Ivan. I told you, I trust you."

He kissed her neck. "I know."

She grabbed her bra and panties. "Thank you, though. You know, for telling me."

His chuckle was decadent. "You're welcome. I wanted you to know who she was. Now, do you need help getting dressed?" He turned her toward him.

She pushed him back. "No. You helping would mean me not getting any clothes on or going to the game."

"And that's...a *bad* thing?"

No. "Yes. We're *supposed* to be going on a date." She dropped the towel and laughed at his expression. Pained. Horny. Aroused. She pointed to the bed. "You stay over there." She slid on her underwear and put on her bra as he made his way there.

"Fine," he grumbled. "My woman wants a date, she gets a date."

She tugged on the shirt. "It's been a while since I've been to one of *Universidad de Chile's* games. Especially a home game." Her pants were next.

"Where are we going again?"

Bailey dug for her Doc Martens, grabbed some socks and sat on her bed near him but not close enough to touch. "*Estadio Nacional de Chile.* It's in Ñuñoa."

He tugged on the end of her hair. "You truly are enthusiastic."

"Love the game, I make no apologies for that fact." Socks on, she reached for one boot. "What's yours? No, wait. Hockey?"

"Something against that sport?"

She tied on her other boot. "No. Quite the opposite. I'm a fan of the game. Not much call for it here."

"So you think you have me all figured out now, *da*?"

Bailey stuck her tongue out at him. "*Da*."

He grinned. "Come on, woman. I still can surprise you."

She shrugged nonchalantly. "Perhaps." She pocketed her ID and some money. "I'm— Wait." She swiftly braided her hair and bound the end. "Ready."

Ivan's laughter was comforting. She enjoyed the familiarity of it. "Come on, you."

They caught a cab to the stadium. Ivan had the tickets and they walked together into the noisy building. The energy flowed into her and beat within her blood. It was infectious. She'd not ever understand how someone could come to a game and not get drawn in. The fans were like a needed pulse. A wave that overtook her, engulfing her. Making her part of the event.

Weaving through the raucous crowd, they found their seats. Up close with a great view of the pitch.

After usual exchanges of handshakes and whatnot, the ref whistled to signal the start of the game. In the end, they had four minutes of stoppage time to add on and the game finished knotted up at two. Her throat was sore and she had enjoyed every minute of it.

She tucked her arm through Ivan's and leaned against him while they departed the stadium. "Have fun?" She posed her question as they waited for a taxi.

"Yes. You know you get extremely foul-mouthed when you watch this game?"

Bailey chuckled as he held the door for her. "I've heard that a time or two." She slid across the seat. "I suppose you're a perfect gentlemen during a hockey game?"

He joined her, gave their destination and said, "Hell no. Trust me, I didn't say it was a bad thing, just pointing it out. I found it kind of hot." He rested his large hand on her thigh, his fingers rubbing the inside of her leg. "Very much so."

She shifted on the seat and cleared her throat. "Thank you for coming with me."

"You wanted to go, how could I say no?"

"Easily."

"I like sports in general. Are you sure you don't want to stop and get something to eat?"

"I'm sure. I ate and drank enough there."

"Bailey, you barely eat. Even when you do it seems you eat so little."

"You've been paying attention to something else then, because I'm a pig."

He leaned close and kissed her. "A very adorable pig."

She smacked him on the arm. "Thanks."

At his place, he paid the driver and walked her inside. He shut his door and locked it behind him. "What now?"

She grinned. "I'm sure there's a spot of wall I've not been up against yet."

His smile wetted her panties and kicked her heartbeat into a much higher gear. "I'm sure you're right." He reached for her and drew her close. "Get over here. I have plans for this body tonight."

Chapter Twenty-One

"Here's to the two of you!" Ivan lifted his glass and toasted the two women with him. "That was some damn good work. And you, Trick, to come up with what you did. You're amazing."

Chrissy and Trick touched glasses with each other and him. They all drank. The bar was loud around them but they were in the back at a table and he was between the two women.

"For a while there, I wasn't sure we'd be able to pull it off." Chrissy stirred her drink as she gazed around the bar.

Trick nodded her agreement.

Ivan understood. During a good chunk of time, the other prototypes weren't even working like the first one had. So the three of them had stopped using anyone else in the lab to assist in the building and had done them on their own. Yes, it had taken longer but they hadn't cared.

Once they had ten working ones, they had put them with the packs. On the final one, after all the tweaks and adjustments, they'd figured out and had it where the wearer wouldn't explode into a ball of fire upon landing.

He'd done the first test on a live person and thankfully it had worked. Today they'd talked to the head of research and development, with the working prototype. After the demonstration, they'd wanted to know more about Trick's addition that removed the static and made it safer.

Ivan had shaken his head and demanded that this remain hers. The patent for it would be hers. So then, the lawyers had come into the room and more discussion had ensued. But what ultimately happened was Trick had the option that the patent would be hers or that Theta Corps would purchase it from her as opposed to just a few devices — that way, production would be much faster for them. In the end, she'd agreed to sell it. And the item had gone into production.

Now they were out celebrating.

"I had moments as well," he admitted. "But we were successful and Trick is now one hell of a rich woman." He toasted them again. "Here's to you, ladies."

"Now all we have to do is figure out what the hell that tingling sensation is when using the bracelet to repel bullets."

"That's next week's project. Tonight, we celebrate then take off a well-deserved weekend."

"I'm in for that. I sure could use a few days of doing not a damn thing."

He laughed with understanding. They'd been going hard for the past month. "We haven't been resting on our laurels, that's for sure."

"No, that's the job for Howland."

That wouldn't get an argument from him. That woman would make a monk swear and give up his peaceful ways.

"What are you all doing here?"

Ivan looked up to see more folks from the lab standing there. "Just out having a drink. You guys want to join us?"

"Sure."

Tables were dragged over and their party of three turned into one of ten. Ivan didn't mind, they were all out to have a great time and there wasn't anyone at the lab that he didn't get along with. *Aside from Howland, of course.*

They ate and drank until well into the wee hours of the morning. He saw the women into a taxi and waved them off before stumbling to his own. At his place, he didn't even shower, just dragged his ass to bed and fell in.

Most of the weekend he stayed around his apartment, doing laundry and catching up on some other things the long hours at the lab had stopped him from achieving. He missed Bailey and, late Saturday afternoon, called her.

The phone rang and rang before it was answered with a "Hello?"

He frowned. "Bailey?" It didn't sound like her.

"No, this is her message service. May I take a message for her?"

Message service? When did she get a message service and where is she? "When will she be back?"

"I'm not at liberty to say, sir, I'm sorry. May I take a message?"

"Just have her call Ivan when she can."

"Any last name to go with that or a phone number?"

"No, she'll know."

"Very good, sir. Anything else?"

Frustration filled him. "No, thanks."

"Have a good night, sir." She hung up and he did as well.

He slumped back in his chair. "Message service? Where are you, Bailey?"

Realizing he couldn't do anything about where she may or may not be, he got back to work. He fell into bed that night ready for a good sleep.

* * * *

Ring. Ring. Ring. Ring.

Ivan reached blindly for his phone as it played a song guaranteed to wake him from any type of slumber.

"Hello?" he said, struggling to wrap his brain around the fact that he wasn't sleeping any longer and coherent responses might be in order.

"You called?"

Bailey. Her voice was smooth and sexy without even trying, and he smiled in the dark.

"I did. I never knew you had a message service."

"Oh, that's just what my phone does when I'm on a job. I usually take a disposable with me."

On a job. He woke up a bit more with that snippet of news. "Where are you?"

"Currently flying over the Pacific Ocean." She shuffled. "I'm sorry, did I wake you? I wasn't thinking of the time difference."

"Forget the time, I'm just glad you called. Can I ask what you're doing?"

"Talking to you."

"Bailey."

"I don't discuss my jobs, Ivan." Her tone had grown hard and unyielding.

"I know." He didn't like it at all. Her doing what she did or with the skill she did it with. He needed to go a different tactic. "Where are you going now? Are you coming home?"

"I'm going back to Chicago."

He reached over to click on the light, squinting when the glare filled the room. "Why not here?"

"I have some contacts to meet."

Contacts. Killing. All of it was just another day at the office for her. "Contacts about what?"

"The disappearance of one of our agents. I don't know if you know him, he works with Valentino. Anyway I had one reach out to me and he said he thinks he may have a lead on him. So I'm going to go talk to him and get what I can from him."

Valentino. So the man taken was damn good at his job also, had to be to work with Valentino Cassano. Whoever had managed to take him must be stellar.

"Will you be in danger?"

"No. But my contact won't deal with anyone but me so I am going." She muffled a curse then there was a clinking of ice. "I don't know when I'll be back in Chile."

"What are you doing?"

"Making a drink."

"So this isn't a commercial flight."

"No. I'm actually being flown by a friend of yours."

His brow converged. "A friend of mine?"

"Yes, Jaydee. She's my pilot."

The phone nearly fell from his hand. Bailey and Jaydee in one plane? Oh, this could be bad. "Are you two getting along?"

"We're professionals, Ivan. Surely you don't think we're up here in the sky rolling around like we were mud wrestlers."

He grinned. "No, but thanks for the image. That will get me through a few nights."

"You so need help."

There was no bitterness in her tone and he just laughed. "Probably." He sobered. "Are you two okay?"

"We'll be fine. I have to go."

"Bailey?"

"Yeah?"

"Be careful."

"You got it. I'll talk to you soon." The call ended.

He tossed his phone down and grunted as he allowed his head to drop back, hitting the headboard. Seriously? Jaydee and Bailey together? This could be very good or extremely bad.

* * * *

Bailey looked briefly at the receiver she'd just replaced. With a shrug, she finished making the drinks and carried them back to the cockpit.

"Here you go." She placed Jaydee's coffee beside her.

"Thanks."

"Ivan says hello."

"He was surprised I was here with you."

Since it wasn't a question, Bailey didn't respond. Instead she took a drink of her juice.

"You mean a lot to him, you know."

Bailey turned toward Jaydee and watched her. The woman wasn't looking in her direction, all her attention was on the task at hand, but somehow she knew she was being observed and judged.

"He means a lot to me as well."

"I don't normally get into people's business because, quite frankly, I don't care. Gio says it's because I wasn't raised like most, so I tend to stay out of things. I don't know. Anyway, my point is, I don't have many friends in the world but Ivan is one of my closest. He is my family. And I will protect him in ways you can't even begin to understand."

"If I didn't know better, I would think you just threatened me." Bailey drank some more juice.

"Don't think I did. Understand I did that exact thing. Don't hurt him or you will answer to me."

"Ivan's a big boy, he can take care of himself."

"He's family."

"So you've said."

"You're not worried about my threat."

"Should I be? I don't know you other than what he's told me. I know your brother-in-law is Valentino. Other than that, you're my pilot."

Jaydee glanced at her. "What do you do for Theta Corps, Bailey?"

"I don't discuss my work."

"I know you don't. You're very secretive about everything. Just like I know you were brought in by Kevin McNeal at the young age of six after having seen your parents die. I know you have homes in Santiago, Chicago and Paris. I know the multiple forms of martial arts you're an expert in and which pistols you prefer to use."

Bailey was impressed.

"I know your apartment in Chile is a five minute walk from Ivan's. He moved there to be near to you. His lab is beneath a farm outside the city. I know you went to Adast to check on a woman who subsequently vanished from the facility before it was cleaned out. I know you saved a young girl in Egypt named Safa and she is being adopted. I know everything there is and I know exactly what it is you do for a living. I know how many times and how often they send you out."

That was just scary. Bailey tightened her grip on her glass. "Your point in all this being what, exactly?"

She turned her head and gazed at her briefly. "That I can reach you. No matter where you are in the world, I can reach you. Don't hurt him."

"Gotcha."

There wasn't anything else she could say. This woman knew what she did and wasn't fazed in the least. In fact, she seemed quite the opposite. Her concern was for Ivan, not her. That alone got her points. Jaydee truly cared about those she considered to be her family.

"You know you're good for him."

Bailey hadn't expected Jaydee to say another thing about Ivan. "I'm good for him?"

"Yes. You get him out of the lab. That man used to be in there for days on end. He's not anymore, when you're around. And you got him to go home."

"So let me get this straight, I'm good for him but you threatened me."

"Just because you are good for him doesn't mean you wouldn't hurt him. I merely shared with you the outcome should you do such a thing."

"Aren't you just a bundle of warmth and good cheer."

Their gazes met. "Not really." She blinked. "Oh, that was sarcasm."

Yes, that's exactly what it was. "I could get to like you, Jaydee."

"You have realized I'm not a threat to your relationship with Ivan?"

"I have."

"Good. That way when you come back to the house you will stay the full time and not leave early."

She reclined back. "Sure. You know, he may not want me to come with him next time."

"You know, he and Lexy used to tell me all the time I had a knack for missing what was directly in front of me because I looked at things only one way. It almost cost me my husband. Don't make that same mistake. That man is in love with you."

"No," she corrected. "He still loves you."

Jaydee shook her head. "Not the same. He lives and breathes to be beside you. How do you not see it?"

"Perhaps because I was taken to his ex-girlfriend's house." Her words had an edge to them.

"He's told you he loves you, right? Ivan isn't shy about sharing his feelings. He's not a man who feels it makes him weak to do that. He's extremely confident in who he is as a person and a man. Therefore, I know he's told you. Why do you doubt? Ivan and I were friends long before we became lovers and were friends after we stopped being lovers. He will always be my friend."

"Yes," she admitted. "He told me." *In his own way just as I did to him in my own way.*

"He doesn't lie. If your problem is that I have slept with him then that's your hang-up. There's nothing romantic between us anymore."

Nothing like being blunt. Well, Ivan had warned her she was straightforward.

"I suppose it is my hang-up. Something I will have to get over."

"Yes, you will." She drank some of her coffee and Bailey finished her juice.

The co-pilot stuck his head in and Bailey got up. "Thanks for the chat." She slipped out and retreated to one of the seats, stopping to put her glass in the dirty dish container and closing it so it would be secure when they landed.

Bailey slept, waking when a light touch brushed her shoulder. She came alert instantly. Assessing her situation, she opened her eyes when she recalled where she was. Still, she didn't rush to sit up. Eyes open, she found Jaydee standing near and looking down at her.

"Everything okay?"

"Of course. We'll be landing soon, thought you might wish to clean up a bit first."

Jaydee actually sounded offended she'd asked if everything was fine. "Sounds good, thanks." She raised her seat and placed the blanket aside.

Jaydee walked back to the cockpit without another word. Bailey rose from the seat and made her way back to the restroom. Once the door had latched behind her, she turned on the water. Using one of the folded white cloths, she washed her face then patted it dry with a towel.

She had kinks in her neck and back, both of which would hopefully work themselves out as she moved around. Bailey checked her watch, focusing on local time. Just before six in the morning.

As she took care of her needs, she tried to decide the best place to meet her contact. By the time she had buckled herself in, she still hadn't decided. He was jumpy and suspicious of everything—not that she blamed him for that.

Bailey stared out of the window as the Chicago skyline came into view. They landed and taxied into the executive airport.

John, the co-pilot, lowered the steps for her with a smile. A dark Suburban with tinted windows lingered just near the halted jet. Bailey shouldered her pack and went to the top step, shivering in the cold air, noticing her other bag already at the bottom.

"Bailey."

She faced Jaydee. "Yes?"

"Good luck."

There wasn't a doubt in her mind that Jaydee knew exactly why she was here. "Thanks for the ride." She headed out and shivered again. She'd not properly dressed for this weather. Winter had already arrived here. The wind bit into her skin with viciousness.

The moment she hit the ground, the SUV's driver door swung open and a tall man, wearing shades and a dark suit, entered her line of sight.

He strode toward her and hefted her suitcase in one gloved hand with ease. Then he reached out to her shoulder pack and she shook her head.

"Ms Hyde, I'm your driver, David. Are you sure you don't want me to take your other bag?"

"I'm sure."

"Okay. I'm to take you to your hotel."

Behind her sunglasses, she narrowed her gaze. "My hotel?" *I have a perfectly acceptable apartment in this city, why exactly do I need a hotel room?*

"Yes. Mr McNeal set everything up."

"I'll be right there."

"Yes, ma'am." He walked away with her bag, heading to the SUV.

Bailey withdrew her phone and placed a call.

"What is it, Bailey?"

"Explain to me why I'm staying in a hotel as opposed to utilizing my apartment."

"Don't argue with me over the phone."

"You're not before me in person."

"Get to your hotel room."

She ended the call and with an eye-roll strode to the idling vehicle. "Let's go," she announced as she slid onto the front seat.

The man put them in gear and drove away. "Most people ride in the back."

"I'm not most people." She closed her eyes, grateful her flight hadn't been a commercial one.

She didn't speak for the entire ride and hopped out the moment he pulled up to the hotel downtown. The driver quickly joined her and handed her suitcase to the bellhop.

"Thank you, David."

"Call me when you need a car. I'm yours twenty-four seven as long as you're here in Chicago." He handed her his card.

"Good to know." She spun on the balls of her feet and walked inside to the main counter. "I'm here to check in."

The man standing there—Phillipe, according to his name tag—smiled at her and gave their standard welcome.

"Name?"

"Bailey Hyde."

He typed a few keys, smiled again and handed her a key card. "Your room is forty-two fifteen. Let us know if we can be of any assistance. The elevators are that way then to your left. Enjoy your stay."

"Thank you. It's okay," she told the bellhop. "I got it."

Exhaling loudly in the elevator, she pressed the button for her floor. Once there, she walked along the carpeted corridor to her door. Key card in hand, she let herself in and froze.

"Good to see you, Bailey. Congratulations on another successful job."

"McNeal. Why am I not surprised to see you here." She wasn't asking, it was a statement.

He appeared all too comfortable lounging in what was supposed to be her room. She dropped her bag and stepped forward so the door would close behind her.

"We needed to talk."

Her suspicions flared and rose along with her eyebrows. "We?"

"Come on in," he called out.

The connecting door opened and in walked Valentino Cassano, Anabelle Lee Jackson and Beauregard Jackson. On their heels was another man she didn't know personally but from his photo, he was the boss not only of the trio who'd just entered but of all Theta Corps. Masters.

"We," McNeal stated.

Shit.

Chapter Twenty-Two

Ivan played with the salad resting in the Styrofoam container on his desk as opposed to eating it. The limp lettuce and floppy vegetables in it were less than appetizing. Regardless of knowing he needed to eat, since he'd not eaten anything thus far today and it was approaching eight at night, he didn't want this.

"Boss," Chrissy said, popping her head in the door. "Come on, have something for you."

"Be right there."

She vanished and he stood, lifting the salad and depositing it in the trash on his way out.

Chrissy led him down to one of their labs and opened the door. Ivan stepped in and froze as he saw what awaited him. Everyone had gathered there. Hot food lined one of the tables and on another sat a large cake.

"Happy birthday!" they cried out.

Shit, he'd been so busy, he'd forgotten his own birthday. "Thanks, guys. This is perfect. Much better than that damn salad, which was the only thing I could find here."

"Now you know why." Chrissy handed him a drink and a plate. "Help yourself."

His stomach rumbled and he eagerly made his way to the food-laden table. "Who told you it was my birthday?"

"Your girlfriend."

In the process of scooping out some meatballs, he paused. "My girlfriend?"

Chrissy propped her hands on the tablecloth next to him. "Yes, she called me and wanted to make sure you had a party, said she knew you had been working hard and would probably forget. Given she is out of town, she still wanted you to have some fun." She nudged him. "I like her, I think we should meet her."

A chorus of cheering rose around them.

"I'll see what I can do," he promised.

Thank you, Bailey. This is just what I needed.

They ate and drank until close to midnight. Even Howland showed up and shared a piece of marble cake with all of them. The time she was there, the joviality faded slightly but it rose again quickly after she'd taken her leave.

He opened cards and had a wonderful time. They cleaned up, said goodnight and everyone went their separate ways. The leftover cake and food remained behind for the night guards to eat.

Ivan rode home and found a package waiting for him outside his door. No return markings. Unlocking his door, he gazed around once more. No one was there. He slid the box inside with his foot then closed the door behind him. He picked it up, carried it to the table and left it there while he went to get a knife to open it.

Carefully, he slit the tape and folded back the flaps. Whatever it contained had been concealed by blue and gold paper. He pulled it out, ignoring the packing peanuts that fell from it, and tried to figure out what it was. Bigger than a book.

A picture, maybe? The item had some weight to it as well.

He rested it on the table and began to remove the wrapping paper. A frame came first and he knew it was a photo. Ivan turned it over and smiled. It was an image of the Scarlet Sails celebration. The ship was a frigate and had the vibrant red sails—it was nighttime and in the background of the image were exploding fireworks. Their reflections lit up the water around the ship. The artwork was breathtaking.

Thank you, Bailey.

Seated in the corner of the frame was a folded note and he opened it.

Here's to you. I wish I could have been there with you on your birthday. Enjoy your day and I hope you like the picture.

~Bailey

The writing wasn't hers but it didn't matter. The words were. He immediately got to work hanging it up. Once it hung in his living room, he made his way to bed. His dreams that night were filled with images of Bailey. The woman who'd come to mean so much to him.

He woke and called her number.

"Hello?"

"I'd like to leave a message for Bailey, please."

"Go ahead, sir. I'm ready."

"Tell her thank you for the gift, it is beautiful and thoughtful. Also I look forward to seeing her soon."

"Anything else, sir?"

"No, that's all."

"Very good. Have a nice day, sir."

"You as well, thank you." He hung up.

It was his day off and he didn't have to get in to work any time soon. But he did want to make it to the market, so he showered and dressed.

Ten minutes later he was strolling through the street, picking up food and taking in the overall feel of the market.

* * * *

The diagrams on his computer spun slowly as he tapped his pencil. Trick sat across from him and they waited on Chrissy.

"I think this will work, Trick. In theory all the pieces fit together. At least they do on the computer."

She smiled and nodded.

"I know the final piece is supposed to arrive today, then we can put them together and give it a go." They were trying the bracelet again to see if they could remove the tingle along the wearer's skin.

Chrissy knocked and entered. "Sorry. It's crazy up there. More trucks than I can ever recall. So, it took me a bit longer than expected to make my way down here. Security is tightened."

"No problem, we were just saying that in theory all the pieces fit."

She laughed. "On the computer?"

"Absolutely. I'm looking at them now. Given we've added in a micro version of Trick's genius, hopefully there won't be any more danger to the wearer."

"That's good. We don't need the wearer catching fire or anything like that just because they have it on their wrist."

"Unless we ship it to the enemy."

They shared laughter then made their way out to the lab and began assembly. While they'd been waiting for the last piece to arrive, they'd dismantled the other one and were comparing every step to each other.

Trick noted down the differences while he assembled the new one and Chrissy did the older version. The work was tedious and long but they kept at it, breaking to take lunch then getting back to it.

Once they both had been reassembled, they handed off the notes to two other workers who would type them up for them while they took a break. All three were back in his office when the printouts came.

Ivan always preferred printouts. He could write on them much easier than he could the tablet. He wanted the hard copy in hand—it was one thing he wouldn't waver on. Those who worked with him now understood that and he never had to ask anymore, they just gave him paper.

With one copy for each of them, he settled back in his chair and reached for his pencil. "Let's figure out what's the same and what the changes are and where they happened."

An explosion rocked the room and yellow alarm lights began to flash.

"What the hell was that?" Chrissy jumped up, followed by Trick.

He hadn't any clue. They were far below ground, so to feel this couldn't be good.

"An earthquake?" he wondered.

"That was an explosion, not a quake. I lived in California enough to know what a quake feels like. That wasn't it."

People were running toward the exit and he didn't move. Their way out was an elevator. They couldn't use one if the ground itself was shaking.

Ivan reached for his phone and called security. "This is Dr Vinokourov. What just happened?"

"Something exploded topside, Doctor. We don't have all the answers yet, our cameras went down with the first explosion."

"So we need to stay put?"

"Yes, the elevators have been shut down. No one is going anywhere until we figure it out and assess the situation. I have to go now."

Another explosion rolled through the walls, shaking everything and everyone within them. Ivan glanced at the women with him. Neither seemed panicked but they weren't pleased either. He relayed what he'd been told.

"We should stick together. Go to your offices and grab what you think you may need if we are given the green to evacuate. Then come back here, we'll stay here. This is the largest space."

They both left and he rubbed his temples. *This wasn't exactly how I planned my day to go.* Fires above ground, and no way out from underground while more tremors shook them.

* * * *

"If you know anything, Ike, I need to know. And as fast as possible."

Isaac 'Ike' Wonder sat across from Bailey in the booth at the small, out-of-the way diner. His suit had seen better days but he was clean and had sprouted a goatee since the last time she'd encountered him. His small eyes darted all around, never settling. His nails were jagged and chipped.

"What's in it for you? Who's this man to you?"

"A friend. He's been missing for a while now and I want to get him home to his family."

He sniffed and ran his hand below his nose, his stringy, brown hair moving in time with the action. "Do you work with him?"

"No." She reached for her coffee and drank. "Like I said, he's a friend."

"Why didn't you come asking me earlier?"

"I've not been in town, been gone on business. I had to make a stopover here just to meet you. Now, do you know something?"

"Maybe."

She didn't fall for it and get upset. This was his way of operating. Ike wanted to push, wanted you to know he had something you desired so he could attempt to extort what he wished as a price.

"You said you did in your message. Now, we both know I don't like my time being wasted. I'm not going to beg. You either know or you don't. So I stay or I walk. Make up your mind."

"I don't know how accurate it is. I heard this months ago."

"Tell me what you know."

He glanced around again before picking at the scrambled eggs on the plate in front of him. "Same price as before."

"You give me information which I find helpful in locating him and it will be more. Otherwise, yes, the same."

He perked up at the mention of more. "You remember that bombing a while back?"

"There are a lot of bombings around the world. Be more specific."

"The one here in the US. It was some federal building, I think. A library. Anyway, the group that took credit for that call themselves The Watchers."

"I remember." She wanted to throttle him and get the answers faster, but Ike worked at his own speed.

"I had a meeting with one of their men, well, not really a meeting. More like he was drunk and I was sitting next to him in the back. He spoke of this man they'd taken from some cover organization."

"Did he say his name?"

"No. Just that they snatched him when he was with family and friends. Took him from Virginia and he was put somewhere in Montana."

"Montana."

"Some secret bunker prison thing they have there. He didn't get more specific than that and I don't know if this person is still there or not. He did say they didn't keep prisoners that long. So his time was coming." He ate some more. "Especially this one because he gave them problems."

Good for you, Ethan.

She reached in her pocket and withdrew an envelope that she slid over to his side. "Thanks, Ike. You hear anything else, let me know. And I was never here talking to you about this, got it?"

He opened the envelope and thumbed through the cash. "Understood."

She tossed some more bills on the table. "Meal's on me as well. Keep yourself safe, Ike."

Bailey walked three steps before he called her name. She turned and looked at him.

"They also mentioned a place they had in Africa."

"Just Africa? Nothing more specific?" *That's not like you're saying somewhere in Rhode Island. The place is a bit bigger than that.*

"Nothing else."

"Thanks, Ike." She pivoted around and walked outside. At the bus stop, she thought about what he'd said and wondered if it was Ethan. She took a seat in the back of the bus and tugged on the sleeves of her coat. "Did you get all that?"

"We heard," McNeal said. "Come back here."

"Yeah, yeah. You're welcome." She hung up and exhaled sharply.

It took her a while to make it back to the hotel and she was cold when she walked across the lobby toward the elevator bay. The fact the head honcho for all of Theta Corps was in her hotel room still felt a bit surreal to her. Not only that, it made her a bit nervous.

Thankfully, the ride up took enough time to allow her to get herself back in control. She was composed as she unlocked her room and stepped in. The men and Anabelle Lee waited for her. They were staying in the connecting suite and Anabelle Lee was using the second bed in this one.

Masters was one hell of an imposing black man. She'd thought McNeal had it in him to be that way but next to Masters, he looked like a teddy bear. The man wore a suit, custom-made for him. She didn't know if Masters was his first name or last. It was all they called him. And she wasn't about to ask. He was her boss's boss.

Valentino wore a dark suit—also custom-made—and had the look of death in his expression. She'd heard since he married he'd softened up a bit. If so, she sure as hell didn't see it.

Anabelle Lee had the color. Her stunning red hair had been gathered and pulled back in a ponytail. Her black leather pants poured into her heeled boots, accenting her already long legs. A light gray leather biker's jacket covered whatever shirt she wore. Dangerous, sexy and eye-catching. Her expression also one that spelt death for the one who'd taken her brother.

Then there was Beauregard. The man was huge, over six and a half feet tall, and he wasn't a skinny tall man but a built one. He could make an NFL or NBA player seem small. He was also the most casually dressed. Currently he slumped in the large chair, arm propping him up almost more than the back.

She saw cowboy boots sticking out from beneath his jeans and he had a dark blue Henley on that did very little to hide the muscles in his body. His blond-brown hair touched his shoulders, his dirty John Deere cap rested in his lap. By all accounts, he screamed 'laid-back' but she wasn't missing the sharpness and alertness in his green eyes. Out of all gathered there, he was the one she would fear the most.

By the time she'd shut the door behind her, he'd gotten to his feet. *He did that yesterday as well, stood when I came in the room.*

"Thank you," Anabelle Lee said.

Beauregard sat once Bailey had shrugged out of her jacket and had taken the last seat in the room. "I don't know how recent it is."

"But you trust him?" McNeal asked with all seriousness.

"I've used him for years for intel. He's not steered me wrong yet. Ike's one of those who people overlook and tend to talk in front of. That's why he gets what he does. Have you checked out the group and their activities? I mean"—she waved her hand—"I know about Mr Cassano's interaction with them and your wife, but I mean other than that."

"Call me Valentino." His voice was smooth and sexy.

"Okay." She glanced back to McNeal. "I wish he could have been more specific about Africa."

"We've got some contacts there. And some headquarters so I'll have those agents touch their contacts as well," Masters spoke, his voice commanding, even calm as it came. He pushed to his feet and stared at her. "McNeal, why is she working for you and not me directly?"

"You said you had a full team."

She could have been with the legendary four of Theta Corps? Bailey hated to admit it, but she was a little star-struck. This group were spoken of in whispers.

"I may have room for more. I've neglected to keep you on my radar. I will rectify that and you will be hearing from me soon."

Bailey stared at McNeal, who looked like he'd just swallowed something foul. *He wants me to stay with him.*

"Thank you for thinking of me, but I'm perfectly happy where I am now within the organization."

Masters looked like he didn't comprehend her saying she wouldn't want to move up to be one of his. His eyebrows converged and he scowled.

Beauregard laughed and stood. "Let her be, Masters. She's happy."

That voice, dear Lord. Her limbs trembled slightly and she was grateful she was seated as his deep southern drawl washed over her.

"Thank you for your assistance, Ms Hyde." Beauregard shared a look with his cousin and the two of them slipped away to the other room.

The man was potent. Masters sat back in his chair and discussion resumed between McNeal and Masters. She remained there, listening and commenting when they turned to her. Those who'd taken Ethan might think the search for him had died down but that wasn't even remotely the case, and they would pay for their sins when caught. She didn't envy them one bit.

Chapter Twenty-Three

"Kissing you is always the best part of my day," Ivan whispered to Bailey as they lay in his bed.

"Don't hear me complaining about it." She leaned forward and flicked her tongue along his skin.

"I could kiss you for hours. Do you have any idea of how you taste?"

Her smile lit up the room. "Nope. I know how you taste, though."

"Tell me more about your trip to Chicago. Did it go okay?"

She laughed. "Why don't you just ask me outright how things went between me and your Jaydee?"

"Is that who your pilot was? I'd forgotten." He grinned and tucked her closer to his body.

She snorted. "Not likely."

"So?"

"Oh, is that how you ask? See, I thought it would be more like, 'Bailey, how did your time with Jaydee go?' and you would kiss me again before waiting for your answer."

"What you said." He kissed her. "And there's the kiss."

"You are such a wuss. We got along well enough. Wouldn't say we'd ever be the best of friends, but we will not kill one another if we're in the same room."

"Good to know."

"She's scary smart."

He tucked some hair behind her ear. "I told you she was."

"She threatened me if I hurt you."

Ivan drew back. "She threatened you?"

"Yes, that's what it was. I thought it was but she said it most assuredly was a threat. Took that small bit of doubt right out of my hands."

"She didn't mean—"

"Trust me, Ivan. She meant every word she uttered. I'm not foolish enough to believe otherwise."

"I don't know what to say."

She wound her arm around his waist. "Nothing to say. She loves you and to her, you're family. That's all the explanation needed."

"And the rest of your trip?"

"Productive. At least I hope it will turn out to be. I got to meet the head of Theta Corps. That was pretty cool. I'd never met him before."

"I still haven't. What's he like? Or she?"

"Big. Very imposing. Has this voice that nearly compels you to listen to what he's commanding you to do."

"But he was nice?"

"Yes. Serious, but again, he runs Theta Corps. I'm guessing he doesn't have a lot of time to hang out and chillax."

"You mean like we're doing?"

"Yes." She rolled them over so she was on top. "Now, enough about me. Tell me about what happened to you."

"Two of the fuel trucks on the farm exploded. They took out the cameras so we didn't know what was going on but we could feel tremors below ground. We weren't allowed to leave for a few hours."

"Holy shit. Was everyone okay? Anyone hurt?"

"Some of the workers died and more were injured. None of us underground had more than minor scrapes and cuts from the impact of the explosions."

She rested her head against his chest. "You said two trucks and there were multiple explosions. So the trucks didn't run into each other?"

"No. It was sabotage."

Bailey raised up, a frown in place. "Sabotage?"

"One of the local drug cartels didn't like that the workers no longer wanted to be their mules and hoped to put the farm out of business."

"Damn."

"So security is being increased and they lost a few of the fields but all shall be salvageable."

"And those who lost their lives?"

"Monetary compensation for the families."

She nibbled on his lower lip. "I'm so glad you weren't injured."

"Me too."

"So what did you do while you were waiting?"

"Stayed in my office with Chrissy and Trick. We continued working. We had bottled water and some snacks so we were pretty well set."

"Nice."

He slid his hands down to cup her ass and held her closer to his groin. "What's on the schedule for today?"

"I have to get some laundry done and clean. Need to pay some bills and pack my bags."

He groaned. "Again?"

"It's my job."

"I know, I know. It is that. Doesn't mean I like you leaving all the time."

"You didn't have to move down here."

"I wouldn't see you at all if I'd not done that."

"I know."

"Can I ask you something?"

"Sure." She snuggled closer.

"Does it ever bother you, what you do?"

Her entire body stiffened and he knew he should have let it go. "Does your job?"

"I'm not following. I'm a scientist."

"Whose inventions can kill."

"Well, yes, they can, but we design them to save lives."

"I'm no different. I was designed to save lives."

"By taking others?"

She rolled off him and got to her feet, staring down at him, the sunlight surrounding her naked body. "I'm not any different than a scalpel the surgeon uses."

"To save lives."

"So it's okay for you to make things that may kill one to save more but I can't?" She hopped onto the floor. "I'm no different than anyone else—my title is just one that makes people think I'm cold-hearted or heartless. Military have the ability to kill as well. Snipers do. But the way you're talking, it's like I'm no better than a serial killer." She shoved into her clothing. "I'm tired of having to defend my work to you, Ivan. I won't do it. And you can't seem to get past what I do. I get it, I do. It's hard for some to understand."

"Bailey, wait a minute here."

"No. I'm done. But before I leave let me explain to you about the last kills I've made. One man was doing things to small villages that could easily rival what the Nazis did at Auschwitz. The next was a woman who sought to run her country so bad she was killing off the families of anyone who dared to speak out against her. She had a favorite pastime. Know what that was? She liked to hang up young girls, mostly in the ages of seven to ten. Why, you ask? Let me tell you. So she could have the pleasure—her words, not mine—of sodomizing and torturing them. It was her 'fun time' to see which ones could hold out. Those that did she would give to her generals to enjoy until they died. The final one was a man who killed off many by trying to turn them into an undetectable bomb, so he could send them anywhere in the world to do his work."

She picked up her shoes and hurried out of his place, slamming the door behind her.

The sound of the door closing with such force snapped him back to reality. He'd watched her storm off yet it had almost been in slow motion. Her words echoed in his head and his gut clenched. Sure, he'd had his belief of what she did. His thinking may have been a bit archaic or antiquated, but to him it was the more viperous and cold-hearted person who killed. And they did that to whom and when they wished, purely because they enjoyed it. Or sold their services to the highest bidder, answering the call to the almighty dollar.

Neither of which identified the woman who'd just left his apartment. Bailey was a warm, caring person. The stuff she kept inside, the people she dealt with, had to be around, all of it could have created a bitter and angry person. Someone dealing with that could just as easily become a person who loved to kill.

Also not Bailey.

"And I was the largest horse's ass to her." He jumped up then dressed in sweats and a T-shirt hurriedly. "Stupid. Stupid. Stupid!"

Boots still untied, Ivan hastened down to the street. No sign of Bailey and he strode at an almost jog to her building. The trip took forever in his mind although he knew it was less than ten minutes away.

He took the steps two at a time up to her door and knocked forcefully. "Bailey."

No response, nor did he hear anything from behind the door. He rested his head against the wood and moaned at his asinine behavior.

Where are you?

Unwilling to give up, he settled on the floor, back to her door, and waited. A noise on the stairs woke him and he checked his watch, astonished he'd been there for five hours. He had risen to his feet the moment a couple walked into view. His heart sank.

Come on, Bailey. You can't avoid your place all day long.

Problem was, she most likely could. Not only that, if she was this pissed and didn't want to see him, she probably would. He'd never seen her as angry as he had before today.

Her golden gaze had glinted unforgivingly, her entire posture had radiated fury.

Ivan smiled at the duo then headed down to the street. Maybe — and it was a faint chance — she'd gone back to his place.

A risky chance that didn't pan out. She wasn't there. This time he made sure to grab his phone. Locking the door, he dialed her number. It went straight to voicemail.

"Bailey, call me back. I didn't mean— Please, just give me a chance to explain."

Ivan wandered amongst the stalls in the market, checking her balcony and window for any sign she'd come home. Did it make him a stalker? He preferred to think of himself as a concerned boyfriend.

He returned to her building when the market vendors began packing up for the night. Same as before—no answer to his knocking, nor was there sound from inside that he could hear.

"I'm such a fucking idiot," he groused.

This wasn't how he'd planned this day to go. He'd envisioned a leisurely morning in bed, breakfast included. Rounds of off-the-wall, toe-curling and mind-numbing sex. Not—definitely not—to be heading home without any knowledge of where she was or—more importantly—how to rebuild the bridge he'd just blown the hell out of.

* * * *

The warm sun streamed down on her face as she played by the edge of the sparkling stream. The water wasn't that deep—right now her toes could touch the bottom. Large frogs sat upon rocks, lending their voice to the day, and stared back at her.

Bailey held a stick, which she used to splash the crystal water and occasionally take a poke at a frog who wandered too close. Beside her on a small piece of gingham sat her sandwich — cheese, her favorite — and a crisp apple.

"Don't forget to eat, Bailey! You mustn't spend all your time playing. Even frog-pokers need their strength."

"Okay, Mama."

Wriggling her lips in distaste, she reluctantly reached for her sandwich. Who wanted to eat when there were frogs to poke and a stream to splash in? Or through.

Her hunger made itself known and she attacked the sandwich with gusto. The energy the food gave had her playing hard again as she pretended to be a knight, fighting a fierce battle. Shoes on the bank resting on the gingham, feet in the sandy bottom of the stream, she waged war. Her opponents were endless but she was the best fighter in the land. Her castle and the princess it protected were depending on her victory.

She swung, struck and danced back out of reach from their swords. Water soaked the hem of her dress but she didn't care, this was for the princess. She had to succeed.

"Bailey!"

Her mother's scream froze her before she scrambled from the water. She ran to where she'd seen them last. They came into view, yelling for her to run away. She stood there, blinking at them. Behind her parents followed three more. Men dressed in all black with scowls. Her father barely slowed, just scooped her up and kept going.

"There's no point in running, Thomas. Where are you going to go? You knew this day would come. It was inevitable, the moment you betrayed me."

They were in the stream and her parents stopped. He set her down and stepped in front of her. She wrapped her hand in his shirt. "Daddy?"

"Keep her back, Milly." He pushed her toward her mama.

Her mother stared down at her then sank to her knees in the water. She smoothed some of Bailey's hair back. "Listen to me, Bailey. I need you to do exactly as I say. Don't ask questions, just do it. Promise me. I need you to be the bravest you've ever been. The knight who isn't scared of anything they face. Can you do that for me?"

Bailey didn't like this. She tried to look at her daddy but her mama gripped her chin and forced an eye connection.

"Run, my sweetest darling. Run and don't look back. Go now." She spun Bailey around and said, "Go now. Remember how much we love you. Always."

As promised, Bailey began to go. She scrambled out of the water on the other side and ran as fast as her little legs would carry her. There were grunts and sounds of pain coming from behind her. She wanted to see. What was happening and where were her parents?

She stumbled and cried out as she hit the ground. She pushed up and brushed off her hands then looked over her shoulder. Her parents had left the water, her daddy on his knees, doubled over and her mama fell when one of the men backhanded her.

Bailey had to protect them. That was what knights did. She ran back toward them. She'd just begun crossing the stream again when the man in the middle gestured at her with his weapon.

"And who is this?"

"Leave my daughter alone," her daddy demanded.

The man sneered and beckoned with the gun. Daddy had told her they weren't toys and to never touch his unless he was there. "Come here, little girl."

She did, ignoring her parents telling her to run away. She only took a few steps then stopped, unsure what to do. Somehow she had to help them. "Who are you?"

"Someone special. And who are you?"

She didn't like him. He made her insides icky. "Bailey. It's my birthday."

His grin scared her. She wanted to hide but she couldn't. Mama had said to be brave. She would do that.

"I'll make sure to give you something special then. Would you like that?" He stroked his goatee.

"Don't you touch my baby," her daddy cried.

"Don't worry, Thomas, I'll make her feel loved." An evil laugh. "In ways you can't imagine." He waved the gun. "Do it."

She didn't know what he meant but the two with him did. They reacted and the area echoed with two loud shots that hurt her ears. The water she stood in was cold compared to the warm liquid that sprayed across her face. Her parents flew back to land in the water beside her. She jumped and looked at them. Their blood mingled with the water flowing past her and on down the stream.

Bailey wanted to scream and beg her parents to get up. But she wouldn't disappoint her mother's last request. She wouldn't disobey again. This was her fault because she'd come back instead of running like mama had told her to do.

The man took one step toward her. He fell. The other two collapsed the next second. She stared at them, their sightless eyes gazing through her.

Bailey touched her face, fingers sliding through something. Drawing her hand away, she stared at the red staining her fingertips. Like her paints. Anger grew inside her. They had no right to ruin her day and take them from her. It rose and swelled like the waves crashing on the shore.

Black boots appeared past her fingers and she glanced up. Him she knew. He sank to his haunches before her and held out his arms. She didn't move, just blinked at him a few times and showed him the blood on her skin.

There was a small room in the back of her mind. She pushed all these memories there and walked to the room beside it. She let herself in this door and sat on the purple bed waiting for her. It was where she went when she was scared. Where nothing could harm her and she wasn't ever afraid. She wasn't ever leaving again. Until she was strong enough to do more than just stand there. As she would grow, so too would her anger. Then people like them would pay the price. They would suffer.

"It was my birthday," she muttered to him before shutting down mentally. "I was supposed to have cake."

He lifted her in his arms and whispered words to her that meant nothing. As he carried her, he tried to keep her head away from the direction her parents were.

"It's okay to cry, Bailey," he said when he placed her in his vehicle.

It might be okay, but she wasn't about to do it.

* * * *

Bailey sat up in bed, sweat dripping down her face and back. Her heart pounded erratically and she struggled to breathe without sounding like she'd run until her lungs had burst.

She reached for her light and clicked it on the moment her fingers found the knob. She'd not had that dream for longer than she cared to admit. She'd locked it away, never wanting to relive those horrific moments again.

Slipping from the bed, she searched for her robe. She drew it on as she made her way from the bed to the kitchen. A hot drink was in order. While the water heated for some tea, she sat on her sofa. Legs up and arms wrapped around her shins, she rested her chin on her knees.

The tremors wouldn't stop and she eventually reached for the blanket draped over the back. Even with that around her, she didn't feel any warmer. It hit her, what she had to do. She pushed up, the blanket falling off her shoulders and landing wherever. Bailey walked to her room, turning off the stove on her way, and stripped.

Her shower was swift and she barely dried off before dressing. Her actions were almost mechanical as she gathered what she needed to take with her. Once it was all in hand, she swung her pack on her shoulder and left the apartment.

On the street, she flagged down a taxi and gave her destination. He stopped her before the airport where she paid and climbed out. Deliberate steps took her inside where she purchased a ticket on the first flight she could have. She didn't complain about being slowed down through security — nothing much mattered at this moment. She needed one thing.

Bailey didn't rest on the flight, she stared out of the window at the starry sky. When she reached her destination city, she went through customs and was welcomed back to the United States. She took another taxi out of the city limits and to a large house seated on three acres. When it stopped at the apex of the drive, she climbed out and tossed him some bills. She made her way to the door over the snow-shoveled walkway and pressed the doorbell.

The door opened and she found herself staring up at the man who probably knew more about her than she did. He raised an eyebrow at her.

"There a reason you're on my doorstep?"

She tipped her head back and asked her own question in return. "Did I ever cry?"

Chapter Twenty-Four

Santiago, Chile

Thankfully, the superintendent of Bailey's building let Ivan in. He'd told him he needed to check to see if she was okay because she'd been sick. The man had met him a few times and hadn't had an issue with allowing him entrance.

Alone in her place, Ivan looked around before making a beeline for her bedroom. He paused in the living room, a blanket hung partway off the couch to gather on the floor. Not like her. She was meticulous about her living quarters.

He picked it up, folded it and laid it back along the top of the sofa. Then he went to her room. The bed, unmade, had him frowning. Something wasn't right. At her closet, he stared in the back, grateful at least in a sense and disturbed in another to discover her bag she took on jobs resting there.

What the crap is going on here?

He picked up her phone and dialed her number. Voicemail.

"Bailey, please call. I'm worried about you. We need to talk."

He went to the kitchen and found it was clean. Ivan stared at her floor safe and wished he knew the combination to see if her weapons were there or not. Unsettled, he closed up her place, lowering the window that had been open an inch and latching it. As he headed down from her apartment to the street, his phone rang.

He answered without looking at the screen. "Bailey?"

"No, this is Howland. I need you at the office. Mine. Now. There's a car waiting for you outside your apartment." She hung up and he swore in a low streak.

Ivan jogged back to his place and found, sure enough, the car was there. He hopped in the back and waited for the driver to get going. *What does this woman need now? I have more important things to do, like find out where Bailey is, than spend time with this harpy in her office.*

They pulled up to the farm and drove to the entrance. Ivan climbed out and walked away, disappearing inside the building. He dug for his card to swipe it when he got to the back room. The wall opened and he stepped into the elevator, waiting for it to take him down to the correct floor.

Howland's office was one of three on her floor. He'd been to hers once before—the thing was massive. Not much in the way of personality, however. He shrugged. *Perhaps that's changed since I was there last.*

He strode up to her door and knocked.

"Enter."

He really didn't want to. Ivan turned the knob, pushed and stepped inside. A cursory glance told him she'd not added anything to make this room more serene.

"Sit."

"Morning to you, too, Howland." He walked to a leather chair and sat.

He faced the back of her chair and he remained silent, waiting for her to turn around. She finally spun to meet him, elbows resting on the arms of the seat she occupied. Howland was an Asian woman who seemed rather unforgiving at times. She liked results and hated delays of any kind.

She must have such a headache. Then again, with that stick so far up her ass what's to say she even feels how tight that appears to be.

Her hair had been drawn back so tightly he didn't think any one strand was out of place. The look, harsh. A perpetual scowl existed on her face and he kept his blank.

"Were we supposed to exchange pleasantries?" She blinked her dark eyes at him.

"Supposed to? Nope, but I was raised with manners." He couldn't help it, this woman just made him want to needle her. Just to see if he could get through that icy demeanor and find a living soul beneath the robot.

Everything about this woman screamed severe. From her hair style to the dark, sexless suit she wore. Many thought her a tyrant and a bitch to work for. He agreed, she was a bitch, but for the most part she stayed out of his way, for he'd shown he wasn't afraid of her.

"Some days I get the feeling you don't care much for me, Doctor." She laced her fingers below her chin. "Miraculously, I don't give a fuck. I'm not here to win any personality contests."

That's not going to be an issue. I worry to see what kind of world it is where you would win one. "The reason I'm in your office on a day off would be what, exactly?"

"You're being temporarily reassigned."

What the fuck? "To where?" *And for what goddamn fucking reason? I have been with this lab since it got off the ground.*

She dipped her head and he noticed a file he'd not seen before on the smooth top of her shiny, black desk. "Everything is in there. You leave tomorrow. That's all. You're dismissed."

Dismissed, like he was a schoolchild who needed to be reprimanded. Keeping his thoughts to himself, he stood and reached for the blue file. "Ma'am." He walked out, shutting the door behind him.

As he made the trek to his own office, the file stayed closed in his hand. He wasn't about to start looking until he was in his place. Leaving tomorrow, that was bullshit.

Waving absently at some workers, he stepped into his office. He kicked the door closed behind him and tromped to his seat. Slapping the file on the desk, Ivan closed his eyes and took several deep breaths. Then he opened them and the file.

Georgia. He was going to Georgia. A smaller town named Danielsville. *Shit, do they even have more than a thousand in population?*

He read on. His flight would leave at five forty-three in the morning. He would eventually end up in Atlanta where a car service would pick him up then take him to Danielsville. That was it—there was no explanation about what he'd be doing there, much less how long he would be there for.

Picking up his phone, he pressed the button for Chrissy's office.

"Hey, boss. Aren't you supposed to be having a day off?"

"Howland called me in."

"Oy, that's not good. What'd she want?"

"I'm being reassigned."

"What?" She sounded exasperated. "How can this happen now? We're just about to make real headway with..." Several deep breaths came over the phone. "When are you leaving?"

"Tomorrow morning. So I have to wrap up my end. If you and Trick can come down to the lab and meet me there, I'll pass everything I have on to the two of you so you can keep going with the research."

"I'll grab Trick and we'll be there in less than ten."

"Thanks."

He ended the call and went to the closet where he withdrew the box he'd had when he'd first moved into this office. He didn't have too much and it didn't take him long to pack his belongings away.

Ivan carried it with him to the lab and set it on a back table before meeting the women by the computers. Trick looked at him with a sad smile on her face.

"What the hell is she thinking?" Chrissy had her hands on her hips, defiance in every inch of her.

"Howland does what Howland thinks best. I don't know when I'll be back, but if you two will keep me in the loop, I will be able to not fall behind. Also, perhaps add suggestions as if I were here."

"Where are you going and what for?"

"The States and I haven't a damn clue." He walked back to his box and grabbed the tablet, which sat on top. "This is what I have that hasn't been shared yet. I worked on this the past two nights."

He took the drive Trick handed him and downloaded the information on there before handing it back to her. They talked for another two hours before he smiled at them both.

"I have to get going, I still have to pack my things."

"I hope you come back soon, Doc. Things won't be the same without you here in the lab."

"All will be fine. You two take care and I'll be back before you know it."

Chrissy smiled. "Sure."

Trick stood and he stuck out his hand. She flicked her gaze from his hand to his face. With a small shake, she jumped in his arms and hugged him. Ivan didn't even hesitate, he just hugged her in return. These two women were like sisters to him and he was going to miss them both, so much.

Chrissy was next after Trick stepped away. He smiled once more at them both then turned away and walked to the door, swiping his box along the way. He never once looked back as he trekked to the elevator.

What awaits me in Georgia?

* * * *

Somewhere in the United States

"You look like you could use this more than I could," McNeal said, handing her a shot of whiskey.

"I don't need a drink. I need to know the answer to my question. Did I even cry?"

"What are you talking about?"

He sat in a large armchair then gestured for her to take one across from him. The flames in the fireplace licked at the stone surrounding them, sparking occasionally before going back to their mesmerizing dance.

"I remember that day."

He rubbed his chin. "What day?"

She downed the whiskey in one drink, eyes watering at the bite it delivered descending her throat. "The one where my parents were killed right before me. Why are you pretending you don't know? You were there. You came to me, carried me to your vehicle. You were the one who told me it was okay to cry. So, I'm here asking you if I did. Answer me, *Uncle*. Did. I. Cry?"

He leaned forward, pulled the decanter off the tray then poured himself a glass. "You know, they said it was repressed, that you'd shut it away just to cope. That it may or may not resurface." He took a sip.

Anger coursed through her. "Newsflash. It did resurface. And I want answers."

"Do you really think that best?"

"Do you really think it wise not to give me what I'm asking for?"

He leaned back and swirled the liquid in his glass. "Are you threatening me?"

"I'm not in the mood for games, McNeal. I've not slept since the dream—nightmare—I should call it what it is—woke me. My patience is damn near non-existent and you don't know what weapons I have on me. Short fuse. Assassin. Tired and wanting answers. Not a good mix for you."

"No."

She wanted to punch him. "No? No what? You're not telling me? You're agreeing it's not a good mix for you? What?"

"No, as in, no you didn't cry. Not once. Not ever so long as I knew."

"Why the subterfuge?"

"I don't follow."

"When I met you as Kevin McNeal, why didn't you tell me the truth about who you were?"

"I thought I was protecting you."

"That's not a viable excuse." Her fingers flexed around the glass.

"You didn't remember me and I took that to mean you didn't recall that day as well. What kind of man would I be if I'd wanted you to remember it?"

She wasn't sure. "An honest one. You groomed me for this. I figured it out on the flight here. My anger, my rage. I had it but I wasn't sure why, just that I wanted to protect others. You took it and manipulated everything so I would do what I do."

He shook his head. "I gave you options. You followed your heart."

Her scoff exploded from her chest. "My heart?"

"Yes."

"Would you have ever told me you were my uncle?" She put her tumbler on the tray. "Had I not had the dream, would you have ever come clean?"

"No."

"Why not?"

"Because it is my job to protect you, not send you spiraling into a dark abyss of the past and things you can't even begin to change. You're to live for the here and now. In the present."

"And foster care?"

"Was a Theta Corps facility, not really foster care. You were safe."

She slumped back and stared at the man she'd believed to be just her boss. What other memories did she have buried in her mind? What did this mean about her identity? Was she who she thought she was?

"The ones who killed them? Who were they?"

"Members of a faction your father used to work for. It was how and where he eventually met your mother and they fell in love."

"What faction?"

His expression grew unmoving. "Don't do this, Bailey."

More rage pumped with each heartbeat. "Don't do what, find out about the ones who killed my parents?"

"Think in terms of revenge. The ones who pulled the trigger are dead. As is the one who ordered it done."

"Still not answering my questions."

"I'm not telling you."

"Why not?"

"Because I think you'll go off the grid and try to exact your own revenge."

How dare he? "How is my wanting justice any different than the times you send me out?"

"That's sanctioned and not done for personal vendettas."

"So you're saying my suffering isn't enough to warrant Theta Corps approving my getting the fuckers out of the way."

"Listen to yourself, Bailey. You're bordering on the edge. If you go over it—" He shook his head. "Don't, please. I don't want to have to send someone after you."

"You would, wouldn't you?"

"If I had to, yes. Someone with your skills, Bailey... You can't be running around killing for no reason."

She jumped to her feet, the chair skidding backwards. "I have a reason, dammit! They killed my parents!"

McNeal stood and walked toward her.

Bailey backed away, holding out her hands. "Don't try to appease me."

"And I told you, Bailey. Those responsible have paid. What are you going to do? Kill their children? Their children's children? That's not how we operate here at Theta Corps."

"Then maybe I shouldn't be part of it anymore." Her words were delivered calmly and without emotion.

She swerved around and approached the door. He called her name but she ignored him, opening it and stepping out into the night. The taxi was leaving but she waved him down and slipped into the back seat.

"Where to?" he asked.

"Doesn't matter. Airport, I guess. No real rush, either."

"Yes, ma'am."

He drove and she leaned against the door, trying to make sense of everything. So many questions she had and so many of them were unanswerable. Right now, she needed to just get away. Find a place and get away from everything before she lost it and went rogue.

Not a bad idea, though. At least that's how I'm feeling right now.

She paid and exited at the airport. Stepping through the sliding glass doors, she stared at the wall of monitors housing the arrivals and departures. A destination. That was all she needed.

A couple went by her talking about how they were going to enjoy their honeymoon in Paris and Bailey figured it out. Time to go home. Another look at the departures and she headed for the airline with the soonest flight out.

This time on the airplane, she settled in, determined to get some sleep. The man who sat beside her thankfully put in his ear buds and lost himself in the game he was playing on his iPad, so she didn't have to attempt conversation.

She kept to herself the entire flight and when she disembarked in Paris, she waited for that familiar feeling of contentment to overtake her. It was absent. She went through customs then walked out of the airport, her backpack her only bag she had with her.

She rode the elevator to her apartment and walked in. This, this was the place she had the most connection to. It housed her art and more of what explained her to her, so she knew she was more than just a Theta Corps assassin, she knew who she was. This place made sense. Sure, she loved Santiago and truly enjoyed Chicago, but Paris beat through her veins.

Still, she couldn't stay long. She knew McNeal and gave herself about two days with no word before he would come looking for her. She had to have time alone to process what she'd learned.

Time to go into hiding.

Chapter Twenty-Five

Georgia, United States

He could smell chicken shit. A lot of it. Ivan scrunched his nose at the powerful ammonia scent as his eyes began to water. *Great, I now have to pass chicken farms on my way to reach my new apartment.*

He followed the female voice that broke up the monotony of the drive by giving him directions. He made note of the location of the grocery store once he'd actually reached the town. *I don't know if I can call this a city.*

The apartment complex was a long brick building. He parked by a run-down sign, which gave directions to the office. He exited and walked along the well-maintained path to the white door. Gazing around, he noticed some people sitting outside, conversing in lawn chairs. Not an odd sight or unfamiliar. Nice to know, actually, that they did that around here as well.

He walked inside, grateful to be out of the nippy air. While it wasn't freezing, for a man who'd just departed Chile, he'd been warmer. A large black man sat fiddling with a taken-apart radio at the front counter. Pieces were spread all over.

"Can I help you, son?"

He stepped up to the barrier, careful not to send any of the small parts to the floor. "I'm here to get the key to my apartment. New tenant."

"Uh-huh." He fiddled some more. "Name?"

Because it's such a thriving metropolis? You have people moving in and out every day? "Ivan Vinokourov."

"I recollect hearing that name. Your company rented it." He stood straight and stared past him out of the front window. "Thought you were arriving with your stuff. Where's your truck? No matter. Right nice of them to send us a new teacher."

Ivan nearly leaned on the counter, only barely halting himself in time. "I'm sorry, teacher? The truck is coming." *I think.*

The man smiled, showing off a brilliant white set of teeth. "Name's Harold. My boy attends Madison County High. He's taking physics this year and will be one of your students. We were all sad when Mr Wheeler had his accident. It was the damnedest thing. Anyway, we needed a good long-term sub and you came with high recommendations." He walked to the small desk in the back by the window. "They said you are one of the best. What are you, like, a professor or something?"

"Or something." *Why does this man know more about what's happening here than I do. How come he knows what goes on at this school? And why the fuck wasn't I told I'd be teaching?* Ivan was having a really hard time wrapping his head around this entire thing and the way it was unraveling. "You know my name because you heard it where?"

"I work at the school as well. Janitor. I hear lots of things."

"You stay busy then. Working both places."

"Have a boy to raise and teach responsibility to. If he can't get a scholarship, he'll need my help to pay for his schooling. I aim to make sure he gets to college and has opportunities I never had."

Ivan was even more impressed. "That's admirable."

Harold scratched his neck. "Too many of our youth are falling in with the wrong crowd. I want my boy to be a success and not a statistic."

"You're a good father."

He shrugged. "I do what I can. Do you have children?"

An image of Bailey flashed in his head. "No, I don't."

"Here we are." He grabbed some papers and a clipboard. "Don't despair, you'll have a few young'uns before too long running around and making you remember the day when you could up and go where you wanted." A wry smile. "They're worth it, though." He picked up his coat from the back of the chair. "I can walk and meet you there—"

"I don't mind giving you a ride."

His grin was wide and he whistled. "Ross, get out here, boy."

A well-built young man appeared. "Yes, sir?"

Ivan noted how he carried himself and gave his own approval, no matter it didn't make a damn bit of difference if he did or not. The young man had manners and he wore his pants up, not with the crotch hanging low.

"This is Mr Vinokourov, he's going to be your new physics teacher. This is my boy, Ross. He's a cornerback on the football team. Mind the counter, leave my project alone and get the phones. I'm doing his walk-through."

Brown eyes ran over him. "Yes, sir. Good to meet you, sir."

"Likewise." Ivan smiled at Ross then led the way to his Chevy Malibu. "This is me."

"Excellent." They climbed in. "We go down to the right then take the first left between the buildings. I'll point out which one is yours."

Ivan did as ordered, surprised to see there were many more apartments than he'd first assumed.

"Yours is there, you can park, yep, right there. This here is the spot assigned your apartment. If you have more than one vehicle, you'll just have to jockey for an open spot elsewhere. The open to all spots don't have the yellow numbers painted in them."

"Got it." He did and killed the engine.

"Come on, son."

For a large man, Harold moved really quickly. Ivan hurried after him then waited for him to open the door. He kept his comments to himself as they completed the inspection.

"Do you need a ride back?"

"I can walk. If you can sign here, I'll be on my way."

"Nonsense, I have to wait for my truck. I don't mind."

They made the short trip back and Ivan shook his hand but stayed in the vehicle. After Harold went back inside, Ivan withdrew his phone. He called the number that was on the sheet given to him by Howland.

"Yes, Dr Vinokourov?" A woman spoke crisply and he pictured a schoolmarm, no room for idle chit-chat.

"I need to speak to whoever sent me here. Now."

"Hold please, for Mr Richardson."

"Yeah." *What the hell, another name I've never heard before.*

"Dr Vinokourov, my name is Paul Richardson. I work for Masters."

There's a name I know. "What the fuck is going on? I'm yanked from my job in Chile and sent here where, according to local gossip, I'm the new physics teacher for a high school. I have an apartment with stuff coming. I would like to know a bit more."

"Didn't Howland explain it to you?"

"She gave me a sheet with my flight time and told me I was being reassigned."

"That woman, some days... No matter. I'm sorry, you should have been properly briefed."

"It would be nice."

"First, let me assure you, there is a truck coming. We didn't want you far from the school so there were no furnished places. You'll be given the basics and we're also sending some suits to teach in. Now, we need you there because they have a student who is incredibly smart and we want to recruit him. You'll most likely see other alphabet groups trying to get to him. We don't want to lose this kid, his potential is incredible. We've not seen anything like it in years. Not to this extent anyway."

"Is this supposed to explain this better? Because I'm now even more confused. Why am I here? I'm a lab rat. I'm not equipped to try to recruit a child."

"Yes, you are, he'll be in your class."

The door opened to the office and Harold's son stepped out. He waved at Ivan and called out to someone else who sat outside.

"Let me guess, his name is Ross?"

A moment's pause. "Yes. How did you know?"

"You put me at the place his father works. I've met him."

"Then you're even closer to success than you were. Good luck." The call ended.

Ivan tossed his phone on the seat. He wanted to pound the wheel and scream. This was insanity. A large straight truck pulled up, with McElroy and Sons Moving in big black lettering on the side. Ivan stepped out to meet the driver.

"Dr Vinokourov?"

"That's me."

"We have your things."

"Let's go then. I'm in thirty-four alpha."

He led the way then stayed out of theirs as they moved the furniture and some boxes in. The men were efficient. Before he knew it, his bed, television and a few other things had been set up. The two bedroom looked so much different from earlier that day when he'd done the pre-moving in inspection.

They left once they had finished. Hell, they'd even brought him some food and had put it away. He stood in his new bedroom and stared in the closet.

"Okay, that's just freaky." All the suits they'd sent were hanging. "This is like they have way too much experience doing this sort of thing. Even made the damn bed."

In the bathroom, he spied exact replicas of the shaving items he used. "Too damn weird." The two men hadn't spoken to him, rarely to each other, they'd just done their job and left.

He walked to the living room and sank onto the leather couch, propping his feet up on the chaise portion he currently used. This was going to be interesting, that was for sure.

Teaching? What was next, going into kindergarten to recruit for Theta Corps? Pre-school?

* * * *

On an island in the Pacific

"In other news today, the government has made a statement about foiling another attack by this terrorist group called The Watchers. Today would have been a huge disaster for there were sixteen buses from local schools taking children to the Jimmy Carter Library and Museum. We are getting reports that the dogs found the explosives mere moments before detonation. Thankfully no one was hurt or injured. Security will be stepped up, tomorrow is a fundraiser there and they are taking no chances."

Bailey clicked off the sound and tossed the remote down. For a while this group had been quiet but lately they seemed to be angling for a headline at least once a month. Supposedly the person she'd retrieved from Egypt would help in bringing down the rest of this group. Not her concern.

Eradicating them fell into the hands of people like Valentino Cassano and those he worked with. She stepped outside and stared along the deck. Beyond that, the white sands gleamed in the sun and the blue waters sparkled.

This wasn't one of her typical places to come. Not that she had a type, given that until Ivan, she'd never even taken a vacation. She loved the ocean and so when this place had come up, she'd jumped at the chance to visit. She'd gone in silent, under no name. She'd bribed a fisherman to bring her here and set her up, which he'd done under his name. He'd brought her a shit load of food so she would be fine in that regard as well. Before he'd left her here, he'd said he'd be back in a week to check on her. Otherwise, if she needed him, to use the radio he'd placed in one of the bags.

She had no intention of calling him. This was *away*. She loved her homes but they were in metropolises and for someone who preferred her solitude, this was more her speed. Her cell phone had been left in her safe deposit box. They couldn't track her and they couldn't reach her.

Selfish?

Ask me if I give a damn.

Her dreams had been more frequent as of late and she needed to get them under control. She was edgy and angry. Still oh so angry.

She left the deck and smiled as her feet sank into the warm sand. "Why is my pain less important than anyone else's? Why wouldn't he have come clean sooner?"

Questions she'd asked McNeal and still plagued herself with. As if she could find the answer she wanted, she craved. She *needed* to bring herself peace within her soul.

"At least enough I stop looking like a raccoon and can go back and do my job successfully. Right now I'm a damn liability to myself and the organization."

She walked out into the water until her fingertips trailed in the surf then she stopped. Her sarong was wet, plastered to her legs. Bailey sighed and began again, heading farther out. Eventually she began to swim and went out about a mile before turning back to shore. Limbs tired when she made it back, she walked a few steps and sank onto the sand, flopping over on her back with a grunt.

The water rose up to occasionally touch her heels but that was it. Once she'd gotten her breathing back under control, she sat up and brushed her hair away from her face. She brought her knees close and wrapped her arms around her legs, resting her chin on them.

Where does all my anger come from? Did I have it as a child? Was my childhood so bad I've blocked out more than just that day?

She didn't think so. She remembered growing up in Paris with other children. Playing, getting into trouble and having fun. She had been here a few days now and still wasn't any closer to having her questions answered. It wasn't easy, admitting this was a problem for her. She couldn't deal with it like she could when she was sent to dispatch other 'problems' in her work. She couldn't use a poison or sight the target and pull a trigger, sending a bullet with deadly accuracy to solve it.

This was much harder than that. She had to open up and stop fighting memories that, for some reason or another, she'd blocked out all these years but that had chosen now to reappear.

She climbed to her feet. "All I know is I have to get this shit sorted out or I don't go back to work. I can't believe I threatened McNeal."

Never would she have remotely considered doing such a thing, but whatever was going on with her had obviously pushed her into new territory. At least here, she was not a danger to anyone. A private island.

She walked back to her villa. At the outdoor shower, she rinsed the ocean water and sand from her body. Then she untied her sarong and draped it on a hook to dry. It didn't take her long to go inside and throw on some running clothes.

After she was ready, Bailey set off. One way or another, she was going to exhaust herself enough to experience a full night of sleep without nightmares. She pushed hard all day long and after a simple fare for an evening meal that consisted of fresh fruit and some cheese, she walked to the master suite and climbed into the king-sized bed. A gentle breeze blew through the sheer curtains, cooling her heated body. Bailey stretched out and closed her eyes, praying sleep would come swiftly for her this night.

* * * *

"Are you sure you want to stay another week?"

Bailey nodded. "It's doing me some good. Thanks for bringing my groceries."

"You need a doctor?" He gestured at her. "You look maybe like you are sick."

"Having some nightmares but it's okay. I'm getting through it."

"So no doctor?"

Unless he was tall and Russian with the name Ivan, she didn't need him. "No, I'm good." She was touched by his concerned look. "I am, truly."

"You remind me of my daughter. I worry. You need me, you call."

She helped him cast off and waved as he pulled away from the dock she stood on. He'd come early because there were some stormy conditions forecast for the next few days. He wanted to take her back with him but she refused. Pivoting on her heels, she strode back to the house and set about putting away her food.

When that was finished, she double-checked the generator in preparation for the storm. Everything looked to be in good order and she retired to the hammock and rested.

"So, are you done with your pity party?"

"You'd better be a figment of my imagination, McNeal," she bit off without opening her eyes. "I don't want to deal with you or your shit right now."

"So that's a no."

She cracked open her eyes and groaned. *Is he fucking kidding me?* Braced against the railing stood McNeal. His white pirate shirt showed off his defined torso while the black pants highlighted the power in his legs. She shook her head and turned away, allowing her eyes to close.

"Is it that I didn't tell you I found you with your parents' blood on your face, you staring at it on your hands, what's bothering you, Hyde? Or is it that you still feel responsible because you disobeyed them and came back when they told you to run?" His words were harsh and his tone callous.

She shot up in the hammock and jumped from it. "Don't you fucking dare!" she seethed. "You don't get to stand there and judge..." She crossed her arms and glared at him. "How do you know this? How the fuck do you know what she told me? McNeal, damn you, for once in your life, tell the *truth*." Her fury was such she vibrated with it.

His expression was sad but she brushed away any and all emotion toward him. He wouldn't let her be. Wouldn't let her try to figure it out on her own. So now he could tell her, to hell with how it affected him on a personal level. Caring had left this vessel a long time ago.

"We all have secrets, Bailey."

"Not you, not now. And especially not about this. Tell me or you will rue the day you ever first taught me to kill."

"More threats."

"No threat. That's a promise, McNeal." She stepped close and shoved her finger in his chest. "Unlike those you send me after, however, you have advance warning. I will come for you if you don't tell me everything. You'll not see it coming, either. You taught me too well."

"You'd kill me."

"I suggest you look at my face. Do you see the circles? The stress? The *fury*? Do not think to push me on this McNeal. I am a hair's breadth away from losing my shit. Completely. As in free-falling from unimaginable heights without a parachute. Tell me what you *fucking know*!" Her voice crescendoed in a high soprano.

Off in the distance, across the waters, lightning split the sky as the tempest rolled closer. If it didn't weaken before it arrived, it would be one hell of a storm. She didn't mind, she felt the same way.

Chapter Twenty-Six

Silence stretched between them. His gaze held hers, unwavering. Bailey didn't care, she wasn't about to let this go. Not this time. The storm moved closer, bringing with it an increase in the wind and the scent of rain.

"You can't outwait me, McNeal. I don't give a damn if the storm rolls over us. I want my answers."

"You want to know how I heard that. I was listening in."

"Why?"

The man finally looked uncomfortable and shifted his weight before settling. "We'd set up a sting. It didn't go as planned."

She canted her head slightly to the side and swallowed, searching for the words. "You mean to tell me that entire day was an op for you and your men? That my parents and myself were being used as bait?"

"Why are you acting so surprised? We do it all the time."

Her smile was bared teeth. "Of course you do. I remember moving a lot. Never staying in one place too long. They were on the run, weren't they? Running from you and the fuckers who pulled the triggers."

McNeal nodded. "We got wind of where they would be, they as in your parents. That you would be celebrating a birthday in that field. News of that got out to the faction."

It was like a dagger to her heart. "So, you leaked it." No way she'd let him get away with saying 'news of it got out'. Her world became tinged in red and she tried to rein her emotions back under control. "So you heard. Where were you? Why didn't you save them?" Bailey was proud her voice didn't waver. It took a considerable amount for her not to clutch her hands into fists. She wanted so much to strike the man before her. Pummel him until he felt even a fraction of the pain and rage she had surging through her, rising like the surf beyond the shore as the storm grew in intensity.

"Our mistake was wanting them alive. But that had been the order, so we hung back. No one thought they would kill your parents. We were too late. *I* was too late."

Another brief glimpse of the man behind the mask. Not that it mattered. She didn't give a damn whether he hurt.

"So you heard my parents get murdered. Or you were close enough to see it." She flexed her fingers. "Which was it?"

"I saw it."

"I'm sure they were glad to have a friend like you in their corner. Set them up and watch them die."

"It wasn't like that, Bailey."

"Of course not. Why didn't you let him kill me?"

"He wouldn't have killed you, Bailey. At least not right away. It was the least I could do to honor their memory — take you and make sure you not only lived and survived, but thrived."

"You used my anger."

"I did."

"And now that you've created what stands before you, you are willing to send a team to kill me if I go crazy and just kill on a whim." She stepped back, needing some space so she didn't hit him. Yes, he deserved it but she wasn't sure she could stop if she began. "How did you find me?"

"Your bag."

"And here I thought I was being so clever."

McNeal just stared at her. The first drops of rain began to fall and she thought about heading inside.

"Who was she to you?"

"Who was who?"

"My mother?"

Pain sliced through his gaze before it was blinked away like water evaporating on a hot sidewalk. "I loved her."

"You loved her. Like, were in love with her?"

"Yes. Since the moment I laid eyes on her, she owned my heart. Didn't matter I could have given her everything. She wanted Thomas and that was also from day one. He was always the one for her."

"How angry did it make you to know your own brother had what you so desperately coveted?"

"Not nearly enough to do what you're beginning to try and discover. I didn't allow him to die because she took him over me."

"Why is that so hard for me to think? You did it then felt guilty so you saved the child."

"Nope. We wanted that faction, Bailey. I admit it was a mistake how things went down. He was supposed to be taken alive and the three of you were supposed to not even know they or us were there."

"How'd that work out for you?"

"Shitty."

Her hair plastered to her head as the rain fell in sheets and the wind whipped around them.

Bailey squinted through the weather at him, longing to say something else, but she whirled around and walked to the villa. She felt him at her back although he didn't speak a word. She walked in and stood in the entryway, dripping on the tiles. The door shut and seconds later, McNeal positioned himself beside her.

"There's a bathroom down that way you can use." She pointed then walked in the opposite direction to the master suite.

Bailey slowly stripped off her sodden attire as she stood in the large bath. She stepped into the large glass shower and shut the door behind her. Adjusting the water temperature, she allowed the warm water to help relax the muscles that had been so tense since the moment McNeal had shown up. Had he not been here, she probably would have enjoyed a long shower. As it was, she kept it brief and stepped back out.

The large towel easily absorbed the water from her skin, leaving her dry. She dressed quickly and padded in bare feet out to the main part of the house. McNeal was there, wearing only his pants as he made coffee.

"You are a lot like your father, Bailey. You have Thomas' drive and dedication to get the job done. Meticulous and particular about how things ought to be accomplished."

She grabbed two cups and set them on the countertop. "How long have you known me?"

"I was near when you were born."

She stopped looking for spoons and faced him. "What does that mean exactly, you were near?"

"I was near. I wasn't in the room but I saw you within a few hours of your birth."

"And you came around from time to time. I remember you there. I never wondered how you always managed to find us, but you did. You never visited the same house twice."

"Nope, I didn't."

"Why did you come by?"

"I wanted them back. Neither wanted to live that life with you. Milly longed to be a mother who could bake with her child and help her with homework. Not dodge bullets and try to stop governmental coups."

She dropped a spoon in each mug, the thunder outside echoing the clang. "So when they died you figured why not carry on the family tradition?"

"There'll never be the right words I can utter which will earn your forgiveness, Bailey. I am aware of that." He faced her. "My question is, will you be able to work with me? Or should I have you sent to work under Masters directly?"

"Good question." How much distance did she truly want from him? Did she want it where he didn't have a say in what assignments she was sent on and if he wanted to know how she was doing he would have to look it up? "I'll have to think about that and see if I want to work directly for him as opposed to you."

* * * *

Georgia, United States

"Merry Christmas, Ivan," he muttered as he poured himself another cup of coffee. Once it was fixed how he liked it, he made his way to the couch and sat with a grunt. He had a small Christmas tree on his coffee table, the colored lights doing their best to bring cheer to his place.

He'd not been able to reach Bailey other than her message service. However, she'd not returned any of them. He stayed busy with teaching but since they were now on break he didn't have it as a distraction.

Paul Richardson hadn't been lying when he'd said Ross was smart. The boy knew his physics backwards and forwards. Problem was, he was under the impression he needed to get out of there on a football scholarship. So he didn't put half the effort into class as he should. Not that he needed to put in more, for he was impressive now in class — still with the extra effort, he would be incredible.

Ivan hadn't figured out how to approach his father about it either. At some point he needed to talk to the young man and let him know there were other options besides sports.

"But it's Christmas. Why ruin his vacation with school talk?" Sure, most seniors already knew where they were going, yet Ross hadn't heard back from the places he had applied to. Or so the rumors said.

He flipped through channels until that grew boring and he turned the entire thing off. Ivan was in the middle of cooking himself some food when a knock came on his door.

He opened it and drew back slightly in surprise. "Wasn't expecting to see you, much less on this day. Come on in."

McNeal brushed by him. "Wasn't expecting to be here."

"What do you need?"

"Bailey."

His heart pounded at the mere mention of her. "She's not here. Trust me, if she were I wouldn't have answered the door."

"I know she's not here and I'm not even going to address that other comment." McNeal paced. "She's holed up on an island in the Pacific."

"So, then given the fact you know where she is, perhaps if she is the one you need, you should be there getting her."

McNeal glanced around the place before settling his body on one of the stools. "Do you remember I told you a bit about her past and how her parents had been killed in front of her?"

"Not something I would forget." Unease began to creep in his blood. What was going on with her?

"She's having nightmares and isn't sleeping well. She looks to be a ghost of her former self. She won't talk to me, well, not in a good way. I need you to go down and check on her. You'll be able to get through to her."

"I don't know about that," Ivan said with a shameful shake of his head.

"What's that supposed to mean?"

"It means I was an ass the last time I talked to her. I may not be the best person to send. Doesn't she have any close people that she works with?"

"Not close in that sense. Not like you are to her."

Ivan shook his head but McNeal held up his hand.

"Son, don't go there with me. I'm not in the mood. We both know the two of you have been having an intimate relationship for a good while now. Since she rescued you is my guess."

"What'd you do to her?"

Dark eyes narrowed on his face. "Why do you assume I did something to her?"

"Because I know how much she respects you and if she's not willing to talk to you, you've done something." Protective instincts rushed over him, nearly taking him to his knees as he tried to wrap his head around this entire thing of her lack of sleeping and the nightmares. "So how about you cut the crap and just come out and tell me everything."

"I'll tell you on the plane."

"Right, of course." Ivan didn't argue with how McNeal assumed he would be going, for if Bailey needed him, and it appeared she did, nothing would keep him from her side. "Give me a few to toss some clothes in a bag."

They were out of the door in fifteen minutes. A black SUV sat illegally parked behind his company vehicle.

"Weren't planning on staying long, I see," he muttered sarcastically.

"Nope."

"I just need to stop off at the office on my way out."

"Make it quick," McNeal said when he pulled up outside the building.

Ivan hopped out without speaking to him. Inside, he found Ross and his father both there. They looked at him and smiled.

"Something you need, son?" Harold got to his feet.

"Not really, just that I'm on my way out until New Year's. I'll be back in time for school, but I have to go check on a sick friend. Anyway, I have some boxes coming, could you just keep them here until I return?"

"Sure thing, or Ross can take them to your place for you. Your call."

"Whichever you prefer. Thanks." He went to the door where he spun back. "Merry Christmas." He dashed through the cold and slipped back into the passenger seat. "Let's go."

* * * *

"Plan on telling me where we're going?" Ivan looked at the man sitting across from him in the cabin of the private jet they were on. "I'm going to go out on a limb and guess she's not just in Australia, despite you saying that's where we are going."

McNeal had a scowl on his face. "I said that's where we were going first, not that it is was the final destination. She is on a private island in French Polynesia."

Of course she is. Although the mere idea of me alone with Bailey on a private island... Let's just say I'm not sure I should be thinking these things while sitting next to this man. "We're on the plane, time for you to come clean."

McNeal ordered a drink and downed it swiftly once it arrived. The flight attendant made herself scarce after taking the glass from him. "She remembered me from before, back when I wasn't her boss but before that. Prior to her being in Theta Corps."

Ivan adjusted the pillow behind his head and reclined his seat. "You knew her from before, you told me that. So she didn't know?"

"Not until recently."

He massaged his temple. "Look, cut to the chase here. I should probably hear this from her, so tell me what it is you need me to do, other than talk to her." He reached for the blanket near him and unfolded it over him. "You say you need her, like, for work? Is she to where she doesn't want to work for you anymore? Or do you need her back to being able to do the job? I don't understand."

"I need her back. I offered her to work under Masters if that's what she needs to do. But" — he raked his hand over his head — "I need her back. This is hard to explain but it will all make sense the moment you see her."

"I'll do what I can but I have to be back by the time school starts. I told you, we didn't exactly part on the best of terms either, so I'm not sure sending me in will be your best strategy."

McNeal pinned him with his gaze. "Honestly, Ivan, I think it's the only one. If anyone has a chance of reaching her it's you. But it has to be done soon or we may just lose her forever."

He hated the cryptic talk. "If she's so bad off and you're fearful of that outcome, why the fuck are you allowing her to remain on the island alone?"

"She's not alone. I have a team out there, keeping an eye on her."

He snorted. "I'm sure that's being taken well."

"It's either that or I take her in."

"You mean try."

McNeal shrugged and Ivan let it go. He wasn't sure what to do exactly, nor how he would be of any help, but he would do whatever he could. He shut his eyes and tried to get some rest.

* * * *

The boat pulled up to the long dock and slowed to a halt. "Here you go."

Ivan hopped out and readjusted the shades on his face. "Thanks for the lift."

"Sure is a busy island for a private one." The driver waved his hand and pushed away before taking off.

Ivan grasped the handles of his duffle bag and with a deep breath began the trek up toward the large and inviting house. Hopefully the occupant would be feeling charitable and not put a bullet in his head even before he'd reached her.

The second his feet left wood and hit sand, he paused. "Bailey? Can you hear me? It's me, Ivan, I'm coming up to the house."

Had she heard him? Was she watching him through a scope on some sniper rifle? What about the others McNeal had said were here? They knew he was on their side, right? He shook his head and began walking again. *I have got to stop being so damn spooked that she is just going to shoot me without any reason.*

At the front door, he knocked then tried the handle when he received no answer. It opened silently and he entered the large building. Beautiful décor. All the best amenities and yet it missed the warmth of what he was used to seeing in the places she typically inhabited.

Bedrooms were all empty and he dropped his bag in the master suite before walking to the back of the house. He opened the sliding glass door and stepped outside to the deck. Following it around, he slowed when he spied her.

Tall, empty bottles of alcohol lay scattered around her as she reclined on a double round chaise-longue. To her left was a sidearm and he gently cleared his throat.

"Bailey?"

Her name hadn't even faded from the air and he found himself staring at the barrel of the pistol. Her face was drawn and she had large circles under her eyes. Eyes that were bloodshot. Saying she looked like shit would have been a compliment.

"I said to leave me alone, dammit. I want to be left alone!"

"I'm sorry, baby, I can't do that. The only way that's going to happen is if you pull that trigger and kill me, right here and right now. Otherwise I'm staying."

"You think I can't do it?"

"I know you can, the question is would you?"

The pistol never wavered and he held his breath. *Maybe I won't be back to teach next year.* He remained still, hands out to his sides as he willed her to see him not as an enemy but as a friend. Lover. Someone she could trust.

Either that or kill me.

Chapter Twenty-Seven

What is he doing here? How did he find me?

Bailey stared through exhausted eyes at the image of Ivan. Hell, she wasn't positive it wasn't another daydream. She'd had them often enough on these binges. She bit the inside of her cheek. No, it wasn't possible. He couldn't be here, so it must be the dreams coming back, trying to fool her by taking his shape.

"Leave before I shoot you."

"I'd really prefer you didn't, baby."

It sounded like him, even moved like him. *No, don't let them close. Keep it away.* "Don't move."

Ivan stopped, hands before him. He gestured to a nearby chair. "May I sit down over there?"

"Sure." Her stomach roiled and rebelled against everything she'd ingested today. She swallowed it back, needing to deal with this first before she let the sickness take over. "Slowly."

He listened and perched on the edge of the seat. "You look tired, Bailey. Have you been sleeping?"

She narrowed her eyes. "You know I haven't."

"Have you been eating?"

"What do you care?"

"I care very much, Bailey. Surely you know that?"

"I know you look like Ivan but you dreams are crafty and sneaky. You'll take any shape to get close to me in hopes I let my guard down."

"Oh, baby."

His two words were whispered so tenderly her hand shook. The demon dreams hadn't cared before. *Perhaps he is real.*

"Ivan?"

"I'm right here, Bailey. Right here."

Her arm was too heavy to hold up the sidearm and it fell to the cushion, bouncing once before settling. He moved closer to her but she didn't have the energy to protest. Ivan crouched beside her and slid the SIG to the other side of the lounger.

"What's going on, baby? Talk to me."

He gathered her close and tucked her into him. She closed her eyes and allowed his scent to wash over her. It was him, truly.

"It all went to hell, just to hell."

"Baby, when was the last time you slept?"

"Can't, the dreams are too bad."

"You need to sleep. Close your eyes and let me take care of you."

A small smile lifted the corners of her mouth. "Already closed."

"Then sleep and I'll keep the demons away."

She was just so tired. "Yes. Can we stay here in the sun?"

"Whatever you want, just sleep."

"Yes, sleep." For the first time in many days, the arms of Morpheus welcomed her.

* * * *

A blanket settled over her, bringing her from the slumber. She stirred slightly and did her best to lift the heavy weight of her eyelids. It was a struggle but she managed to do this task and found a handsome man bending over her, love and tenderness in his eyes.

"What time is it?" Her mouth was dry and cottony.

"Shy of six. Are you hungry?"

Not really. The thought of food was stomach turning. She shifted and looked beside the lounger. The first thing she noted was her weapon was no longer there. The second was that all the empty bottles she'd been gathering from her binge drinking were gone as well.

She shook her head then tugged the blanket up around her shoulders. A wind had picked up and was actually cool over her exposed skin. "How about a drink?"

"How about a shower instead?"

She sighed. "I am kind of rank. Okay, I can do that." Still exhausted — and more than a bit intoxicated — she wobbled the few times she attempted to rise.

Ivan didn't comment, just removed the blanket he'd put there and scooped her up in his arms and strode inside. Part of her wanted to argue but the glint in his eyes warned her to keep it quiet.

He didn't slow at the shower, instead opened the glass door and stepped inside. Keeping her in his arms, he turned on and adjusted the water, which sluiced down over both of them. Once he seemed content with that, he placed her feet down and assisted her to stand on her own.

Her limbs were shaky but the warm water felt so nice on her skin. She turned her head to stare at the man behind her. His shirt was plastered to his chest, allowing her to see the defined muscles. He settled his hands on her shoulders and angled her back to face the spray. She had a moment of refusal but, damn it, this felt too good and she closed her eyes.

His fingers dallied along the back of her neck and she experienced a tug before the top of her bikini fell from her to land on the shower floor. He continued down her sides to the ties at her hips and deftly removed the bows so that piece of material, too, soon joined her top. When he removed his touch, she swayed but he soon returned.

The rich scent of her bath wash filled the air. A light kiss of vanilla combined with a provocative blend of dark berries, like plums and black raspberry. Ivan began bathing her, using long strokes and small circles with her loofa. She kept her eyes closed as he continued, remaining where he'd positioned her. His touch was incredible but she didn't have the energy to pursue anything more. As it was, the longer this took, the more she shook. Not from cold but because she'd not had any substantial food for a good while. Alcohol wasn't conducive for keeping her in top shape.

She opened her eyes when he leaned close and shut off the water. He'd removed his clothes as well and she couldn't help but appreciate his body. Ivan assisted her out of the large shower and stood her on the mat where he ran a large towel over her then wrapped it around her, tucking in the end by her breasts. She waited while he quickly dried himself.

"Come."

It was the first word he'd spoken since suggesting she take a shower. He held out a hand and she took it. Ivan led her up to the bed and indicated she should sit there. He tossed her a bathrobe then rooted around in his bag for a pair of shorts.

With her in the robe and him in the singular item of clothing, they went to the living room where he sat on one of the couches before tugging her down with him. Silence reigned as he wrapped his arms around her and cradled her.

Bailey drifted in and out of consciousness as she didn't fight the exhaustion she'd been running from for so long now, it seemed. Each time she woke, Ivan was there. Holding her, touching her. Keeping the demons at bay.

He barely said a word, other than offering her water. She never once witnessed any condemnation in his gaze or any judgment. This time when she woke, her head was clearer than it had been and she stirred in the warm cocoon he had created around her.

"What day is it?"

His arms tightened briefly. "Two days since I arrived. Thursday."

She rolled so she could see him, his scruff highlighting his chiseled jaw. His eyelashes in this light looked dipped in gold and as usual that glacial blue of his gaze made her heart skip a few beats.

"Why are you here?"

"Because you needed me."

Anger flickered anew. "Is that the only reason?"

"I'm not going to fight with you, Bailey. You can yell all you want but I won't fight with you. I want you to tell me what happened with these nightmares."

She pushed her head into his chest, so she wouldn't have to see his eyes. "I'm supposed to be strong."

"You are. Never doubt it."

"I'm weak. I let some damn dream derail me from what I am supposed to be."

He moved his hands over her back. "And what exactly is that?"

"A person who doesn't let dreams kick their ass."

"Hmm."

She sniffed. "Hmm, what?"

"Well, I just thought you were human, like the rest of us, capable of having moments of weakness."

"I've not had them before."

"It happens. To all of us. There comes a time when we're hit with the fact that no matter what we had imagined ourselves to be, how strong, powerful, whatever, that we are nothing beyond human and we have to succumb to that knowledge."

"I shouldn't have to."

"Why not? Because your parents were killed in front of you? Because you feel betrayed by McNeal and what he's done and hasn't told you?"

When he put it that way, she sounded foolish. She sobered and lifted a hand to settle upon his warm skin.

"I want to kill him."

"I don't blame you. He's an ass and, worse, he's a manipulative ass."

"You know what he did?"

"Not all, no."

"He used me."

"People do that from time to time."

"When he told me my need for revenge wasn't important, I lost it. How could he say that? Did you know they were killed on my birthday? I hadn't remembered that. We were supposed to have cake after lunch. I never got the cake." Her chest felt so empty.

In a sense, she supposed it was foolish to complain about not getting the cake, but she had long since been confused as to how she should react. Ivan didn't respond — she was happy he didn't. She knew he was listening but she didn't want any judgment, just wanted to get it off her chest.

If he had the chance to wrap his hands around McNeal's neck and squeeze the very breath from his body, Ivan would take it. *The bastard.* What kind of man used people like he did?

He ensured to keep his body relaxed, not wanting to share his own anger with her. She needed to let go and move on. He still couldn't even begin to express how deep his fear had been when he'd first stumbled upon her. The haunted look, shadows and lifelessness. That wasn't even taking into account the drinking.

However, she had been responsive to him, thus far. He continually moved his hands in a soothing motion on her back, bunching and straightening the material as he went.

"Cake," she muttered. "There wasn't cake. Just blood." Her entire body shuddered. "Blood on me, my dress, my hands and face. Spilling into the water of the stream, staining the hem of my dress."

Lord help him, he longed to take all the pain from her and give her nothing but wonderful memories. He knew he couldn't but damn it, he'd never felt as helpless as he did being unable to take away her pain.

What had that been like for a six-year-old child? To have her afternoon ripped apart by gunfire and death.

"He came," she continued. "I saw his boots first, he stepped into the stream, sending the red farther away. They were black and he crouched down so I could see him. He covered my hand with his and lifted me into his arms. I knew him, I felt safe. He carried me away and to his vehicle. As he buckled me in he told me it was okay if I cried." Another tremor racked her. "I didn't. I never did."

"Never?" Ivan couldn't stop the question from slipping free.

She shook her head, the motion moving her hair back and forth along his skin. "Nope. I've not cried since before that day. Not a single time. Does that make me a bad person, that I didn't cry when they died?"

He gripped the material covering her. "No, and don't you even think it."

"What six-year-old doesn't cry when they witness their parents die before them? Me, that's what kind. There's something wrong with me. All I felt was anger. And shame. Shame I'd not listened to my mother and anger that man took them from me. I wanted him alive so I could kill him myself."

His fingers found skin as he continued to rub her back.

"And he manipulated that hatred."

No need for him to ask who the 'he' was she meant. He had his own beliefs on the wrong way that McNeal had handled this but it wasn't time for him to air his own anger. This was about letting her work through this and being there for her.

"I don't know how he got me to forget him."

"You were a child who'd experienced a horrific tragedy, Bailey. Your mind was protecting you and closing out that day. And that part of your life."

"I should have known when I felt like I should know him."

"You need to stop being so hard on yourself about this. Cut yourself a break."

"I wanted to kill him for using me." Her fingers gripped his sides. "He was there that day they died. He used my parents as bait and watched them die. The woman he loved, he did nothing to save. Why am

I supposed to believe I mean anything to him? He says I do but I don't believe him."

"I would take it all away if I could, Bailey. I'm sorry."

She stiffened. "I don't want your fucking pity."

"It's not pity, Bailey. I don't pity you in the least. I'm sorry you had to endure what you did but I don't pity you. Look at what you've become. *Who* you've become."

"Someone who just goes out and kills, apparently not a good person."

"So McNeal isn't the only stupid fucker. I shouldn't have said what I did, either, but I did. I can't take it back. I wasn't looking at it from your point of view. But you're right. You're a soldier and you follow orders."

"I wasn't looking for your approval." Her tone had grown sharp.

"Wasn't caring if you were or not. That was actually an apology for my asinine behavior."

"What kind of guy apologizes as well as saying and doing nice things?"

"One who was brought up the right way." He gazed around the room. "Just because I don't walk around cussing and cupping my dick every other second doesn't mean I'm less than a man, Bailey. I may be a scientist but I'm in no way a pussy. My mother raised me to be respectful, polite and admit when I was wrong. I'm man enough to do that. It doesn't threaten my manhood to say those words. I'm a genuine person, I love my friends and will do what I can to keep them safe. For the woman I love, why the hell wouldn't I apologize if I was wrong? Just to appear like I'm more alpha? I know I'm an alpha male, I don't need to act like Tarzan. Most guys I know who want to be that way are more of a 'pretend to be Tarzan but act like Jane'."

He leaned back and tipped her head up so he could stare at her. Her eyes were still haunted and it ripped at his gut in ways he had never known an emotion could.

"You're not like any man I've met," she admitted.

"Is that a good thing?"

"I don't want to disappoint you."

He shook his head. "I'm not following. How would you disappoint me?"

"Look at me," she cried.

"I am. Still not seeing what you think I should be obviously seeing."

"I had a nightmare and went on a drinking binge."

"You're right. Hang on"—he lifted her arm—"nope, not there"—drew back the collar of her bathrobe and stared down—"not there either although there is temptation in there"—he brushed a finger along the whorl of her ear—"here it is. Do you know what I see?" He kissed behind her ear. "A sign that indicates you're human and, like I said before, allowed to act like one."

Her chuckle, however slight, warmed his soul.

"I'm still so angry at him."

"Is there a time limit you're allowed to be angry?" He pulled back and stared at her, completely serious. "I mean, why can't you let it work itself out?"

"I threatened him."

"I know, he told me."

"He also said if I went off the deep end he would send people after me."

"You're a dangerous woman, Bailey. You frighten him."

"Why are you here if I'm so dangerous?"

Ivan framed his hands along her face and handled it how it handled life. Straightforward. "Because this scientist is in love with the dangerous woman before him."

"Even though I'm not prepared to deal with my feelings?"

"You're not a prickly Saguaro cactus, Bailey. Quite the opposite."

She rolled away from him onto her back and stared up at the ceiling. "I don't know what I want to do anymore."

"Tired of what you're doing or not sure anymore?"

"Some of both. I'm scared I will want to exact my own revenge."

"He killed the ones who did this, yes?"

She nodded.

"So what would the revenge be against? McNeal himself?"

"I don't know. I just wanted to do something."

He lay beside her and laced his right hand through hers. "Then do this—live your life. Be happy. Don't let them control how you live your future."

"And if I don't go back to work for Theta Corps?"

"Then you don't." He stared at the blending of their skin and the beauty it created.

"It wouldn't bother you?"

He brushed his lips over her knuckles. "So long as you're happy, that's what I care about."

She opened her eyes and reached up to touch his face with the pads of her fingers. It was gentle. Loving. Exploratory.

"Your eyelashes are tipped in gold. I thought it was my imagination but it's not."

"It's so they can match your eyes."

She chewed on her lip and avoided eye contact. "I don't know what to do."

"Come with me back to the States."

"And do what?"

Good question. "Well, you could rest and figure out what you wanted to do with the next step of your life. I will be teaching during the day but the nights I promise will belong to you and you alone."

She held his gaze again. "Teaching?"

"Yes. I'm in a small town in Georgia teaching high school."

"Something happen at the lab for you to leave?"

"I was reassigned for a while. They are looking at—"

"They're recruiting."

"Yes."

"How big of a town?"

"Not big. There aren't even a thousand in the town. The school is for the entire county. There wouldn't be much for you to do at the apartment, but you are always welcome to come with me."

"Is it nice there?"

"It is."

She yawned and snuggled back into him. "Okay then. When do we leave?"

Ivan was thrilled he had gotten her to agree to leave with him. "Soon." He closed his eyes and held her tight. "Soon but not right now."

Chapter Twenty-Eight

Ivan walked to the door and opened it to admit McNeal. Past him, he could see the boat moored to the dock. Two armed men waited down by it but McNeal stood alone.

"She's in the backyard." He closed the door after him.

"Good work." McNeal brushed by him and Ivan ground his teeth. "Glad you could get her to stop whatever it was she was doing."

He ground his teeth. "McNeal."

The man turned back to him. "Yes?"

Ivan delivered a right hook to his jaw, baring his teeth in satisfaction when McNeal stumbled backwards. Shaking off the sting, he glared at the man who'd regained his balance. "You hurt her again, McNeal, and it will be you and me. The kid gloves will be off. She can poison or shoot you but I can liquefy your bones, organs and skin, making it so there is no trace of you left for a single person to find." He walked off to lead the way outside.

Bailey waited on the double lounge and Ivan went to join her. She didn't get up to meet McNeal, instead she curved into Ivan as he draped his arm around her shoulders. He brushed a kiss over her head as McNeal took a seat.

"You wanted to talk, McNeal." Bailey still maintained an edge to her voice. "What happened to your face? It looks like someone finally got the best of you."

"Your boyfriend there decked me."

Bailey looked up at him before reaching for his hands. "Did you hurt yourself, Ivan?"

"Have you made a decision, Bailey?" McNeal asked.

"I'm going with Ivan to Georgia for a while. No jobs until I figure out if I want to work for you or Masters."

The expression on McNeal's face was priceless. He didn't like this at all but he didn't argue.

"Anything else?"

"I don't need anything from you." She shifted on the lounge. "We'll be ready to go tomorrow. We want the jet as well. You can show yourself out."

"Are we going to talk about—?"

"Goodbye, McNeal," she said with no room for argument.

Ivan waited to see if he would resist. McNeal did not. The man rubbed his jaw, his fingertips touching the spot Ivan's fist had connected with when he had slugged McNeal. Then he rose and walked back through the house, no words of farewell or anything of the sort. One moment there, the next gone.

Silence reigned between them for a moment before she rose up slightly and stared at him, her left eyebrow raised. "You punched him?"

Ivan shrugged unrepentantly. "He deserved it. Besides, he is lucky that's all I did to him."

"But... He's McNeal."

"You threatened him."

"I kill people for a living. You work in a lab."

"Still a man."

She nodded. "Yes, you are." Bailey settled her head back upon his chest. "Yes, you are."

* * * *

They were alone on the flight back to Georgia—not even McNeal was with them. Ivan didn't give him another thought—he would find his way back how and when he did, it was no longer his concern.

Now they'd gotten a vehicle, one that had somehow been in the long-term parking lot. Who'd put it there he hadn't a clue, but it was a Ford Edge. He drove as Bailey reclined in the passenger seat.

She'd slept most of the way, waking to partake in some real food. There had been moments of anger and some of withdrawal. She constantly remained amazed that he hadn't left her somewhere or pushed her out over the ocean. Ivan realized he couldn't explain it to her but the understanding why he was supporting her and being there for her would have to come in its own time.

When they slept together, it was wrapped tightly in one another's arms. Since being back with each other they'd not had sex and he wanted that level of intimacy with her again but as with the rest of her recovery, it would come in time.

He gazed askance at her. She had her head against the window and toyed with the seatbelt across her lap.

"You okay?"

"You weren't lying when you said small town, were you?"

"Nope. It's nice, though. The apartment manager is a very nice man whose son is in my class."

"He's the one you're supposed to recruit."

She said it so casually he was taken a bit by surprise.

"Why would you say that?"

"I know how they work. You think it's a coincidence they put you up there in that place only to find he works where you do as well as lives where you live and his son is in the class you happen to be taking over for until the end of the year?"

Bitterness leaked free. Ivan put his attention back on driving as they continued down the two-lane road.

"No, I know it wasn't. I was just wondering why you thought that?"

"I listen and I hear things. Plus, given how it went down with my parents, I wouldn't be surprised if somewhere in the grand Theta Corps scheme they have a plan for me to be here with you. If it wasn't planned out then they have a contingency for it."

He didn't begrudge her the doubt spilling from her. They had earned her distrust.

"Well, I for one am glad you're here with me."

"Is there anything to do around here?"

He slowed as they entered the town. "Athens isn't too far away. There's a lot to do there."

Ivan let it go that she'd not once responded to him saying he loved her. Or just now how she'd brushed it off he was glad she was there with him. He knew she had feelings for him, felt it deep within him. But it would be something different to hear her actually say it.

"Athens." She sat up a bit. "I know Athens."

He wasn't sure what to make of that. "Wonderful." Ivan slowed and turned into the apartment complex and stopped at the office. "I'll be right back, need to see if I have any packages."

"Okay," she said, settling back against the door.

Ivan hurried in, bracing against the cold wind. Ross was behind the counter and he stood when Ivan walked through.

"Hi, Doc," he called out.

"Ross, any packages for me?"

"Nothing recently. I put all the others in your place. Good to see you back."

"Ready for class?"

"I think so. Looking forward to the last part of my senior year. I just wish I knew if I'd been accepted by a college or not."

"You know," he said, seizing the opening, "there are other options."

"Not really. You don't understand how important it is to my father that I go to and finish college. I'll be the first one in the family to do so."

"I do understand. Maybe you and your father can come by and I can talk to you about what I mean. I don't want to do anything behind his back."

"I'll let him know. Thanks, Doc." He tipped his head to the side. "New vehicle?"

"Girlfriend's. She's staying with me for a while."

"Oh, Doc's got a honey. She a teacher too?"

"No."

He flashed a grin. "Can't wait to meet her."

Ivan chuckled and waved while he headed out. As he shut the door behind him, he paused, catching a glimpse of Bailey. The late afternoon sun shined through the glass, surrounding her with a golden halo. It caressed her skin like a lover. In that moment, she looked at peace and he wanted nothing more than to keep it on her.

"No packages? I was just about to come in and see if you needed help carrying them out." She rolled her head on the rest to watch him as he slipped behind the wheel.

"He's already taken them to my place." He cleared his throat. "Our place."

"Them. How much stuff did you order?"

"Some things for class that the school didn't have." He started the engine and got them headed toward his apartment. Ivan parked in the closest free spot that he found and cut off the engine. "Here we are."

She unbuckled her belt and opened the door. Bailey climbed out, her backpack in hand, and looked around at her new place of residence. At least for however long she wanted to stay with him.

He wrapped his arm around her waist, leading her to the door.

"First floor. How's the crime around here?"

"Crime isn't horrid here. First floor is okay. We'll be fine."

Her smile was brief. "Sorry, habit."

"You're not working, Bailey. Resting and recouping."

She held up her hands, shrugging. "Sure thing."

He unlocked the door and gestured her inside, trailing her. Off to his left sat the boxes holding the items he'd ordered for the school. Bailey turned to face him.

"Yes?"

"Where am I sleeping?"

"Hopefully with me, but if you'd like to be in the other room, we can get you a bed."

The corners of her lips twitched. "Not going to demand I share your bed?"

"As if it would do me any good. No, I am not going to demand you do that. I don't own you, Bailey. No matter how possessive I feel toward you." He lightly brushed his knuckles over her cheek. "And I'm seriously fucking possessive toward you."

"I'm sure I'll like your bed just fine." She whirled back around and sauntered off, hips swaying enticingly.

Maybe I'm getting the Bailey back who lights up my world with her smile.

He allowed her to go explore and he left his bag by the door, opting to check out the boxes. Ivan had just put the fourth one on the table when she reappeared. He looked briefly then his head snapped back toward her so fast it spun. She wore nothing. Absolutely nothing.

His cock responded instantly, rising to the occasion with no hesitation.

"Bailey?" Christ, his voice sounded more like a frog croak than a human question.

"You might not be demanding, but I'm feeling more than a bit. You. Naked. Now. I want you inside me." A sly smile. "Unless you're too busy."

He dropped the knife and stepped toward her. "Too busy? Not even close."

Bailey watched him approach. Ivan moved like a predator. He wasn't like some of the men she knew who at times were over the top in their alpha tendencies. He wasn't anyone's bitch, that was for sure, but he also didn't need to shove his masculinity in someone's face.

As he neared, he tugged his shirt free from the waistband of his jeans, lifting it off over his head. When it fell, she never took her gaze from him, allowing herself the pleasure of seeing his tanned, cut physique. The deltoids, abdominals, obliques, pectorals and more, each working in harmonious tandem with the others, creating the visual feast for her to enjoy. The six-pack she'd enjoyed licking caramel off when they'd been in his apartment called to her now.

She'd not been feeling particularly sexy as of late, more like a loser. But here she'd felt stirrings and had decided 'what the hell' and was going with them. From the looks of his fierce expression, he was on board.

Longing shot through her. Her nipples tightened and a low throbbing began in her clit before it spread up and throughout the rest of her body. His long fingers tackled the button on his jeans even as he toed off his shoes, not bothering to untie them.

Bailey paused in the middle of his bedroom and watched him, waiting for that moment he would be bared to her, completely. He shoved off his pants and continued approaching her, kicking free of his jeans as he moved. His boxer briefs were black and she zoned in on his groin. The defined ridge there had her whimpering in desire and he'd not even touched her yet.

Primal need flared, adding an almost eerie look to his gaze. It burned her, branded her, possessed her. She didn't care. Deep down, Bailey knew the truth, whether it was voiced or not, whether she wanted to acknowledge it or not—she belonged to this man.

There was no one else for her who would understand her like he did. Who wouldn't feel intimidated by what she did for a living. Who would take her good with her bad as he did. He loved her for what and who she was on the inside.

She reached for him and stopped when he shucked his final article of clothing. He'd removed his socks at some point, she wasn't sure when. *Don't really give a damn either.* His cock was long and thick, rising proudly.

Her tongue snuck out and dampened her lips as she fixated on his length as he walked toward her, not stopping until the velvet-over-iron length was snug in her hand. He flexed his hips, rubbing himself along her skin. She tightened her grip, allowing her thumb to smear the pearly drops of pre-cum over the bulbous head.

His guttural moan was unidentifiable to her but it still warmed her. Fire licked at her veins and skin. Searching. Seeking. Feeding.

Ivan cupped her breasts, rolling and tugging on her nipples. He moved down her body, fanning the flames as he went. Her legs shook as she worked his cock faster. Along her hips and over her belly, he smoothed his palms.

She swallowed hard when he moved behind her and dropped to the floor. His warm breath fanned along the small of her back. He nipped at her skin and she jumped, trying to turn toward him. He refused to allow it.

Long, slow licks along her skin had her dropping her head back in pleasure and scrunching her fingers into fists as she tried to remain upright. He nudged her legs wider apart and slid an arm through, so his palm rested against the flat of her belly.

His right hand gripped at her hips as he continued his loving ministrations and his left dug into her flesh surrounding her belly button. He used his strength to keep her up, for her legs were trembling like matchsticks in a storm.

Higher and higher he pushed her need. She rocked along his arm, seeking any type of friction she could get from him. He didn't stop what he was doing, in fact, if anything he went slower. Longer, more languid laps along her heated skin. Grazes of his teeth that had her mewling, begging for release.

She dug her nails into her palms, unsure what else to do with her hands. Her world spun nearly out of control as the passion overwhelmed her. She teetered on the precipice but he wouldn't let her go over. He knew her and would back off when she neared, leading her back down. Then he would start all over again.

Her words wouldn't come in any semblance of order and it took her a while to realize she was speaking French. Switching back to English, she begged, "Please, Ivan."

Her pussy was so wet and craving, her gut hurt. She needed what he could give her.

Slowly he stood, dragging his arm out from between her legs in a torturous manner. His kisses ran up her back and to her shoulders before he dipped his head and lapped at her breasts, the flat of his tongue swiping along her taut nipples.

He moved to stand in front of her, his cock poking her belly. She wrapped her hand around it and he moaned low in his throat while capturing her mouth in another toe-curling kiss.

Ivan lifted her in his arms and carried her the rest of the way to the bed, his lips mashed to hers, his tongue surging and dancing in tandem with her own. He laid her back, his larger, stronger body covering her.

She didn't wait any longer and guided his cock to her pussy. The broad head pushed in easily. Her hand fell away as he drove in with his hips, filling her completely in one stroke.

Words escaped her as passion reigned supreme. Her body shattered and she came around him. That was what she'd needed. She didn't care—he wasn't done with her and she knew she would be coming again.

She closed her eyes only to open them again when he tapped her cheek.

"Watch me, Bailey."

He drew back, slowly, deliberately. Then back in with that same agonizing speed.

"Faster," she cried.

"No. Slow. Easy. Watch me make love to you." He kissed the tip of her nose. "Watch me so I can see every reaction you have to what I'm doing to you." He laced their fingers and positioned their hands above her head. "You and me, Bailey Hyde."

She knew this wasn't about just the here and now. He was claiming her forever. There was an edge to his words that allowed no doubt to her belief of what he was doing. Bailey tightened her grip on his hands.

"Yes."

That was all she said. All that needed to be said.

Ivan, as he'd promised, made love to her. When they finally succumbed to sleep, she could hardly keep her eyes open. Her dreams were pleasant ones and she never once woke to a nightmare. She did wake to him eating her out and her cries echoing off the walls.

Her fingers dug into his scalp as her back bowed, hips arched off the bed and she cried, "Ivan!"

He didn't relent and when she finished coming on his tongue, he rose up and slid inside her with a fierce stroke.

"Now," he muttered against her lips, sharing her taste with her. "Now, we go fast."

He hooked her legs over his shoulders, angling her so he could power deeper, and began to piston his hips. Hard strokes. Deep strokes. Unrelenting.

She couldn't see him—the room was dark as pitch but it didn't matter. His fingertips bit into her hips as she undulated with his driving thrusts. Their heavy breathing filled the air as she came once more, his name again spilling from her lips.

He slammed into her three more times before she moaned as thick ropes of his cum filled her.

No condom. It hit her as his release triggered another of her own. They hadn't used one previously either. Something else she didn't care about.

His body sank onto hers as he pressed her deeper into the mattress, his lips along the side of her neck. She wrapped her arms around him, telling him without words she wanted him to stay where he was. She didn't mind him on her, it made her feel safe and protected. And there he stayed, still buried deep inside her.

Chapter Twenty-Nine

"Are you sure you don't want to stay?"

Bailey paused with her hand on the door of the Ford Edge. "No, I'm good. You talk to them and I'll be back later. I'll bring something to eat so don't worry about cooking."

Ivan smiled. "Have fun, Bailey."

The one he got back in return was incredible. She'd found herself again. This was the Bailey he remembered. There were no more dark circles under her eyes and she no longer appeared on edge. The serenity he was used to seeing surround her had returned.

"I plan on it." She hopped inside and, with a wave, drove off.

As she left, he spied Harold and Ross approaching and he waited for them to arrive before going back inside. Soon they all sat in his living room.

"What's this you wanted to talk to my son about?" Harold stirred his coffee and helped himself to a few of the sweets Bailey had baked before she left.

"Opportunities."

"I'm not following."

He glanced between father and son. "I mean instead of a way out with football. The people I work for, the company I represent, has shown great interest in you, Ross."

"I thought you were just a teacher." Harold sounded accusatory.

"I'm more than that. I work in a lab most of the time but teach when needed. I've spoken to my employer at length about you and how brilliant you are." He kept his attention on Ross.

"I have to go to college—football is my only chance." Ross gestured at his father. "It's the only way he won't be in debt forever. And my one real opportunity."

"Not true. At all. Let me ask you something. Would you like a career in physics? Have a lab of your own and people working under you?"

"That would be awesome, but I have to finish school."

"And you would. My company would fully fund your education, undergrad, grad, however far you wanted to go. There would be no expense to you or your father. They will also provide you with a place to live, but you'd have to be working with them when you weren't in school. As in, that would be your job. You could still play football if you desire. Your choice."

They stared at one another and he sensed they were coming around to his side. Ivan poured himself a bit more coffee and ate a cookie.

"I know the lure of the NFL is great, all the money. But do you have a guarantee you'd be there? A lot can happen in college to a player, which can end their football career before it begins. With my company, you wouldn't have to worry about the damage to your body. And it wouldn't matter if you played and got hurt, we would still want you. We wouldn't expect you to pay for treatment like colleges do now. You and your father would be completely covered, insurance-wise."

Ross whistled. "Dude, who do you work for?"

"A government agency."

"For real?" Ross leaned forward. "Like the CIA or FBI?"

"Not quite. We have facilities all over the world you could opt to work at once your schooling is done. Or perhaps you'd care to go to school in another country. France. Spain. England. Wherever. We can make it happen."

"Let me get this straight. You're offering my son a job, now. One that will completely pay for his schooling no matter how many degrees he wishes to acquire? And all he has to do is work for you? He can go anywhere in the world?"

Ivan nodded. "Yes."

He leaned forward and placed his arms on his thighs. "Mr Collins, we value intelligence at this company. And we pay well for it. The money he would make in the NFL, should he get there, would be nice but that's years away, given he has to be out of high school for three years before he can enter the draft. Then there's the physical punishment. How long will that money last when it is going to injuries accrued on the field of play? Or the wrong crowd who's upset because of a win or a loss?"

They shared another look and Ivan kept going.

"There's not that risk and the money would be arriving as soon as you are part of the company."

"Isn't this illegal? Asking him to work for you?"

"It's a job, Mr Collins. No different than him working and going to school. Our business isn't illegal. I'm just offering another career choice. One that will benefit him financially, take care of his schooling and offers the option to travel."

"And if I say no?"

"Then you said no, Ross. There's nothing untoward about this offer."

"You really think they want me?" Ross scooted forward a bit more.

Ivan picked up another cookie. "I know they do. You have an uncanny and unique way in how you look at physics and the world surrounding it. That kind of insight and dedication would be greatly appreciated."

"What kinds of things do you work on?"

"More than you could possibly imagine. Before I came here I was on a few things, including but not limited to, dark matter, wormholes, that kind of thing." He finished his coffee. "I don't need an answer now, but the sooner, the better. And please, no mention of this to anyone at school. Do you have any more questions?"

They did and he spent the next few hours talking to them and trying to allay any uncertainty they both had. When Bailey opened the door, he was shocked such time had passed.

"Oh," she said. "I'm sorry, I didn't realize you were still meeting."

"No problem, Bailey. You remember Mr Collins and his son."

"I do, nice to see you both again." She shut the door behind her and carried the bags to the kitchen.

Ross looked in her direction. "Does she work with you?"

"With me? No. Same company, though."

"Can I go ask her a question?"

"Sure thing."

Ross rose and walked to where Bailey was putting the food away. Ivan watched her stop and give the young man all her attention.

"I'm concerned this is too good to be true," Harold said, drawing his attention back to the man speaking.

"I'm sorry you feel that way." He reached into his wallet and withdrew a card. "This is my boss—feel free to call that number and ask her any other questions you may have." *I hope to God Howland is better than I would expect her to be in this type of situation.*

Harold stared at it, flipping it back and forth before shoving it in his pocket. "I will."

"And if you have any more questions, let me know. If I don't know the answer, I will do my best to get it and report back to you."

Laughter from the kitchen had him looking over there. Bailey and Ross were laughing together and looking all chummy. Ivan approved—he loved watching Bailey happy.

Harold rose and said, "Thank you for taking the time to explain things to us. I think we should go and discuss a few things ourselves." He scooped up some more cookies. "I'll just take a few to go."

"Please, take them all," Bailey said, walking up. "We have plenty more where they came from."

"Far be it for me to argue with a lady." Harold winked and did as she'd suggested.

The two men left and Ivan turned back after he'd shut the door behind them. Bailey sat on the chaise portion of the couch. "So, how'd it go?"

"He's definitely interested. Was amazed we'd pay for the schooling and all that so long as he was working for us. I tried to emphasize that, unlike football, it wouldn't be dangerous to his body. And Ross really perked up when I mentioned dark matter and wormholes."

"You have until the end of school, right?"

"I think they would take him any time. The boy doesn't even realize how smart he is. All he wants to do is make his father proud of him, but he hides his intelligence to fit in at school. I see it in class because the light goes on and I know how quickly he gets the answer."

She reclined back, propping up on her arms. "I thought you said there were tests where it looked like he struggled."

Ivan walked over to her and straddled her, lowering his head to hers for a kiss. "There are. But I've been putting extra credit questions on the bottom, stuff we do in the lab and, Bailey, he never misses those. Ever. No one else even comes close to getting it right and it's not stuff we've discussed in class. So I know he's deliberately dumbing down what he does in class. He's afraid of being an outcast."

She hooked her legs up around his hips and tugged him down, so their pelvises met. "Good thing you're there for him then."

He trailed one hand up her side to cup the underside of her breast. "If you say so."

"I think you're getting distracted."

"Only think? I'm doing something wrong if you only *think* I'm getting distracted." He flicked his tongue against the corner of her mouth. "Way wrong."

"Probably. I could use another example." Her breath sounded thready.

"Just one?"

She gave him a wry grin. "Or three or four. Hell, maybe ten or more." She wrapped her arms around him, rubbing her breasts into his chest.

"I'm liking that." He captured her mouth, bending his arms so she was pressed back into the cushion. *Yeah, I'm liking that idea a lot.*

* * * *

"Did you make a decision?"

Bailey stared across the large desk at the man behind it. Kevin McNeal. Her uncle. Her boss. And, until recently, the focus of her anger. She blinked and put her foot in the seat beside her, leaning her head against her knee.

"Why did you save Lynn?"

"She needed saving." He laced his fingers and leaned back in his chair.

"Is she your daughter? Is she my cousin?"

A few charged moments of silence lingered between them. "Yes."

"Is that why you wanted her to stay with me?"

His jaw tightened then relaxed. "Yes."

"Does she know who you are?"

"No."

"So yet another woman who doesn't know your relationship status in regards to her." She shook her head. "Does it make sense to keep so many secrets?"

"I liked you better when you didn't ask so many questions."

"And I respected you more before I found out about the subterfuge. Where does that get us? No-fucking-where."

"What is the meaning of this visit, Bailey? Did you make a decision?"

"I did."

He waited then raised his brows. "I'm not going to beg for your answer. Tell me or leave and I can make it for you."

She narrowed her gaze. "That's the problem— you've thought you had the right to make decisions for me. It's what got us here to the situation we're in now."

"This isn't the *Care Bears* or *Barney*. Shit happens and we're not always happy about it."

"You'll never admit you were wrong, will you?" She waved off any answer he may have been about to make. "I don't care. I don't need to hear it. Your approval isn't my goal. I'm back to work as of now. I will go where you send me, but I think it best we stay out of one another's way. You keep interfering with my life and I will go work directly under Masters." She pushed to her feet. "That's all I have to say. Now, I have to get back in time for high school graduation."

She left his office and walked outside into the early June New York weather. The car she'd arrived in waited. She slipped into the passenger seat and shared a look with the driver. He immediately left, taking her back to the airport.

Bailey dozed on the plane ride and when she landed, she drove fast to make it in time for the ceremony. She stepped into the auditorium and listened to the names of graduating students being called. Working her way up, she stood along the back wall with some of the other overflow attendees. Ten students after she arrived was Ross.

She put her fingers in her mouth and whistled, cheering him on. He lifted his head and saw her. His smile was blinding and she knew if she could find his father in the gathered crowd, his smile would mirror Ross'.

The principal stepped up to the microphone before dismissing the class and said, "We have a very special award to give to one of our graduates. All of you know, our physics teacher, Mr Wheeler, got sick earlier this year and his replacement, Dr Vinokourov, will be presenting this award."

Bailey crossed her arms and watched as Ivan strode up to the podium. He looked dashing and sexy even wearing the robe as he did. She knew what lay beneath it.

"It has been my honor and pleasure to teach physics at this school. I spent my time here surrounded by wonderful people and a tight-knit community. I wasn't a stranger for long. The physics department held some tests throughout the year that were utilized to identify those with an extreme aptitude for the subject. We found one. Ross Collins, please come up here."

The place exploded in cheers and they stood as Ross walked back up to the stage.

Ivan smiled at him. "Don't look so worried, you're not in trouble." Laughter moved through the room next. "It is with great honor that I am able to extend this to you. I've known how you struggled to figure out what school to attend and that you've sent out some applications. In my hand I have here not only your acceptance but your full-ride scholarship to the Massachusetts Institute of Technology." He held it out. "Congratulations, Mr Collins."

If the cheer had been loud when Ross had been called back up, now it deafened. The amount of support and love poured through the room as they whistled and called his name.

Ross shook Ivan's hand and waved before departing the stage to another standing ovation. Bailey waited in the wings as the ceremony concluded and all the hats were tossed in the air. The party spilled outside as the new graduates hugged, took pictures and cried with friends.

She found Ivan off to the side and she slipped her arms around his waist. "Hey," she whispered.

"You did make it. I was afraid you wouldn't be back in time." He turned and kissed her.

"I wouldn't miss this. Look at you, beaming like your own children were up there."

Their eyes locked and she saw the desire in his.

"They are mine, in a way. I'm very proud of them." He placed his hands on her hips bringing her in close. "I wouldn't mind having some of my own."

"I think you would be a hit. The man who gave birth."

"With you, woman. With you. How'd your talk go with McNeal?"

"I'm still under him but he's going to steer clear of me for a while. He also said Lynn was his daughter, so I guess I now have a cousin."

"Are you okay with that?"

"Not anything I have a say in. It's how it is."

"I have to admit, for a while I thought he was your father."

"I'd wondered that too, but when I realized he was my uncle it made sense."

He grumbled in Russian and she tugged on his robe to get his attention.

"What?"

"How soon can we leave?"

"Hot and bothered by looking at me in this robe?"

She laughed. "Yes."

Someone called for him to get a picture and he stepped back. "Soon, I'm sure."

"Good," she replied. "I was thinking we could practice making children." With a wave, she left him there, standing staring at her.

* * * *

Santiago, Chile
Seventeen months later

Bailey stood on the balcony of the apartment. Ivan was supposed to be home soon and he would see what she'd been doing all day. She'd arrived back from a mission two weeks ago and was recouping.

She watched him park his bike then stride to the door. She remained where she was, waiting for him to enter.

"Hey, babe, I'm... What is going on here? Bailey?" He appeared at her side. "Why have you packed the place up? Would you look at me?"

She did. The sun glinted off his blond hair and made his tanned skin appear golden.

"We're moving."

He blinked and stared at her. "We're moving? You love this apartment. Why are we moving?"

She captured his hand and pressed a kiss to the back of it. "I'm pregnant."

His eyes grew wide then a grin followed. "Are you sure? How far along? Why didn't you tell me? When did you find out?"

He dropped to his knees and pressed a kiss to her stomach.

"Stop," she said. "I've known since I got back. I didn't tell you because you've been stressed about your work. The one night I had planned to tell you" — she shrugged — "you fell asleep before dinner was even done cooking."

"I'm so sorry," he said, staring up at her. He pushed to his feet with a frown. "You're not going out again."

She didn't mind his demand. "I've told McNeal, he knows. Until the child is born, I'm not active anymore. I picked a place still close to where your lab is but it's got more room."

"I don't know what to say, Bailey."

"Just tell me you're happy."

"More than you can ever know." He kissed her, long and drawn out until she sagged into him. "One more thing."

"Uh-huh." If he kissed her like that again, she'd agree to damn near anything.

"We're marrying before this child arrives."

"Whatever you want."

"I want you," he muttered before he slanted his mouth over hers again.

She succumbed to the need and the love she had for him. Wrapping her arms around him, she smiled when he lifted her. He stopped once she lay on the bed and stared into her eyes.

"I love you, Ivan."

"I love you, too, Bailey."

As he slowly undressed her, she wasn't sure what their future would bring but she was all in. He was the one who made her life worth living, despite their differences. As he slid inside her, she held him as tight as she could. He was hers. From now until eternity. What more could she ask for?

About the Author

Aliyah Burke is an avid reader and is never far from pen and paper (or the computer). She is married to a career military man, and they have a German Shepherd, two Borzois, and a DSH cat. Her days are spent sharing her time between work, writing, and dog training.

Aliyah Burke loves to hear from readers. You can find her contact information, website details and author profile page at http://www.totallybound.com.

Totally Bound Publishing